NO GOOD DEED

A NOVEL

JACK WALLACE

atmosphere press

Published by Atmosphere Press

Cover design by Felipe Betim

Atmospherepress.com

for Joanne

CHAPTER ONE

MONDAY

Kim pushed up on one elbow to check the time on the microwave clock. The blue numbers read 4:45. She lay back on her mattress and stared at the ceiling. Afraid of oversleeping, she'd been awake most of the night. The countdown had begun: fifteen minutes before her escape. She raised herself on her elbow again. Fourteen minutes.

The basement room was windowless, but a small lamp on a rickety table across the room gave enough light for Kim to peek out of her sleeping bag and ensure none of the other women were awake. Since they all arrived home most nights well after midnight, they were not likely to stir this early.

Sukee was sleeping beside her, only the top of her head peeking out of the red nylon sleeping bag, black hair spilling across her pillow. Kim considered nudging her and saying goodbye but decided their whispers might wake up June and Ji-hu, sleeping on mattresses a few feet away. She couldn't take that chance. Ji-hu would sound the alarm. Besides, Sukee begged her not to leave. With tears in her eyes, her friend said the men would find her and beat her, or worse.

Nine minutes. Kim traced the steps in her head. Ji-hu held the only key to the basement door. The men trusted her with it, and she kept it in the pocket of her satin jacket. Kim stroked Sukee's hair. "Bye, my friend," she whispered, then crawled from her sleeping bag and pulled on slippers, tiptoed to Ji-hu's jacket hanging on the back of a ladder-back chair, found the key, and eased up the basement stairs. While clutching her small purple purse that held six hundred dollars of mostly wrinkled twenties, she worked the key in the lock.

Kim paused with her head sticking through the partially opened door and listened for any movement. Min-jun's bedroom door was cracked open, his ragged snoring providing a steady beat. Kwan's door was closed. She tiptoed to the front door of the house.

This was her last chance to change her mind. Once she opened the door, she had thirty seconds before an alarm would sound. Min-jun and Kwan would grab their pistols and burst out of their rooms to check for any intruders. Then they would hurry to the basement to count the women. Once they discovered she was gone, they would rush to the van and drive the streets searching for her.

Kim bit her lip as she twisted the front door lock. She pulled the door open and slipped out into the pre-dawn darkness. Shivering in the April morning chill, she shut the door and ran across the street.

She breathed faster. Her side ached as she sprinted between houses and darted across streets. Two more blocks to White Bridge Road and the bus stop for downtown Nashville. She paused beside a large tree near a one-story brick home. Doubled over, she gulped for air. She had not run any distance for the four years she had been in the United States.

When her heart quit racing, Kim dodged around a tire swing hanging from a branch and hurried across the front lawn of the house. Her stomach lurched as she saw headlights slowly approaching. "Kwan and Min-jun," she muttered.

As she dashed to the corner of the house, the eave light flashed on, exposing her for a few seconds before she ducked into the shadows at the side of the house. She glanced over her shoulder. The car had slowed almost to a stop. Had they seen her? Then she realized a board fence at the back corner blocked her path through the back yard. She squeezed behind a holly bush, the leaves prickling her bare arms. She held her breath and tucked her hands under her arms to still the shaking.

The sound of the car's engine grew distant. Kim scooted from behind the holly bush, ran to the neighboring house, and found a clear path to the next street. Tears blurred her vision as she weaved between houses, putting distance between her and the mysterious car. She paused to catch her breath beside a two-story brick home on the last street before White Bridge Road.

The bright streetlights up ahead were her beacon. She peeked around the corner. After checking for headlights, she dashed the short distance down the street to a strip of restaurants and stores on the corner of White Bridge Road.

Loose gravel poked through her thin slippers, but she hardly felt it. She checked over her shoulder again as she ran, fearing a van would wheel off the main road and roar across the parking area. The street was clear. She darted into a recessed entrance to a shoe store. The streetlight didn't reach into the cavernous space, and it appeared to be the best place to hide. For how long? She didn't know. But she could see the bus stop at the corner. She hoped it wouldn't be long before the bus arrived. If the sun came up soon, she would be visible to the street.

Kim hunkered down and wrapped her arms around her knees, trying to make herself as small as possible. With her back pressed against the store entrance, she watched for the bus.

CHAPTER TWO

Something about early mornings in the spring, even a Monday morning, invigorated Christopher. The heater on the ten-year-old Buick sedan was turned on high. Both front windows were rolled down. Cold air pushed in around his neck and head, despite his gray hoody and Chicago Cubs baseball cap.

At this hour, the suburban Nashville neighborhood was quiet. The Lumineers sang "Ho Hey" on the Roots Radio station. Christopher hummed along as he crept slowly through the deserted neighborhood streets, slinging *Tennesseans* out the passenger window and then the driver side. After nearly two years of this morning newspaper delivery route, he had the rhythm down, rarely missing a driveway. *Not a bad arm for an over-the-hill almost forty-year-old*, he thought.

He idly scanned the darker areas of the lawns. This older West Nashville community had big yards with mature trees, hedges, and thickets, and he occasionally saw a fox or a coyote on the prowl. Just last week, three deer, appearing out of nowhere in the mist, dashed across the street in front of him.

A sudden movement near the next house caught his eye. It was still too dark to see much, but he thought it might be a person. He slowed for a better look. As the shadowy figure reached the side of the house, a motion detector spotlight flashed on. In the few seconds of light, he recognized the form of a slender woman before she darted quickly around the corner. He eased the car to a stop and strained to see more, but she was out of his line of vision.

Why would a woman be running across a yard in the dark? She seemed in a hurry to hide. Was she trying to break into the house? He considered whether to turn into the driveway and knock on the door. No, better not to get involved, he decided. Just do my job. He continued slowly down the street, reaching into the bin of rolled-up newspapers in the passenger seat, bracing the steering wheel with his knees as he alternated throwing hands, slinging with his left, then his right.

Christopher turned right at White Bridge Road and drove a short distance, passing a bank and a liquor store, then parked in front of Bruegger's Bagels, the only business he could count on to be open at 5:30 AM. He was usually their first customer, getting his morning coffee and raisin bagel each day and leaving a stack of *Tennesseans* beside the cash register.

"Morning, Chris. The usual?" The woman behind the counter, in her mid-thirties, a little plump, skin the color of mocha, gave him a friendly smile. He preferred to be called Christopher, but never bothered to correct her.

"Morning, Stella. Yep. The usual. What's new with you today?" Christopher laid the newspapers on the counter.

"Same old, same old. Left my old man in bed. Told him he better get on up and fix breakfast for those three children of his and get them off to school. I be calling him in about twenty minutes, waking him up again, I expect." She handed Christopher his raisin bagel and a large black coffee. "Here it is. Strong and black, like I like my men."

"Yeah, well, like bagels, you don't know what you like till you try other flavors."

"Who says I ain't tried already?" She cocked her head at him and put her hands on her hips.

"Whoa, you *are* feeling sassy this morning." Christopher stirred in a packet of sugar.

"It's spring. Might as well feel your oats. I hope you're looking for a little romance for yourself." Stella winked at him.

"No romance. Still broke and broke down." Christopher

looked around to make sure there were no eavesdroppers. The store was empty except for the other early-morning employee in the rear getting bagels out of the oven.

"What, you been divorced for about two years, ain't you?" Stella stood at the cash register and wagged her finger at him. "Man, you need a girlfriend. You're due for some loving. I can't see your bank account, but I can see you, and you ain't broke down. You look mighty fine. You need me to help you find someone? I got women friends who might be interested."

Christopher laughed as he inched sideways toward the entrance. "I appreciate the offer, but I have my hands full working two jobs and trying to help raise a rebellious teenage daughter. Later, Stella." He slid out the front door, bagel and coffee in hand.

It had been a while since he'd been with a woman. Stella was right about that. But he was too old-fashioned to go for an easy hookup. He'd had a rebound relationship last year, lasting only a couple months, that ended badly. Still, he should probably put himself out there and let someone like Stella know he was interested in dating. He was finally doing okay financially. And his daughter, Amy, rarely stayed at his house, so that was not a problem. He longed for the days when she loved riding in the car with him, talking about her school friends or herself, and what she wanted to be when she grew up. Now, when she was with him, she mostly stared at her phone, often with earbuds on.

Almost to his car, he noticed a slight woman huddled in the darkened doorway of a shoe store two businesses down. She was curled up, head down, knees against her chest. Christopher didn't want to stare or meddle, so he directed his attention at unlocking the Buick. As he reached to place his coffee in the drink holder, he wondered if she might be the person he had seen running between the houses earlier, a few blocks away. He paused halfway in his car, rattled his keys, straightened up and turned to face the woman.

"Miss, are you all right?" He took a few steps in her direction.

Fearful almond-shaped eyes stared back at him. She slowly nodded but kept her arms wrapped around her sides.

"You sure? You're not hurt, are you?" He took a step closer and then stopped. She was trembling, and he didn't want to spook her. She looked young, maybe late teens. Maybe a runaway?

"You trying to get somewhere?"

"I wait for bus," she said, pointing to the bus stop on the corner.

Christopher looked at his watch. "I don't think it comes until 6:30. That's almost an hour. Are you headed downtown?"

She nodded. "I go to Greyhound station." Her accent indicated she was not American. He wondered how much she knew about bus routes and ticket purchases.

"What time does your bus leave from there?"

She shook her head.

"You don't know?"

She shrugged one shoulder. "I get on bus to Atlanta."

Christopher rechecked his watch, looked out toward the street, then turned to the woman. "Look, I have time to take you to the Greyhound station. Why don't you ride with me? I'm almost finished with my paper route. I can have you there before this city bus comes along."

She glanced down the street, her brows knitted with worry, then back at him. After studying his face for a moment, she said, "Okay."

He headed to his car. The front passenger seat held the remaining newspapers, so he opened the back door. The young woman remained hunched at the store entrance. "Come on," Christopher said, motioning her forward. She peeked down the sidewalk, then ran to the car, almost diving into the rear seat. She scrunched down in the far corner.

He started the car, then twisted around to talk. "I need to

deliver newspapers to houses on two more streets." He waved his arm over the bin with the remaining papers. "It'll take about fifteen minutes. Then we can head to the bus station. You want half this bagel?" He held it up.

She shook her head.

"Do you live around here?" Christopher looked at her in the rearview mirror. She didn't respond. She appeared Asian, but he couldn't guess her nationality. Chinese? Vietnamese? He wondered if she understood much English, why she wanted to go to Atlanta, and why she seemed scared, but he didn't ask. He noticed the small purse she clutched. Was this all she brought for her trip? No sweater or jacket for a cool spring morning. She must have left in a hurry, he speculated.

After a few more minutes of slinging papers, he said, "I'm done. We'll head downtown to the Greyhound station." He watched in the rearview mirror for any response, but there was none. He drove out of the neighborhood and onto White Bridge Road toward downtown Nashville.

Sunrise was almost an hour away, but darkness had faded in the east over the city skyline. Christopher slowed down as they neared the bus station and eased over to the left lane. A maroon minivan swooped by him and turned left into the bus station parking lot. As he moved to the center turn lane, he heard a half-scream and a word he didn't understand, followed by "No, no!"

In his rearview mirror, he saw the girl staring at the parking lot with a horrified expression on her face. He slowed to a crawl and watched a wiry man in jeans and a t-shirt hurry from the passenger side of the maroon van toward the bus station.

He felt a punch on his shoulder. "No, don't go there!" He glanced back. She had moved behind him and hunkered down.

He stepped on the gas pedal and drove past the bus station. He glanced over to see if he'd attracted the attention of the van driver. The driver stared straight ahead at the front of the station, talking on a cell phone.

A block later, Christopher turned right on a side street and into an empty parking lot.

"Are those men after you?" He twisted sideways to face the young woman. She slumped again in the far corner.

She nodded. Her eyes showed her fear.

Christopher drummed his fingers on the passenger seat headrest as he looked out the window, unsure of what to do next. He had his day planned, which didn't include spending a chunk of time carting this unknown girl around. Still, he couldn't abandon her here. If these men were looking for her, she needed help.

"Do you want me to call the police? They can come here and make sure those men don't hassle you or prevent you from getting on the bus to Atlanta."

She shook her head. "No police. The men still catch me if they know I go to Atlanta."

Christopher twisted his mouth as he thought about her dilemma. She needed to get away from the men. For now, he may be her best shot to help her catch that bus to Atlanta without the men knowing her destination.

"Do you want me to take you back to your house?"

"No," she said, her eyes wide. "They live there. They will beat me."

This sounds like a domestic situation, Christopher thought. *There's probably a shelter for battered women in Nashville.* Should he drop her there? She seemed determined to get to Atlanta. How would she get back to the bus station?

He considered letting her spend the morning at his house while he worked, then bringing her back in the afternoon. At first, he rejected the idea, not wanting to get that involved with her situation. He was cautious by nature, and a domestic issue could be a hot mess, if that's what this was. Still, he was raised to help people in need. His dad had often gone out of his way to give someone a ride or buy gas. Do the right thing,

Dad always said, and you won't go wrong. Maybe the right thing to do was to spend a few more hours helping her find a way to get to Atlanta. He could spare the time.

"Okay, I don't think they'll stay at the bus station all day. Probably just this morning. I need to get back to my house. We'll come back in a few hours. If they're gone, you can get your ticket to Atlanta. How's that sound?"

She looked at him, eyes wide, and didn't respond. Christopher wondered if she understood, but as he started to say it again, maybe simpler this time, she said, "Okay."

He turned out of the parking lot and drove toward an interstate on-ramp that led west. His house was a twenty-minute drive from downtown at this time of day.

▪ ▪ ▪

"She is not at the Greyhound station." The minivan driver spoke Korean into his cell phone.

There was silence from the person at the other end of the conversation for a moment. "But that is where she was headed, according to the other girl."

"Yes, Boseu. Sukee may know more. I can go question her again."

"No. Get the girls to Orchid Spa. Leave Kwan there at the bus station. She may show up later. I'll send Sung-ho to help search." The voice on the other end was raspy, as if from years of cigarettes, but the tone was authoritarian.

"Okay, Boseu."

"When you find her, get rid of her," the raspy-voiced man said. He ended the conversation.

CHAPTER THREE

"I'm Christopher. Christopher Jones." He studied the woman in the rearview mirror. "What's your name?"

She stayed huddled in the corner of the back seat and stared at the passing landscape. "Kim."

"How long have you lived in Nashville?"

"I live here almost two years," she replied, finally meeting his gaze in the mirror.

"Where did you live before?"

"San Francisco. I want to go there."

"Oh. So, you're going to Atlanta and then on to San Francisco, right?"

She nodded.

"How long did you live in San Francisco?"

"Two years."

"And where did you live before then?"

"Korea."

"Did you come to the United States to work?"

She nodded, then turned her head to look out the window again. Christopher picked up on her lack of interest in more conversation. As he glanced again, he couldn't help but wonder about the men looking for her. What was their connection? Was it a Korean family dispute? How much more should he do to help her? He decided not to question her any further. He would take her to the Greyhound station in a few hours, and that would be it. His home-based computer repair business would keep him busy the rest of the day.

He exited the interstate onto Ashland City Highway and continued toward his house, or, in reality, his mom's house, out past the Nashville suburbs and near the county line, where most of the homes were surrounded by several acres of land. Many had been farmhouses built in the 1940s and 50s, but very few remained working farms.

His parents bought the house and ten acres when Christopher and his older sister were in elementary school. Christopher didn't have good memories of the long bus rides to and from school. He remembered being alone for much of his childhood and adolescence. During his junior high years, some of his school buddies would come to his house because he would take them for a ride on his dad's John Deere tractor, or they would prowl in the woods at the rear of the property. They seemed less interested in tractor rides when they reached high school.

He moved back into this house a little over two years ago when he and Barbara separated, living with his mother as she faded into the nether world of Alzheimer's. He once again had that familiar feeling of isolation from the rest of the world. But, as an adult and an introvert by nature, he minded it less.

The mailbox at the road said Jone. A slick mark remained where an "s" once stuck to the black metal. Christopher thought the missing "s" was appropriate since there were once four people named Jones living here, then two, and now only one. Last year his mother moved to Abraham and Sarah's Place, an assisted living facility with a memory care unit.

An old Airstream camper sat behind the house with its shiny metal nose barely visible from the driveway. Christopher had not been inside the camper in more than a year. He suspected field mice had moved in and set up housekeeping.

He drove the Buick up the long driveway and parked in front of the red brick bungalow. The chain-link fence wrapped around the house, with a gate at the end of the walk within a few feet of the gravel drive. Gracie greeted each visitor at the gate with a fierce bark, but her wagging tail usually belied any seriousness as a watchdog.

Christopher got out of the car. "Hush, Gracie." He opened the gate, blocking the dog from scooting past his legs. He turned to the young woman as she opened the car door, eased out, and warily looked at the large yellow dog with floppy ears. She kept a hand on the door, ready to jump in the car if the dog lunged at her.

"She's harmless. And old." He looked down at the dog pushing against his leg, nose up and sniffing. "Gracie, this is Kim. Be nice." He grabbed her collar.

Kim's eyes were wide as her gaze moved from the dog to the house with the dark porch. She stood frozen. Christopher raised a placating hand.

"Look, I can tell you're scared. Do you want to wait in the car rather than come inside?"

Kim's eyes searched Christopher's face as if looking for signs of deception or malicious intent. She must have found some assurance because she slowly shut the car door and approached the gate. "I go in," she said.

Christopher was relieved that Kim had decided to come into the house. If she'd opted to wait in the car, it would have made it challenging for him to go inside and work for several hours. "Come on and get acquainted with Gracie. Let her sniff your fist, and she'll be fine. She won't bother you."

Kim held out her fist. "Is she... what kind of dog?" she asked.

"I think she's a Golden Retriever mix. Amy, my daughter, and I found her near here, beside the road, about two years ago. She looked old and malnourished. I think someone just dumped her there. We brought her home, and with a little vet attention and patience, she's better now. She's been a good dog."

After sniffing Kim's hand, Gracie turned and walked to the front porch, her tail wagging slowly. Christopher and Kim followed.

"Come on in," Christopher said. He unlocked the front door. "I bet you're hungry. Let me see what I have in the fridge."

As he said the words, he realized he had very little that might appeal to a young woman, especially an Asian woman.

He led the way through the living room to the kitchen behind it. As he flipped on the light, he looked around. Only a few crumbs from last night's deli sandwich were on the worn Formica countertop. He wiped up the crumbs, but there was not a whole lot he could do to spruce things up. It was an old kitchen with the original knotty pine paneling and cabinets.

On one wall hung a large clock with an imprint of the iconic face of Jesus. The slogan below the face said Make Time for Jesus. The other wall held two rows of plates from ten national parks, his mother's collection from family vacations. Christopher wondered if Kim knew any of the names: Yellowstone, Yosemite, Grand Canyon, Zion, and Arches.

The appliances were at least twenty years old, and the kitchen cabinets were the originals. His dad's favorite saying was, "If it's not broken, then why replace it?" Christopher tended to agree. Good lord, he was becoming his father.

"Would you like some coffee?" Christopher asked, looking over his shoulder at Kim as he washed his hands.

She stood in the doorway, appearing unsure about entering the kitchen. "You have tea?" she asked.

"I think so. My sister brings some with her when she visits from Louisville." He dug around in a cabinet and spied a small box that said, Earl Grey Tea. He pulled out a tea bag, held it up, and pointed at a tea kettle on the stove. "I'll heat water. How about toast and scrambled eggs?"

A few minutes later, Kim sat at the chrome kitchen table, sipping hot tea and eating small bites of egg and toast, carefully chewing as if to make the taste last. Christopher told her he would be back and ducked up the stairs to check the condition of the bathroom and his daughter's bedroom. Amy was supposed to stay with him every other weekend since the divorce, but it seemed many of those weekends were only short visits or missed altogether. Like most teenagers, she preferred hanging with her friends rather than spending time with her dad. Her growing disconnect and disinterest left him yearning for the little girl who gave him spontaneous hugs and enjoyed a good tickle. He still had a collection of her drawings, most of them signed, "I love you Daddy."

He returned to the kitchen. Kim sat silently at the table with an empty plate in front of her. "You look a little tired." She nodded slightly.

"Let me show you the bathroom and maybe a place to rest. We'll wait a few more hours before we head to the bus station. I'll check the afternoon departures to Atlanta."

Kim followed Christopher up the stairs. He pointed to the bathroom and then showed her Amy's room. After assuring her he would knock on the door when it was time to go, he hurried downstairs to the dining room and booted up his laptop.

Christopher started his home computer business three years ago after his information technology position with Hospital Corporation of America, a hospital management company headquartered in Nashville, was eliminated.

He provided computer support for small businesses and people who worked from home. Most of the work involved cleaning off malware and viruses, defragging, updating, and loading more memory or new software for clients who didn't have the know-how or patience to do it. Since he was willing to go to homes and small businesses, many calls were more instructive than actual repairs. He'd learned to be patient, especially with older customers who hadn't grown up using computers.

Occasionally, he brought the machines home when there was a total system crash or a stubborn problem. The dining room table was his workspace. There were three computers in various states of repair on the table now, along with two other systems of his own—an older HP desktop and a new MacBook Air laptop.

It was a business based on a few regular customers and word of mouth for adding new clients. Unfortunately, it didn't pay as much as he'd hoped. At first, he had more expenses than income at the end of most months. He struggled to pay child support and tried to negotiate with his ex-wife a temporary reduction until his business improved, but she refused, suggesting that he tap into the account he and his sister set up for his mother's care. His dad's life insurance and investments gave his mother a good nest egg. Christopher promised his sister that he'd make a monthly contribution to that account as his business grew, and he wasn't going to do anything that would abuse his sister's trust in his management of the account. He'd added the newspaper route almost two years ago to supplement his income. Juggling the two jobs required some organization, but his business was improving, and he was finally getting ahead financially. He'd considered giving up the paper route, but he liked the mindless routine, and it got him out of the house. He was a morning person, so the early hours were no problem.

Christopher studied the Greyhound website. Buses left for Atlanta every four hours. Perhaps the two o'clock departure would be best. By then, the man watching for her at the station would probably have given up. There was an overnight bus out of Atlanta for San Francisco with several connections. It looked to be a three-day trip if she rode buses all night. Christopher leaned back in his chair, stretched, and looked at the ceiling. The cost was around three hundred dollars for the whole trip, and she needed money for food, even if she slept on the bus or in the terminal. How much money did she have in the small silk purse? What about a photo ID? According to the website, she needed one to purchase a ticket.

He shook his head. These were not his problems. He had plenty of his own. He would get her to the bus station and make sure no one waited there to harm her. That's the best he could do.

CHAPTER FOUR

After she heard Christopher's footsteps going down the stairs, Kim checked the bedroom door to be sure she was not locked in. She peeked out in the hall, then shut the door and locked it from the inside. She sat on the edge of the single bed and looked around the room. There were photos in frames on the dresser. Most were snapshots of a teenage girl with friends. One picture showed the girl with a woman, probably her mother since they both had blue eyes, turned-up noses, and wide smiles. Another photo included the girl when she was younger, the woman, and the man downstairs. A large poster of *One Direction* was thumb tacked to the closet door. Kim recognized the English pop boy band from articles in the stack of old *People* magazines in the basement room where she'd lived the past two years.

The courage she had this morning was gone now, replaced by a sense of foreboding and fear. The Greyhound station seemed to be a dangerous place. She was afraid to return there, but what else could she do? This man downstairs—was he like the other men? Only interested in her body? Would he keep her a prisoner here in this house? Her feeling of desperation grew. It seemed like a long drive from the city to this place. If he harmed her or locked her up, no one would know. She narrowed her shoulders and shivered as her mind filled with fear.

She remembered reading a story in a magazine about a girl held captive by a man who kept her locked in a storage shed for years and forced her to be his sex slave. Kim couldn't imagine how the woman survived, living isolated and alone all that time. At least there were three other women at the house where she lived, including Sukee, her friend. Here, she had no one.

Her eyes welled with tears, and she curled up, hugging her knees. No, she told herself, no more crying. Be strong. She stood up and wiped her eyes. No, she would not be a captive ever again. Not without a fight.

She went to the dresser and began to open the drawers. She found only t-shirts, underwear, and jeans for a girl about her size. She moved to the bedside table, pulled open its one small drawer, and found a worn pocketknife with a yellow Post-it note rubber-banded around it. She unwrapped the note and read: *Amy, this pocketknife belonged to your grandfather. He would want you to have it. Love, Dad.*

Kim stuck the Post-it note back in the drawer. She opened the two-inch blade, propped her left foot on the bed, slid the open knife into the legging of her tights, and tapped her foot lightly on the floor to be sure it would not slide out. A look of determination came across her face. She would fight to the death rather than go through the enslavement and abuse she'd suffered the past four years. She reclined on the bed and leaned against the headboard, feeling a small sense of control over her future.

The knock on the door woke her. She sat up, alarmed at first. Last night she hadn't slept much, so she'd fallen into a deep sleep. The knock came again.

"Kim, there's a bus to Atlanta leaving in an hour and a half. You want to try for that one?"

She walked to the bedroom door, unlocked it, and cracked it open. "Okay."

Christopher peeked in. "Do you need anything?"

Kim shook her head. "I am okay."

"Come on downstairs when you're ready. It's about a thirty-minute drive."

CHAPTER FIVE

Christopher pulled into a parking lot a block from the bus depot an hour later. "We'll park here, out of sight," he said to Kim. "You can wait while I go check it out and see if someone appears to be looking for you." He left her hunkered down in the back seat as he walked to the Greyhound station. Hopefully, this would only take a couple of minutes to verify there was no need for her to be afraid. He could wish her safe travels and get back to his planned work for the day.

As he pushed through the front door, he spotted an Asian man in jeans and a tight t-shirt standing in a shadow against the far wall. He was older but with a trim physique. Was this one of the guys looking for Kim? Christopher ducked into a group of travelers milling around the middle of the station, not wanting to attract attention. He glanced at the man again, then strolled to the ticket window and studied the schedule on the electronic board, standing with his hands in his pockets, thinking about what he should do.

"Excuse me." Christopher leaned in the window. A thin, bald man with skin the color of coffee sat at the ticket counter, head down as he hunched over his newspaper. "If I want to buy a ticket to Atlanta, what sort of ID do I need?"

The man looked up over black-rimmed readers, a bored expression on his face. "Driver's license."

"What if I'm not a U.S. citizen?"

"Passport, visa, or a green card," the man replied.

Christopher nodded, jingling his change in his pocket. He couldn't leave her here, with the suspicious man in the shadows. He decided his only option was to return to the car and tell Kim the situation. He glanced once more at the far wall as he turned to leave. The Asian man stared back.

After Christopher reached the car and told Kim about the man, she shrunk further into the corner of the back seat.

"Don't be afraid," he said, trying to sound reassuring. "We'll come up with another plan. Let's go back to my house. You can stay there until we figure out our next move." Kim didn't answer him. She stayed huddled in the back seat and stared out the window.

As they headed toward Interstate 40 from downtown, Christopher decided he needed to know more about her situation if he was going to devote a large part of his day to helping her.

"Do you have a visa or a green card?" he asked as he looked in the rearview mirror.

"I have visa at house. The men keep it."

"I guess you don't have a passport or any other form of photo ID, right?"

She shook her head. "They have passport."

"That may pose a problem with buying a bus ticket."

He tried to think of a way around that dilemma. Would a Greyhound station in a smaller town require a photo ID? Since 9/11, probably every form of interstate transportation has tightened its policies.

Should he call the police and turn the problem over to them? If he did, it might complicate matters, and it would probably add a delay of several days to Kim's departure. Besides, she'd asked him not to do that.

Maybe he could help her get a temporary copy of her visa. Surely there was a system in place for people who lost them.

The only other solution he could think of was to go to the house where she lived and ask for her passport and visa. *Maybe they would be reasonable*, he thought. He could offer some money, maybe one hundred dollars. Worst case, they would refuse and question him about her location. He could park away from the house so the men wouldn't know Kim was with him. He would stay outside, not go in the house. If they were Asian, they probably wouldn't mess with him, an American citizen.

"Do you live near where I met you this morning?" Christopher asked as he studied her in the rearview mirror.

She nodded yes.

"What's the name of the street where you lived?" Christopher asked.

"Cedar."

"Cedar Street?"

She nodded.

Christopher knew Cedar Street. It was on his paper delivery route. "What's the house number?"

She shrugged and shook her head. "I do not know number, but I know house. It has red bricks, a brown door, four windows on front and four on back, and basement with no windows. I live in basement."

"If I take you to Cedar Street, can you point out the house where you lived?" He watched her face in the rearview mirror.

Her response was to stare at him, her eyes wide. He took the White Bridge Road exit off the interstate.

Christopher looked for a house that fit Kim's description as they drove slowly down Cedar Street. He saw a red brick house on the next block that seemed a possibility.

"Is this the house?" He pointed at it and watched her in the mirror as they drove slowly by. Kim peeked above the window in the rear seat, then quickly ducked down. She looked at Christopher and nodded slightly. Christopher pulled to the side of the road a half block away and turned to Kim in the rear seat.

"Do you think, if I tell them you are with me and ask them for your passport and visa, they might give them to me?"

She vigorously shook her head. "No!" Her eyes were wide,

brimming with tears. "They are bad men. They will hurt you. They will hurt me if they find me."

Christopher rubbed his chin and looked back at the house. "You're sure about not calling the police?" he asked. "Seems like they could demand these men give you your passport and visa."

"Police will ask me about the spa. Min-jun say we will be in jail for many days if police catch us. I must get far away. To San Francisco."

Christopher shifted the Buick into gear and drove away from the house. Her fear made him uneasy. Should he get involved at all? Could he be in danger? Probably not, if they didn't know she was staying with him. He drove slowly out of the residential neighborhood, unsure what to do next. His computer jobs needed his attention today, but this girl, Kim, needed his help. How could he help her get her passport and get on a bus to San Francisco? Was she prepared to travel for three days on a bus? Christopher thought again of his dad. He wished he was still alive. He always seemed to know the right thing to do. With a sigh, Christopher decided he did know the right thing to do: Get back to his house, get online, and find out how to replace her passport and visa. If they could do it tomorrow, then he would do what he could to help her get far away. It might eat up a lot of his day to help this girl, but for now, she seemed his responsibility.

CHAPTER SIX

Christopher parked in front of the Target store on White Bridge Road and told Kim he would only be a few minutes. He went inside and returned with a few items in a large Target bag.

"Here." He handed the bag to her. "You need more clothes than what you're wearing."

Kim opened the shopping bag and pulled out a pale blue t-shirt, a thin gray cotton sweater, and black stretch pants. There was also a small yellow canvas travel bag for carrying clothes.

"I pay for this. How much?" She held up her small silk purse.

"No, no." He waved her off. "I paid for it. You don't owe me anything. It wasn't much."

She stared at him, questioning, then nodded once. "Thank you."

Christopher started the car as he watched her in the mirror. "I would've bought you tennis shoes, but I didn't know your size. I think everything else is stretchy enough that a size small will work. That's what my daughter would wear. You seem close to her size."

They stopped at a Publix grocery store. Kim waited in the car while Christopher bought a roasted chicken, potato salad, and a pre-packaged Asian salad for dinner, along with milk, tea bags, and eggs for breakfast. Not long after they arrived home, they sat again at the kitchen table, eating dinner, this time a little more comfortable with each other.

He was curious to know more about this woman, now that he had spent most of the day with her, and it looked like she would spend the night in his house. "Why are those men looking for you?"

She stared at him, mouth half-open with chewed chicken, then looked away. She swallowed and still didn't reply. Christopher raised a placating hand. "I understand they want to harm you, and I don't want that to happen. I just want to know your situation. Were you married to one of the men?"

She shook her head. "I work for them. I make them money at Orchid Spa. I give massage, make men feel good." She pronounced massage as if it were three syllables, emphasizing the last, making a "J" sound.

"Did you live with them?" Christopher leaned forward on his elbows; his brow furrowed.

Kim set her fork down and twisted her hands together. "Yes. Girls live in basement of house on Cedar Street. Men live upstairs."

"There were other women who lived in the basement? How many?"

"Four," Kim said. She held up four fingers. "We live in one big room."

"You all lived in the basement?" Christopher asked. "Did it have a bathroom and furniture?"

"We have two mattresses, TV, CD player, table, four chairs. Suitcases for clothes. Bathroom and kitchen upstairs. Sometimes door locked, sometimes not."

Christopher thought about her description of her living space. It sounded like a barracks or a prison. "Why did you leave Korea and come to San Francisco?"

"For job. My family is poor. I the oldest. Three sisters and one brother. Too many girls. Mother, she sick." Kim's eyes became unfocused. She looked over his head as if she could see all the way to Korea and her former life.

"I want to go to university, but Father, he have no money to send me to university, only my brother. I sixteen, must work or get married." She glanced at Christopher, then looked away and continued her story.

"We live in small village, long way from Seoul. Father, he

look for someone to marry me. Old man in nearby village, he want to marry me. He can pay Father money that will help my brother go to university. Another man came to village, say he can get me job in America. I will make good money. I pay him back. I tell him yes. He pay my father."

Christopher stopped eating, laying his fork on his plate as he listened, concentrating on understanding every word she said in her accented English. "So, the man helped you get a job here in the United States?"

Kim nodded. "I leave with man to go to America. I do not know that job is at massage parlor until I get to San Francisco. I think it is at restaurant or maybe store."

"Did they tell you how much money you owed?"

She shook her head no, her hands folded in her lap.

"So, you don't know how much more you need to pay or if you've paid them back?"

Kim looked down at her plate, bowing her head as if in prayer. Then she looked up at him with pleading eyes and shook her head.

"They keep you working at the massage parlor for how many years?"

"Four year."

"How do you get paid?"

She raised and lowered one shoulder. "I make money, but Kwan and Min-jun say we must pay them for rent and food. We must make five hundred dollars each day for them. After we pay five hundred, we keep half of extra money, other half go to them."

Five hundred a day or more seems like a lot of money, Christopher thought. Yep, more going on at the spa than just a massage. "So, how much did you get to keep each week, on average?"

Kim flipped a hand. "Maybe one hundred. Sometimes more, sometimes less. Sometimes they take more than five hundred if customers not happy."

"Where do you keep the money that is yours?"

"In my purse. I keep purse with me all time, lock in my suitcase at night, so no one steal."

"Did you get to spend it? I mean, could you buy things you needed?"

"We go to Walmart on Sunday. Girls wait in car with Min-jun, one go in with Kwan. Then next girl go in with Kwan. We buy things we need."

"So, you decided to get away from these men. How did you know about the Greyhound bus station?"

She leaned forward and narrowed her eyes as she looked at Christopher. "I decide I will escape. I ask customer I see many times about bus to San Francisco. He check schedule and come back, tell me to ride city bus to Greyhound station. I can buy ticket to Atlanta. Then I can buy ticket to San Francisco. He tell me cost." She balled up her fist and softly pounded the table. "I make plan and save money. Last night I escape. I run to bus stop."

She paused for a minute, looked down, and then met his gaze. "I will not go back to spa, give massage, have sex with men. I rather die."

Her frank admission to having sex with customers confirmed Christopher's suspicions. He pushed back his chair and stood up. He went to the sink and stared out the window, hands in his back pockets. So, she was a prostitute. But not willingly, more a victim. This was sex trafficking. Something he only knew about through TV and online stories. He considered once again if he should call the police and let them handle it. Perhaps he needed to know more about her plans before he made that decision.

He turned and looked at her from across the room.

"Why do you want to go to San Francisco?"

"When I live there, old woman bring food to spa for us. She tell us many Koreans live in San Francisco. They have families, they work good jobs, make good money, help each other. Sometimes they help girls like me, she says. They help me find good job, go back to Korea if I want."

"But you have to get there first," Christopher said. "You are brave to do that on your own." He folded his arms and thought about her situation. She was a victim, but she had a plan to escape. If he called the police, would that start a process that would sidetrack her plan? Should he continue to help her get to San Francisco, since that was what she wanted? Maybe her most immediate need, besides food and shelter, was some form of ID. Either way, she needed that. He decided to access the Internet and learn how to replace a Korean passport or visa. Then he could decide if he could help her get her passport, or just turn it all over to the police.

"I'll do a little research on how to get you a replacement passport. Do you want to watch TV or rest a little, maybe take a shower?" he said.

"I go take shower."

Christopher watched Kim climb the stairs carrying the travel bag with the clothes he'd bought her. She had narrow hips and thighs, small breasts, more of a woman than Amy, though, at fourteen, Amy was developing those curves. Her young girl bras would probably fit Kim. She was twenty, six years older than Amy, but in his mind, they seemed close in age. They were both young, vulnerable girls. Except Kim had been a prostitute for the past four years. How had that experience warped her view of the world? Of men? He shook his head as he turned toward the dining room and his computer. He needed to get online and research how to help the young Korean.

▪ ▪ ▪

Kim closed her eyes and let the water wash over her as she luxuriated in the floral smell of the shampoo and the feel of the soap as she rubbed it over her body. Some of the fear she'd felt since her early morning escape slipped away, following the sudsy water down the drain.

The clothes purchased by the man named Christopher were nice, and she was glad to have clean pants and a new top. He was different from the men she met daily at the massage parlor. Her years of interacting with men at the spa gave her an intuition of the evil ones, the troubled ones, and the devious ones. Some made her scared, and others made her feel superior. They all used her, and she despised them all. Christopher, she didn't despise. He made her feel safe.

When she got out of the shower, she pulled on her new tights and t-shirt, but didn't slide the pocketknife in the elastic cuff. She took it to the bedside table, carefully wrapped the Post-it note around it, and placed it in the drawer. She selected a worn book from the stack on the desk, one written by Laura Ingalls Wilder, and settled on the bed to read.

CHAPTER SEVEN

Christopher booted up his laptop, got online, and Googled, "How to replace a lost Korean passport." After a few keystrokes, he found the information he needed and learned that replacing a passport or visa from South Korea was not easy. It required appearing in person at a Korean Consulate, and the closest office was in Memphis. Okay, there had to be a way to get Kim's passport from the guys at the house. Who could make that happen? Could the police? What if the men denied they had it? What if they had destroyed it?

As he pondered that problem, he reviewed her story about how she got to the U.S. in the first place. Did it ring true? He decided to research the spa business and any possible connection with South Korea.

Two hours later, Christopher leaned away from his computer, stretched, and placed his hands on the top of his head with his fingers interwoven. His mind spun with the stories he'd read about sex trafficking and South Korean women.

He'd learned that the connection between the United States and Korean women used as prostitutes dated back to the Korean War and the years following when American soldiers stationed in South Korea found prostitution services readily available. During the 1980s and 1990s, South Korea became a destination for sex tourists. Men from all over Asia, Australia, and the United States traveled and participated in the open sex trade and trafficking of Korean girls and young women.

Christopher read through several articles, quickly learning how entrepreneurs began exporting the business, especially as South Korea passed laws during the early 2000s criminalizing and stigmatizing the sex trade. The Republic of Korea, as it's officially known, was now a prosperous nation, particularly in the industrialized provinces. However, women were still coerced into the trade through debt and promises of jobs and opportunities. They were sold and traded, trafficked to Japan, Western Europe, the U.S., and even to Nashville.

Christopher paced the dining room. He thought about Amy, his daughter. She was just two years younger than the Korean woman upstairs had been when she was forced into the horror she'd endured for the past four years. Amy was expressing her independence in typical teenage girl fashion. Somehow, she'd acquired a small butterfly tattoo on her right shoulder blade, and last week Barbara complained they'd had a big argument when Amy declared she was getting her nose pierced. Christopher feared this was only the beginning of her rebelliousness, and he felt like a failure as a dad. He and Amy used to be close, but since the divorce, the chasm between them seemed to widen with each passing week. She seemed reluctant to talk at times, not opening up about her thoughts as she once did so easily. The young girl who used to hug him and say she loved him seemed oblivious to any loving touch from him. With all her school activities and friend get-togethers, she hardly spent any time at his house.

He wondered how much Amy knew about prostitution and sex trafficking. Dangers lurked out there, especially on the Internet. It was probably time to talk with her about it, but he felt inadequate to begin the conversation. Barbara, his ex-wife, never asked for his input, so he didn't know if she talked with Amy about internet perverts and their con games on young girls.

He shook his head. He obsessed over the past two years too much. Focus on the problem at hand. This Korean girl was twenty and knew what she wanted: her freedom. He tried to help, but her situation had become a bigger problem than he initially thought. He would figure something out tomorrow, get her help, and get back to his computer business. He had bills coming due.

Christopher glanced at his watch. It was nine PM, his usual bedtime. He needed a decent night's sleep before his four-thirty alarm, so, after taking Gracie outside for her last pee, he headed upstairs to his bedroom. Maybe after a good night's rest, he would better understand how to help Kim.

CHAPTER EIGHT

TUESDAY

The next morning, Christopher decided to call Metro Police, despite Kim's worries. He had mulled it over while delivering newspapers. A crime had been committed against this young woman, and he should report it because that's what a good citizen would do. And they might be able to recover her passport and visa from the Koreans. Now he sat at his kitchen table with his second cup of coffee and phone. He heard Kim stirring around upstairs as he dialed the emergency number on his phone.

"Nine one one, what's your emergency?"

"I'd like to report a sexual assault and kidnapping."

"Sir, who's been sexually assaulted and kidnapped?"

"A young woman. Her name is Kim. She's staying with me, but she told me she was held against her will and forced to have sex with men at a massage parlor."

"Is she in danger now? Is she injured?"

"No, she's safe. She wants to leave town, but she's afraid. She thinks some men are looking for her."

"Who are these men?"

"The men who held her hostage and forced her to work at the massage parlor."

"Sir, I'm going to have someone call you back. Where are you? What's the best number to reach you on?"

Christopher gave the operator his name, address, driver's license number, and cell phone number. Five minutes later, he received a phone call from a police officer who said he was on his way. After a few minutes, Gracie barked and ran to the front door. A knock followed.

"Gracie, park it." Christopher pointed at the dog bed as he walked to the door. Gracie reluctantly went to her bed.

Two uniformed officers stood at the door, one maybe in his early thirties and the other in his mid or late twenties. The younger officer hung back, his hand on his service revolver.

"Are you the person who called and reported a sexual assault and kidnapping?" the officer nearest the door asked, peering around Christopher to look in the living room. The name on his shirt was Jeffrey Hudson.

"Yes. You can come in if you like." Christopher pushed the door wider and stepped back.

The police officer asked for Christopher's driver's license. He reviewed the information on the license and then handed it back.

"Sir, are you alone?" the officer asked as he stepped in. The other one remained just outside the open door, his hand still on his weapon.

"There's a young woman upstairs getting dressed. She doesn't know I called you."

"Would you mind asking her to come down?"

"Not at all." Christopher stepped to the foot of the stairs and called, "Kim, can you come down here?"

Kim appeared at the top of the stairs and started down, abruptly stopping when she saw the officer standing behind Christopher.

"Don't worry, I called them. Come on down. I want you to talk to them."

Kim slowly descended the stairs, holding onto the handrail, eyes wide and her mouth pursed.

"Ma'am, are you okay?" Officer Hudson asked her.

She nodded.

"Are you here of your own free will?"

She didn't reply, still looking at the officer and back at Christopher.

"Kim, tell them you came here because I tried to help you," Christopher said, his voice soft and encouraging.

"Sir, I'll ask the questions if you don't mind." The officer stepped toward Kim. He extended his arm in front of Christopher as if to bar him from contact.

"He help me," Kim said. "I come here with him. He not hurt me." She folded her arms across her chest. Her voice, though soft, was firm.

Officer Hudson looked at her, his gaze shifting from her face to her neck and then her arms, as if looking for bruises or marks. He looked back at his partner and nodded. The second officer stepped in and shut the front door behind him but stood near the door, his feet apart and his hands resting on his equipment belt.

"Let's sit down," the cop said, pointing to the seating area in the living room. Christopher and Kim sat on the worn olive brocade sofa, and the officer sat in the leather La-Z-Boy chair facing them. He took out a pen and a small pad from his chest pocket.

"How about telling me how you met this woman?" He pointed the pen at Christopher.

The officer listened, taking a note occasionally, as Christopher explained how he and Kim met. Afterward, the officer asked Kim to state her full name. "Soon Yee Kim," she replied. Christopher realized he'd called her by her last name. She'd told him to call her Kim. Maybe it was a Korean thing.

"How long have you been in the United States?" Officer Hudson asked.

"Four year."

"Did you come here to work?"

Kim told the story of her journey from her small village in South Korea to the U.S. with hopes of a well-paying job.

"But the job was at a massage parlor, right?" Hudson asked.

"Yes. First San Francisco, one year, then San Diego, one year. San Francisco again. Then Nashville."

"Why did you come to Nashville from San Francisco?"

"In San Francisco, one night, police come, take us away, put us in jail. We get out next day. Two men take me and four more girls to a van. We ride in van two days to Atlanta. Stay there four days." She shifted in her seat and twisted her hands. "We ride in van to Nashville with different men. We meet Kwan and Min-jun in Nashville. They tell us we work for them at massage parlor. We live at house on Cedar Street two years, work at Orchid Spa every day but Sunday, and we have to earn much money." Kim stopped her story and waited with a resigned look, as if she expected to be arrested again.

"Do you have a visa or a green card?" the cop asked Kim.

She nodded yes. "Visa."

"May I see it?"

She shook her head. "I not have it. The men keep it at house."

"She needs to get her passport and visa back from those men," Christopher chimed in.

Officer Hudson thought for a moment, tapping his pen on the notebook. "Why were you arrested in San Francisco?" he asked.

Kim hesitated, looked at Christopher, then back at the officer. She said in a low voice, "They arrest us for prostitution."

The police officer studied Kim for a moment, then said, "Okay, you came over here to the U.S. voluntarily, and you came to Tennessee after you were arrested for prostitution in San Francisco, which probably means you failed to show up for your court date, and you've continued to work as a prostitute here. You admit to that."

Kim looked at Christopher, who stared back at the officer in disbelief.

"Look, this woman was kept against her will in a basement here in Nashville. She was *forced* into prostitution." Christopher tried to control his anger.

The officer shrugged. "I believe you. The problem is that to arrest and convict someone, we need evidence, not just her testimony. Those men will claim she's here of her own volition, and what she's doing is of her own free will to pay off her debt. They'll say she's supposed to give massages, not have sex with customers." He placed his pen and notebook back in his shirt pocket and stood up, still looking at Kim. Christopher stood, too, his body tense.

"Ma'am, there are shelters in Nashville for women who are escaping from situations like yours. Do you want me to contact them? If they have room, I could take you there."

Kim shook her head.

"You don't appear to be in any danger at this moment. I'm going to talk with one of the vice squad detectives. I'm sure they'll be interested in your story and will be in touch." He turned toward Christopher, then hooked his thumbs on his equipment belt as he chose his words carefully.

"Sir, it's my assessment that you are not holding this young woman here against her will. We have only her word that she's in the country legally, but that's enough for now. We aren't dropping this. We're deciding it's not an immediate emergency. Am I right about that?" He waited for Christopher to answer.

"She's safe here, for now, I guess."

"The vice squad handles prostitution. They'll take over from here."

Christopher could feel his face heat up. "What about the men who held her captive and have her passport? Can't you arrest them or go to that house and ask for her passport?"

"Vice squad will address that. A detective will be in touch shortly."

"I hope so. She needs help that I can't give." Christopher's voice was tense. "She wants to go to San Francisco, but she can't travel without some form of legal identification."

"I understand," the officer said with a nod. "It may be best to contact someone in immigration at Homeland Security as to how she gets another passport."

Christopher already knew it required more than that. He showed the two officers out, shut the door, and turned to Kim. Her eyes were wide as she stayed on the couch, her feet tucked under her thighs.

"That didn't turn out how I thought it would," Christopher said. He paced around the room, reviewing the conversation with the officer. Kim's prediction that she would be arrested if the police got involved had almost come true. Rather than see her as a victim of sexual slavery, they seemed more focused on her admission to prostitution. It could have resulted in her arrest. He rubbed the side of his face. Maybe the detective with the vice squad would see it differently and go after the Korean guys for sex trafficking rather than arrest Kim.

CHAPTER NINE

Christopher fried an egg for Kim and served it with toast and strawberry jam. While she ate, he washed the skillet and wiped the countertops as he thought about his next steps.

"I need to make a few calls. Do you like to watch TV?"

She nodded. "We have TV in back room at spa. We watch all day."

"What do you like to watch?"

"I like news so I can learn about America. Other girls like Doctor Phil, Kelly, Jerry. I hate Jerry. Everyone yell, cry." She placed her dishes in the sink, went to the living room, and turned on the TV.

Christopher located the number for the South Korean Consulate in Memphis and began the chase through their government bureaucracy to see what it would take to get Kim another passport to replace the one left at the house on Cedar Street.

While he was on the phone with the South Korean Consulate, he received a call that rolled into voice mail. After being handed off to three different people, he finally made an appointment with a Korean official in Memphis for Monday at eleven o'clock—six days away. That was the earliest appointment the harried bureaucrat had available, and he sounded as if he was doing Christopher a favor to schedule it that soon. He said if Kim had been issued a passport and visa, he could confirm fingerprints and probably issue replacement documents on the spot, but she had to be there in person.

Christopher hung up and thought about Kim's passport dilemma. If he had to, he could take Kim to Memphis next Monday and put her on a bus from Memphis to San Francisco that afternoon and get home by late evening. It would be a long day, but it could work. Of course, that meant she would probably stay with him until then, unless he found some place else. This was turning into a huge time suck. But he had to help her. It was who he was. It was how he was raised. He almost felt his dad looking over his shoulder, whispering, "*Son, always do the right thing, even if it costs you.*"

Christopher walked into the living room and explained to Kim what he'd learned, then checked his voicemail. The message on his cell phone was from a detective named Simpson. He dialed the number.

"Simpson." The man's voice was terse. After Christopher identified himself, the detective asked a few questions and said he would be there shortly.

An hour later, Kim and Christopher watched out the large picture window as three men in suits and ties stepped from a dark sedan, opened the gate, and walked to the front porch. Gracie barked and ran to the door but went to her dog bed when Christopher gave her the command.

The older man, who appeared to be around fifty, was thin with weathered skin and a cigarette voice. He introduced himself as Detective Simpson. Christopher thought the detective's wrinkled suit had likely not seen a dry cleaner in a while.

"That's Detective O'Reilly," Simpson said, pointing to a younger man, probably mid-thirties, strawberry-blond hair cut short.

"How are you, sir?" O'Reilly said, extending his hand. He wore a light gray suit, and a starched blue shirt.

"This is Assistant District Attorney Forbes," Simpson said, pointing to the youngest of the three, dressed in a black suit, white shirt, and polished wingtip shoes. Christopher invited them in, introduced Kim, and grabbed two kitchen chairs so everyone could sit.

Forbes, the Assistant DA, took charge. He opened his leather portfolio and removed a pen from his suit jacket. "Officer Hudson told us how you two met and how Kim got to Nashville, but we would like to hear it again." He pointed his pen at Christopher. "Let's start with you."

Christopher told his story, how he'd found Kim hiding while she waited for the city bus. He described the Asian man in the Greyhound bus station and driving by the house on Cedar Street, then ended with Kim's story as she told it to him last night.

"Have you ever been to the Orchid Spa?" O'Reilly asked him.

"No," Christopher replied. "I've never been to any spa or massage place."

"Kim, tell us in your own words about how you came to the United States and to Nashville," Forbes asked as all three men focused on her.

In halting English, she related her saga once again.

"Are the men who stay in the house the same ones that drove you from Atlanta to Nashville?" the youngest detective, O'Reilly, asked.

Kim shook her head no. At his request, she described the two men who were the usual residents at the house.

"One man, he comb his hair back, all shiny and stiff. His name is Min-jun. Other man, Kwan, he is strong." She made a fist and clenched her arm. "He have short hair and mean look."

"Have you seen other men from Korea at the house?"

Kim nodded yes.

"Can you describe them?" O'Reilly asked.

"Two men come by many times. They sometime stay overnight, drive us to other massage spas. One has scar here." She drew a line of about an inch on her jawbone. "Other man, he is short, have a round face."

"Did you meet any other Korean men?" O'Reilly asked again as he leaned forward.

She hesitated before continuing. "Another man come twice, late at night, but not stay. He is older, more old than you."

She pointed at Detective Simpson. "He stand real straight, like general. He have scar on lips, maybe from knife cut." She drew a line with her finger through both lips, on the right side of her face. "Other men call him Boseu. He is boss. I serve him tea but not look at him. He is scary."

"Do you think he is the boss?" O'Reilly asked.

Kim nodded.

"That's a good description, the knife scar on lips, erect posture. He's probably a former military officer," Forbes said, looking at O'Reilly and then Simpson.

"You went to other spas?" Forbes asked Kim, "Where were they?"

"They were long drive, maybe one hour, maybe two. One in Deekson, one in Cookesville, the men say."

"Dickson and Cookeville, like we thought," Forbes said, nodding at O'Reilly. He turned back to Kim and Christopher. "Okay, here's what happens next. Kim, based on your testimony, we can get warrants and raid this massage parlor in Green Hills and the house in West Meade. We can shut that massage parlor down and arrest everyone there for prostitution, but we need more evidence, or they will open again in another location with different girls. It's like a game of whack-a-mole." He shook his head.

Christopher understood what he was saying, but by her look of confusion, he knew Kim had no clue.

"O'Reilly and I are on a human trafficking task force," Forbes continued, "and we've worked on this for over a year." Forbes looked at O'Reilly as if seeking confirmation, then continued. "We're after the main man, the boss. We believe he lives somewhere nearby, and we hear he controls several massage parlors in Kentucky, Tennessee, and Georgia. That's the man we want to catch. He and his henchmen have moved into these areas by eliminating the competition with force. They're killers." Forbes slapped his palm on his knee for emphasis as he focused on Kim.

Kim curled her shoulders and wrapped her arms around herself, her eyes wide.

"We think he has other legit businesses, restaurants, one here in Nashville, maybe other cities," Forbes said. "He launders some of the money from the massage parlors through them."

Forbes rubbed his thighs. "We need to find him, and we need a witness connecting him to the massage parlors. Then we can get a warrant and raid his businesses. Hopefully, we'll get other witnesses and evidence of human trafficking. But he probably has a good lawyer and will be hard to catch and convict."

He pointed his finger at Kim. "Your testimony is the first big break we've had. We need you to be available over the next few days. We'll talk again soon."

"She needs her visa and passport," Christopher said. "If you raid the house, please look for her documents so she can get to San Francisco."

"Okay," said O'Reilly. "Do you need a place to stay? We can find you a safe house, maybe through one of the agencies in town."

Actually, that would be good, Christopher thought. He needed to focus on his business and generate some income. His child support was due in ten days.

Kim glanced at him, then shook her head and spoke in a soft voice to the detective.

"I stay here for now."

Christopher, surprised by her quick response, turned to her. "Kim, it could be several days before you leave. Maybe one of the women's shelters would be better. I have to work, and you'll be here by yourself during the day."

Kim's eyes searched his. Christopher saw her worry and uncertainty, so he held up a hand. "But if you want to stay here, I'm okay with it, at least until you decide you're ready to move someplace else."

"I stay here," she said again.

"Okay, but let us know if you move someplace else," O'Reilly said.

After a few more questions, the three men stood up, and the assistant DA thanked Kim for her information. Each officer handed out their business card, and O'Reilly underlined his cell phone number.

Christopher sat back down on the couch after they left. He processed the conversation and decided he'd done the right thing by calling 911. A solution for getting Kim's visa and passport seemed to be in the works, but Kim looked at him and said in a soft voice, "I do not want to testify about Boseu. He will find me and kill me. I want to leave here and go to San Francisco."

"I know," Christopher said. He felt an urge to give Kim a reassuring pat, but she was curled up in the far corner of the couch. He wondered what he'd gotten himself into. It was getting more complicated, and the detectives didn't seem that interested in helping her get to San Francisco. They mostly wanted her here in Nashville as a witness. If they found her passport, would they hold on to it to keep her from leaving? That would mean she was held against her will once more unless he could help her get a replacement. The appointment in Memphis next Monday might be the best way to get her a replacement passport and a bus ticket to San Francisco, but if he did that, would he be in trouble with the police?

He was no hero, but he felt a strong tug to help this troubled girl. He thought about Amy, his daughter, and, God forbid, if she were ever in desperate need of help, hopefully, someone would step up and come to her aid. He would pay it forward and continue to provide shelter for Kim. Worst case, till next Monday, six days away.

CHAPTER TEN

WEDNESDAY

Christopher returned from his newspaper delivery and sat with his coffee and the morning paper at the same yellow enamel and chrome table where he'd slurped up many bowls of cereal as a teenager. He jumped up when a scream came from the living room.

"Look!" Kim said, pointing at the TV as he ran in. The local news was on, and the video showed a man and three women walking into the Metro Police station, all handcuffed. Christopher grabbed the remote and rewound the newscast to the story's start.

"Late last night, police raided a massage parlor in Green Hills and arrested three women and one man on charges of prostitution," the news anchor said. The picture flashed to a strip mall in Green Hills, narrowing in on the glass door of a storefront. The painted sign read The Orchid Spa.

The news anchor said that later the police served a search warrant on a house in the West Meade suburb of Nashville. According to the report, the detained women and the man lived in the house. The shot panned to a red brick rancher; the same one he'd driven by yesterday with Kim. A brief clip followed of the Metro Police Public Affairs Manager as he read a statement that said the raids were based on new information, part of an ongoing investigation into illegal activity connected with this massage parlor and possibly others.

Christopher rewound the news story again, freezing it at a

close-up shot of the women and the man under arrest.

"Do you know these people?" he asked.

"Yes, they live in house with me." Kim hopped off the couch and moved closer to the TV. "That man's name is Min-jun." The short, stocky man wore his hair slicked back in a shiny pompadour.

"That girl," she said, pointing at one of the women, "her name is June." She pointed at the next woman. "That girl is Ji-hu, and that one is Sukee. She is my friend." Kim stared at the still picture of the four individuals frozen on the screen. The man had a sneer on his face as he leaned forward with his hands cuffed behind him, escorted by a police officer on each arm. The women, their faces down, hands cuffed, huddled together as if clinging to each other.

Christopher watched Kim. She was horrified at first, then her eyes filled with tears. "What will happen?" she asked.

"I'll call Detective O'Reilly and find out," Christopher told her, trying to sound reassuring. He left a message, and within a few minutes O'Reilly returned his call.

"We didn't find any evidence of captivity at the house," he said, "and we didn't find any passports. It was clear the women were sleeping in the basement, but they told us they could go up to the kitchen and the bathroom when needed. The door could be locked from either side, but one of the girls had a key, so we can't prove they were locked in the basement." He paused, then added, "We depend on Kim's testimony if we go after human trafficking charges unless one of these girls will tell us something different."

"What happens next?" Christopher asked.

"They'll probably all get out on bail sometime late this afternoon or evening. They have a good lawyer, and he's already working on it. Bail is only fifty thousand, and that's no big deal to these guys."

Christopher thanked him for his call, hung up, and relayed the information to Kim.

She sat silently, then asked, "Can I go see Sukee?"

"I'll call O'Reilly back and find out."

O'Reilly's phone went to voice mail. Christopher left a message for him to call back. He waited thirty minutes, then tried Detective Simpson's cell phone.

"Simpson." It was the same terse voice from the day before.

Christopher explained the request. There was a brief silence.

"I'll make it happen. Come on down. Tell the front desk officer to page me."

▪ ▪ ▪

An hour later, Christopher sat at a table next to Kim as she talked in Korean to a young Asian woman. They were in a twelve-by-twelve room in the Criminal Justice Center. A uniformed female correctional officer leaned against the doorframe with her arms crossed. Detective Simpson stood outside a large plate-glass window. He'd told them they had thirty minutes and warned them not to touch the woman and to always keep their hands on the table.

Movement outside the window caught Christopher's eye. He saw O'Reilly walk up and start what appeared to be a heated discussion with Simpson. Christopher couldn't hear the conversation but could tell by the gesturing and body posture that O'Reilly was not happy. He stormed away, and Simpson turned back to the window, his expression unchanged.

Kim and Sukee talked until the correctional officer in the doorway said their time was up. Christopher didn't understand the conversation, but he could tell they were close friends. Twice they reached across to grasp hands, and the correctional officer had to warn them not to touch. He considered their working conditions, their life in the basement for the past two years, the isolation from society. Their friendship must have developed out of that desperate need for someone they could trust, someone to confide in.

"O'Reilly looked mad," Christopher said to Simpson as they walked down the hall from the room after the guard led Sukee away to her cell. He looked over his shoulder at Kim, but her head was down as she followed them to the front of the jail facility.

Simpson glanced over at him, his eyes hooded. "Yeah, he felt like he should've been the one to set up this meeting. I told him you tried him first."

"Why?"

"I think he would've preferred to coach Kim a little, maybe tell her to get Sukee to give corroborating testimony about being held against her will. Also, to find out if she had any more information on the big boss."

Kim was quiet as they drove away from the Criminal Justice Center. Rush hour traffic kept Christopher focused until they got to the interstate and headed west. He glanced at Kim, waiting to see if she would share some of her conversation with Sukee. She finally spoke up as they exited onto Ashland City Highway.

"Sukee wants to go to San Francisco with me. She says they get out of jail tonight, go back to house. She want to run away tomorrow. You get her, bring her to your house, okay?"

Christopher glanced at Kim, then back at the road. "She's going to run away from the house where you lived in the basement?"

"Yes."

"She wants to do like you did, early in the morning before dawn?"

"Yes. Ji-hu has key to basement door. Kwan and Min-jun trust her—she has been with them long time. She dropped key when police came, and Sukee picked it up. The men do not know. She says tomorrow she has to move to another city, maybe Deekson, and live at spa. She must run early tomorrow. She will leave, run to next street and hide, wait till she sees your car. She will jump out to street and get in car."

"I don't know, Kim, it sounds risky." Christopher slowed down as he thought about it, looking for ways the plan could go sideways. But, if all he was doing was driving the same streets as his newspaper route, and if he saw the young Korean woman, offering a ride was probably low risk.

"I guess it could work," he said, "but why doesn't she tell the police she wants to go to San Francisco? If she tells them she's being held against her will, they will help her, probably get her to a safe place now."

"She say to not trust police. Somebody at police tell Boseu. He know everything police know."

Christopher's head snapped around, and he slowed almost to a stop on the empty road as he looked at Kim. "She said some person at the police station knows this boss guy and is telling him everything? There's an informant?"

Kim nodded. "Kwan come talk to them in jail. Boseu is mad because he did not know about the raid, but he know everything now. Kwan tell Sukee and other girls if they say wrong thing, Boseu will know, and they will die."

CHAPTER ELEVEN

The detective sat in his car in the parking garage two blocks from the Criminal Justice Center, cell phone pressed to his ear. It was in the evening, and his dark sedan was parked away from the few remaining cars in the garage.

"You should have told me about the raid," the raspy voice said.

"I didn't have a chance. I was with other detectives and cops almost every minute from the time the raid was planned yesterday afternoon until we pulled it off last night," the detective explained, his words tumbling out. He wiped sweat from his forehead. "Besides, only a few of us knew up until the hour before. If it looked like you were tipped, we would all be under suspicion." He clutched the phone tightly as he looked around again to be sure no one was watching him.

There was silence on the other end, then a response. "Still not acceptable. If you had told me, we could have discussed how to make it appear we didn't know."

"I'm telling you it was too risky for me to make a call. If someone had seen me, they might've asked who I was talking to. If my lieutenant got suspicious, he might try to trace my calls."

"No one can trace this phone to me," the raspy voice said.

"Listen, you have bigger problems than the raid. Kim, the girl that ran away? She's talking. She's described you and placed you at the house with the others. That's what you need to worry about. But I know where she's staying and how you can get her."

There was silence on the other end of the line, then the

raspy voice said, "We will get Min-jun and girls from jail tonight. You come over tomorrow. We will talk about Kim."

"I'll be there after I get off work." The detective waited for a response but only heard a click. He flung the burner cell phone against the passenger side window and watched it bounce onto the floor. He pounded his fist against the steering wheel. How could he get out of this bind he was in? The toll for his indiscretions last year seemed to increase with each passing month.

Visiting the spa in Dickson was stupid. Going back again even more foolish. Somehow, they'd learned he was a detective in the Metro Nashville Police Department. The envelope with his name on it showed up in his mailbox a few days after his second visit. There were two photos of him going in the front door of the spa, and two more of him inside, sitting on a massage table in a small room, naked, smiling at a woman in a kimono with her hand on his groin. There was a phone number attached to the photos.

He'd called the number and was instructed to go to the empty lot behind the Bank of America on Church Street and park next to a black sedan. And to not come armed.

This was probably a shakedown by the spa owner, he'd figured, but that guy had no idea who he was dealing with. After all, he had many years as a street cop and now four years as a detective. He'd dealt with plenty of rough guys who thought they could intimidate him.

He took a small recorder and a plan to turn the tables and threaten to bring the weight of law enforcement against whoever this was. After all, blackmail was a felony.

It didn't go as planned.

The driver, an Asian man, climbed out of the black sedan and motioned for him to get out. Without saying a word, the man did a quick pat-down and found the recorder. His smile was unfriendly as he pulled the small instrument from the detective's inside jacket pocket and tossed it in the driver's seat. He opened the back door and pointed in. As the detective climbed into the car, he felt the driver's gun shoved into his back. He hunched his shoulders, fearing a bullet to follow.

The man in the back seat was Asian, with wrinkled, leathery skin and slits for eyes, but clearly the boss. The old man only glanced at him before placing a cell phone box on the seat.

"You will carry this phone at all times," he said softly, his voice raspy as if from years of smoking. "I will call from time to time. You will call me if you know anything that could affect my spa business. If you give me good information, I will pay you. You can continue to visit the spa in Dickson, no charge."

The detective didn't try to intimidate the man. He could tell it wouldn't fly.

"I need to think this through," the detective said as he tried to buy some time. Perhaps he could negotiate better terms.

The Asian man gave him a stare. "There is nothing to think about. You do this, or you will die." There was no bluster in the statement. The tone was matter-of-fact, with no room for any other interpretation.

The detective's face paled. He turned and reached for the door but froze as the man in the driver's seat looked at him in the rearview mirror, then held up a pistol. These men were not the usual thieves, drug peddlers, and pimps he routinely faced. Without a doubt, they knew where he lived and his role in the Metro Police Vice Squad. It was a deal with the devil, but he instinctively knew these men had killed before, and they would kill again without hesitation. He reached across the car seat and took the phone from the older man he now called Boseu.

CHAPTER TWELVE

After he ended the call with the detective, the man called Boseu rose from his desk and strolled to the large window in his office. He stared across the columned front porch, enjoying the view of the well-landscaped lawn across the back of his two-story southern-style mansion in Brentwood, a wealthy suburb south of Nashville. He allowed himself a little reflection on his rise from a pig farm in rural South Korea, where he was born as Cho Lee. It was a long journey, but, by any measure, a successful one, rising from a poverty-stricken boyhood to become a wealthy businessman in America.

His mother urged him to escape the near subsistence life on their farm by joining the army. He enlisted at age seventeen. Thankfully, it was a few years after the Korean Armistice Agreement was signed. He escaped the near wholesale slaughter of Korean boys and men on the front lines in the closing years of the "police action," as Truman called it.

The leaders of what became North and South Korea didn't declare an end to their war, so periodic skirmishes and incursions continued. There were opportunities for adventure and promotions for brave young men.

He'd quickly become involved in secret missions into the North Korean side of the DMZ. His superiors recognized his cunning and bravery. He did not shy away from torturing and executing captured North Korean soldiers to obtain intelligence. As he once explained to a fellow soldier, killing pigs was excellent training for killing any North Korean soldier, which he didn't value as highly as a good pig.

By his late twenties, it was clear to him that the senior

army officers were the de facto rulers of South Korea. Most had accumulated wealth through selling goods and services to the American soldiers based in South Korea. One of those services was prostitution. They eventually moved their businesses, including prostitution, into Japan and the rest of Asia.

A senior Korean officer made him the enforcer for his prostitution ring, and he began to study the business of trafficking young Korean women to other countries, and decided the U.S. was his future. He worked on his English skills. After he finished twenty years in the Korean army, he resigned his commission, quit helping others make their fortunes, and set out to make his own. He moved to the United States.

He'd spent two years as an enforcer with a former Korean officer colleague based in Los Angeles who controlled the Asian spa business in southern California. He learned where the opportunities were in the United States and soon focused on the Southeast. There were only a few Asian spas in those states, controlled by local Korean or Chinese families. There was no regional player with enforcers that could prevent him from moving in.

He located to Atlanta, taking two former soldiers with him—men with strong-arm skills he knew from his time in the Korean army. Within a year, he'd taken over two Asian spas in Atlanta by "encouraging" a local Korean family to get out of the business. Within five years, he added spas in Georgia, Tennessee, and Kentucky. He became known throughout the Korean communities in those states as someone you did not want to cross. If you did, you would disappear.

By the early 2000s, other Korean organizations had moved into the rest of the eastern U.S. Through careful negotiations, they established territories and worked together to set up a pipeline that supplied young Korean women to the spas. They were all making fortunes.

He turned away from his window and returned to his desk. There were still occasional business setbacks and challenges, but he knew how to deal with them: aggressively and decisively. This current problem with the raid on his spa would be resolved within a day or two. Money took care of all problems here in America, just like in Korea. And when he located the runaway girl, Kwan and Min-jun would eliminate that problem too, with no hesitation.

CHAPTER THIRTEEN

THURSDAY

The young woman crouched behind a large boxwood near a driveway, a few feet from the edge of the street. Though early morning, it was still dark.

She tensed as she saw headlights slowly approaching. It was a large car, just like Kim had described, and a wave of relief flooded over her. She stood up and moved around in front of the shrub, stepping near the street's edge as the car approached.

The engine roared, and the black sedan accelerated. Before the woman could jump back to safety, the front of the car hit her, throwing her over the hood. She bounced off the windshield, cartwheeled over the vehicle's top, and landed in a ditch. Her head bounced off the hard ground. The sedan slid to a stop. A man jumped out of the passenger side and ran to the woman. He looked at her for a moment, then stomped on her neck. There was a crunch of bone.

The car reversed, stopping next to the man. The driver hurried to the rear of the sedan as the trunk lid slowly rose. The two men picked up the limp body and dropped it on a tarp in the trunk. They got back in the car and drove slowly down the street. There was no movement in the windows of silent houses. No curtains pulled back. No porch lights flashed on. No one bore witness to the sudden end of the young woman's life.

■ ■ ■

Christopher parked the Buick in front of his house and stepped through the gate. The sun was below the eastern horizon but close enough to brighten the morning sky. Gracie waited still as a statue on the front porch.

She always followed him out each morning when he left before five, squatting in the grass and doing her business, then settling on the porch when he drove off, waiting for his return. This morning, he must have had some nervous energy because she leaned into his leg as he patted her goodbye on the top step.

She sat on the porch now, mouth open and tail thumping. Her arthritis made climbing the steps difficult, so she rarely greeted him at the gate. The vet said her mobility was progressively worsening, and her kidneys showed signs of failure. Probably within a few months, he would have a hard choice to make. Christopher dreaded that decision.

"Hi, Gracie. I'm glad to see you, too." Christopher leaned over and scratched behind her ears, getting a faster thump of the tail. "Yeah, it's time for breakfast. Let's go in and talk to Kim. She's going to be sad."

Kim was sitting on the couch, feet tucked under her. She looked at him, then tightened her lips and lowered her head. She didn't say anything.

"I'm sorry. Sukee didn't show up," Christopher said, standing inside the front door. "I drove down every street twice but didn't see her. I guess she couldn't get out."

Kim nodded, then looked out the front picture window. Christopher went to the couch and sat near her. His feeling of relief over not having the extra responsibility of another Korean woman for a few days vanished as he watched sadness and grief wash across Kim's face. He knew she was worried about Sukee, afraid that she wouldn't have another chance to leave before the men moved her to a new town and a new massage parlor, trapped with no resources to help her and no clear path to escape. Christopher reached over, placed his hand on Kim's shoulder and gently patted her. Her body sagged a little. He slid over and put his arm around her shoulders, allowing her to lean into him as tears flowed down her face. Gracie came over and placed her chin in Kim's lap.

▪ ▪ ▪

The man spoke in Korean as he talked into the phone. "We took care of the runaway, Boseu. No one will find that maechunbu."

"Good," the raspy voice responded. "Tonight, we will find out where the other girl is, and we will make her disappear."

CHAPTER FOURTEEN

Christopher spent the rest of Thursday morning returning customer calls and lining up a few appointments for computer analysis. He'd missed one deadline to return a repaired computer because of the events over the last three days. He needed to refocus on his business. His customers were few, and their references and good ratings were essential to his business growth.

Kim stayed in the living room watching TV, mostly CNN, but occasionally she flipped to the nature channel.

When Christopher took a break to go to the bathroom, he found tights, thong underwear, and the blue t-shirt he'd bought her, all wet and hanging over the shower rod. Maybe he should have offered to put them in the washing machine. Should he put them in the dryer? He decided she'd already taken care of her needs.

"I know Yellowstone Park, Yosemite Park, Grand Canyon. Where is Zion Park, Arches Park?" Kim asked Christopher as they sat at the kitchen table, eating lunch. He'd fixed sandwiches from leftover chicken. She'd made a broth from the chicken carcass, then added onions, carrots, and a potato she'd found in the pantry. The aroma of chicken soup filled the kitchen.

Christopher followed her gaze and looked over his shoulder at the souvenir plates on the kitchen wall. "Zion and Arches are national parks in Utah," he said.

"America has nice parks, pretty scenery. I see many pictures in magazines, read about them. Someday I want to go to Utah, visit the parks." She slurped soup with a large spoon.

"My parents visited those parks, but I have not. You see the camper in the back yard?"

Christopher pointed out the kitchen window. "After my dad retired, they traveled to national parks every summer, on the road for several weeks, pulling that camper behind their pickup truck. They had a sign hanging in the rear window of the Airstream that said: *Martha and Bud Jones, Living the Dream.* They'd camped in ten national parks before my dad died."

Looking at the camper, Christopher remembered that September day, four years ago, when he helped his parents unpack from their last trip. His dad complained to him, not of chest pains, but about how his mother couldn't remember anything, couldn't read a map, and no longer helped with the driving.

The heart attack came in late October while he was raking leaves. By the time Christopher arrived at the hospital, the old man was not conscious, struggling to breathe on a respirator. Two days later, he died. It was a shock to Christopher. His dad had seemed to be in good health, only seventy and just four years into enjoying his retirement.

"Sometimes I feel like Dad is still here, in this house," he told Kim. "Like he's in this room. I'll turn around quickly and expect to see the old man sitting at the table with a bemused expression in his eyes, behind smudged horn-rim glasses."

Christopher paused and looked out the window. "I miss him. He was a good man, always helping others."

"You just like him," Kim said.

"Thank you for saying that, but I have a long way to go to be as good," Christopher responded. Kim dipped a piece of bread in her soup and looked at him thoughtfully. "Is your mother still alive?"

"Yes, but she's not well."

"She is in hospital?"

"She has Alzheimer's disease. You know what that is?"

Kim looked up at the ceiling, thinking for a moment before answering. "She has forgotten everything."

Christopher nodded. "Most everything. It's a gradual loss."

He told her how his mom had seemed not to comprehend how sick his dad was when he had his heart attack. The events of that time came flooding back as he talked. As his mother continued to decline, he'd decided to take six weeks off from work under the Family and Medical Leave Act. They seemed to handle his absence well at work, maybe too well.

Christopher shook his head as he refocused on Kim and came back to the present. "About six months after my dad died, she started wandering out of the house. One day, on my way to see her, I found her walking down the middle of the highway, cars swerving to avoid her. She told me she was looking for Bud, my dad. I finally moved her to Abraham and Sarah's House, a nursing home for people with that disease. I see her every week, but now she thinks I'm her husband. She calls me Bud."

"You are good son," Kim said. She sat motionless across the table, her hands in front as if praying. Christopher continued spilling out the events of the past four years.

Human Resources at his job told him he was RIFFED, a Reduction in Force, one person among hundreds let go due to lower profits. Barbara blamed the loss of his job on his unwillingness to deal with his mother's illness. She said he should've found a memory care place for her sooner and sold her house to pay for it. Their marriage already had problems, so his job loss was the final straw. They officially separated as the second anniversary of his dad's death approached and were divorced six months later.

He moved into his parents' house. At first, he slept in his old bedroom in a twin bed, with boxes of his clothes stacked against the wall. After a few weeks, he faced the reality that this living arrangement was long-term. He cleaned out his dad's closet and bureau and took everything to Goodwill. He unpacked his clothes from boxes and moved in. Not ready to deal with his mom's possessions, he cleared off the top of her dresser, stuffing her mirror, hairbrush, and makeup in the drawers. Her robe was on an upholstered chair as if she was only gone temporarily.

Christopher stopped talking. He realized he'd told Kim more about himself in fifteen minutes than he'd told anyone else in the past two years.

Kim came to his side of the table and patted his shoulder. She collected his plate, picked up the tea kettle from the stove, and moved to the kitchen sink. As the water ran, she looked out the window, standing still. Christopher watched her glide across the kitchen, realizing she was wearing one of Amy's t-shirts, a black one with VANDY printed in gold letters.

Kim turned off the water, then focused on a small one-foot-high plaster statue of Michelangelo's *David* on the windowsill. She raised her hand and tentatively lifted a small piece of cloth, slightly larger than a postage stamp, attached to the statue over David's groin.

"My mother did that," Christopher said.

"Michelangelo, he famous in Korea. We study his paintings and statues in school. We study famous sculptors and painters from Europe. Renoir, Degas, Picasso." She rattled off the names and pronounced them correctly. "Van Gogh, he is my favorite painter."

It dawned on Christopher that Kim was educated and perhaps more sophisticated about the world than he'd thought. Her broken English masked a sharp, inquisitive mind.

"Sounds like you learned a lot about other cultures in school."

Kim set the kettle on the stove and turned to look at him. "Korean schools are good. We learn science, history, arts, technology. Koreans believe their schools are better than American schools. We learn about China, U.S., European countries. American students only know about U.S., not much about

China, nothing about Korea. Korean teenagers learn English. American teenagers only speak English."

"How many years did you go to school?"

She looked up at the ceiling as she counted in her head, translating the number into English. "Eleven."

"Were there still more grades, or years, in Korean schools, or did you finish?"

"One more grade if you need, then college. School is hard in Korea. If you want to go to college, you must study. I study many hours each night. I was top student, made good grades. I stop school after eleven years. I want to go to college, but my father, he say no."

She shook her head and turned back to stare at the statue.

"My mother bought that statue of David in Florence, Italy. She and Dad went there on their twenty-fifth wedding anniversary," Christopher said. "Since then, she must've looked at that statue every morning for twenty-two years."

"But she no like to see his deek," Kim said, pointing to the makeshift loincloth draping the front of the statue.

Christopher laughed. "I guess not. It messed with her mind in some way. Or maybe she covered it up when her ladies' group from the Mount Zion Baptist Church came over. She only glued the top of the cloth, though. Maybe that allowed her to peek if she wanted to." He wasn't sure if Kim followed everything he said, but she turned around and smiled at him as if she did.

After she poured hot water over her tea bag, Kim sat across the table, leaning on one elbow as she stirred her tea. She looked up at him.

"You know how to go to Deekson?"

"Yes, I know how to get to Dickson."

"You must go there and find Golden Sun Spa. It is near interstate. You go in and ask for Sukee?" Her forehead was wrinkled, her eyes pleading. "I must help her get away."

"I don't know about that, Kim. Who is at the spa? You

think Sukee might be there, but would one of the Korean men be there too? I'm not sure I want to mess with them."

Kim shook her head. "They don't stay there. Just old lady and three girls. The men come by, stay for few hours at most. You can look for red van. If it's there, you leave, maybe come back later."

Christopher turned it over in his mind, weighing the danger against Kim's desperate plea. He felt himself getting drawn into her need to find her friend. It was probably a long shot, but why not try?

"I guess I could go there. Do you want to go with me or stay here?" he asked.

"I stay here in case Kwan or Min-jun are there. There is a camera outside of front door. It hangs down." She held her hand up, her fingers circled. "Looks like light. Sometime the old lady sits in back room, watch screen to see who come to door. Sometime she go out, check car when customer inside the spa."

"Are there cameras inside?"

Kim shook her head. "Not in rooms. It would make customers not stay. There is big teddy bear with camera in mouth." She held her hand three feet from the floor to show how large it was. "Sometime they put the bear in room with customer, take pictures. They turn music up, snap pictures from back room with remote button. You watch for teddy bear. Tell girl to take it out of room. You can do that," she said, nodding at him.

"Okay, if I find Golden Sun Spa and I go in and ask for Sukee, what do I do next?"

"If she is there, you tell her I am here with you and ask if she wants to leave with you. She probably say yes. Old lady and three girls live in back of house. Old lady answers doorbell, but she not move fast, she not drive. She walk to store every day. If red van is not there, Kwan or Min-jun are not there. Sukee can run out the door, get in car with you, come here, go to Memphis Monday for passport. We both go to San Francisco."

Christopher rubbed his chin and thought about her proposal. This could be more complicated than driving familiar streets in the early morning darkness and looking for Kim's friend. Or it might go down pretty easy. It sounded safe enough, as long as the minivan wasn't there. He looked at Kim, shrugged, and nodded. "I'll give it a try."

"Good." Kim clapped her hands together.

"But if the red van is there, or it feels unsafe, I may head for the door."

Kim's smile faltered. Christopher felt a momentary twinge of guilt for sounding cowardly.

CHAPTER FIFTEEN

As he drove west on Interstate 40 an hour later, Christopher reviewed Kim's description of the Golden Sun Spa. It was in a small white house behind the big truck stop near the interstate. He knew the truck stop at that exit, visible from the interstate. The red neon open sign at the house would be on since the spa was only closed from two AM till ten AM. Truck drivers and travelers visited more frequently at night. Three or four girls lived there, she said. They worked ten-hour shifts or more. There were mattresses in a room in the back of the house, and one or two usually slept.

The older woman answered the door, Kim told him. A man who worked for Boseu came by daily but rarely stayed for more than an hour or two. He remained in a small room in the back and never answered the door. One of the girls would always answer if the old woman had walked to the store.

Kim told Christopher to say he wanted to stay a half-hour and pay sixty dollars. When he and the girl were in the room, he could whisper and tell her to get Sukee. Sometimes the old woman would listen at the door, but she wouldn't hear anything if he whispered.

After he found the small white house with the open sign and parked, Christopher took sixty dollars from his wallet. He locked the wallet and his cell phone in the glove box and looked around before getting out of his car. The paved area between the truck stop and the house was at least a hundred yards wide, with a few cars parked near the truck stop. He noticed a white panel van parked maybe fifty yards away, but no maroon minivan. A fence prevented vehicles from driving around to the back of the house. His car was the only one in the front. He sat for a few minutes, considering if he wanted to go through with this, then decided he'd come this far, so what the hell. He'd never been inside a massage parlor, but it wasn't illegal to get a massage. That was why he was there, so what was wrong with paying for a rubdown? He hurried to the front door, rang the doorbell, and pushed in when the door lock release buzzed.

The waiting room had a linoleum floor and four plastic chairs. A gaunt woman with Asian features and gray hair pulled back in a bun stood behind a small window in a wall a few feet inside the door.

"You want massage?" she asked.

"Yeah, I guess so," Christopher said.

"One hour, eighty dollar."

"I only have sixty." He held up three twenties.

"Eighty dollar."

He shook his head, staying on sixty as Kim had told him.

The woman finally took the three twenties.

"Thirty minutes," she said in a snappy voice. She disappeared from the window and opened a door nearby. She grabbed his arm and pulled him down a hall to a small room. A massage table covered with a sheet took up half the room. A straight-backed chair in the corner and a small table were the only other pieces of furniture. A boom box on the floor played soft music that sounded Eastern. Two tall bottles of lotion and a box of Kleenex were on the table.

"Take off all clothes," the old lady said. She turned and walked out, shutting the door behind her. Christopher leaned against the massage table, unsure if he wanted to get undressed. He finally removed his shoes, pants, and shirt and kept his socks and boxers on. He laid his clothes on the chair and sat on the massage table. What was he doing here? He realized his fingers were nervously tapping the table. A few minutes passed before a young Asian woman wearing a pink kimono and lacy underwear came in. She smiled at him.

"Hi. My name Jade. You want table shower?" Her voice was pitched high.

"No," Christopher said.

"Okay. You no want to take off underwear and socks?"

"No, I think I'll leave them on."

Her smile faltered. "Okay. You lay down on your tummy."

He motioned for her to stand beside him. She hesitated, then eased over close. Christopher touched her shoulder and leaned in to whisper in her ear.

"I'm a friend of Kim's. You know Kim?"

The young woman tilted her head back as she looked up at him, her eyes big.

"You know who Kim is?" Christopher asked again.

She nodded.

"She's staying with me. I'm trying to help her get to San Francisco. Her friend is Sukee. You know Sukee?"

A frightened look came into the girl's eyes. She nodded.

"Is she here?"

She shook her head.

"Do you know where she is?" Christopher whispered near the young woman's forehead. She shook her head no again.

"Do you know how I can find her?"

The girl motioned for him to lie down on the massage table. "You get on tummy." Christopher looked at the table and back at her. She nodded at him several times, pointing to the table. He reluctantly stretched out on his stomach. She poured lotion into her hands and rubbed it on his back. After a couple of minutes, she leaned in and whispered.

"Two girls from house in Nashville come here this morning. They in back. They say Sukee ran away today while still dark. Kwan and Min-jun go out in big car, look for her. They came back soon. Girls hear them talk to someone on phone and say they found her. They leave in car later. Girls not see Sukee. The men come back. They say Sukee went to Atlanta.

Everyone scared. The two girls from house say they probably go to Atlanta tomorrow or next day."

The girl insisted that he stay the full thirty minutes. Christopher didn't mind. The back rub felt good, and her hands were warm. She massaged his legs and shoulders, rubbing in the lotion.

"You roll over," she said.

After he did, she looked down at him with her hands resting lightly on his stomach.

"You want happy ending?"

It only took him a few seconds to realize she was suggesting a sexual act. He figured that was when most guys negotiated the extra services. He felt sleazy being in this spa. "No, I need to get going," he said as he hurriedly sat up, embarrassed that the massage and the insinuation of sex slightly aroused him.

She told him to get dressed and then stepped out of the room. His mind churned as he put on his clothes. How would Kim react to this news of Sukee? He tried to think of other questions to ask Jade but couldn't come up with anything.

He drove away from the spa, oblivious to the window rolled down in the white van parked across the lot. Inside, a man with a long-lens camera snapped multiple pictures of him and his car.

▪ ▪ ▪

On the way home, Christopher processed what he'd learned. Evidently, Sukee did run away from the house, but the men went after her and caught her. She was in Atlanta now and beyond his ability to help. According to Kim, her opportunity to escape from the men had probably evaporated with this move.

Could he find other resources to help Kim find her there? Maybe someone with contacts in Atlanta? Bert, his former best friend, might know someone in Atlanta since he worked in the protection business.

Christopher knew that Bert's company, Solid Rock Security, provided protection to music stars and celebrity types in Nashville, along with managing security at concerts and special events. He was good at networking and probably had connections in Atlanta. Christopher thought about how Bert joined the company as a security guard after a four-year stint in the army. He'd steadily worked his way up as the business grew, and his two tours in Iraq seemed to help his career. Soon after he returned from his second tour a few years ago, the security company owner retired and made Bert the managing partner. There was no doubt he was making good money. No, he probably wouldn't have the time or interest to help a young woman in trouble.

Christopher didn't talk to Bert much anymore. The last friendly conversation ended a year and a half ago when Bert said he wanted to ask Barbara, his ex-wife, out. Yeah, he'd told him to go for it, but it was less than a year after their divorce, and his feelings were still too raw. Bert should've known better, but he started dating Barbara. Three months later, Amy told him they were engaged.

No, he was not calling Bert. He'd deal with Kim by himself.

Damn, he'd forgotten to call Barbara and tell her this was not a good weekend for Amy to stay at his house. His cell phone was still locked in the glove box. He was almost home. He would call then.

Christopher drove up the driveway and parked, wishing he had good news to share with Kim. He knew she'd be watching out the front picture window. She'd see his mission was not successful. He grabbed his wallet and cell phone from the glove box. As he walked up the sidewalk, he checked his phone. There were three missed calls, one voice mail from Barbara and a voice mail and text from Amy.

CHAPTER SIXTEEN

"Dad, where have you been? Why didn't you answer your phone?" Amy stood at the open front door as he walked up the porch steps. Christopher could see Kim on the couch behind her.

"Amy, what are you doing here?"

"Mom has a meeting after work tonight, and Bert is busy, too, so Mom picked me up from school and brought me here. She called you and left a message. I let myself in with my key, and then I called you when I got here and texted you a little while ago. You never called back." She stood with her hands on her hips and a pout on her face.

"I just now saw the messages. I was dealing with a problem and didn't have my phone on me. I see you met Kim."

Amy glanced over her shoulder, then back at her father. "Yeah, we talked a little. Can I talk to you?"

"Sure." Christopher was still standing on the porch. Amy stepped outside, shut the door, and crossed her arms as she looked at him.

"Dad, is she your girlfriend?"

Christopher put up a hand. "No, she's not my girlfriend. She's someone I'm trying to help. She's in trouble and needs a place to stay for a few days until she can get to San Francisco."

Amy's pouty look changed to a worried one. "What kind of trouble is she in? Are the police looking for her?"

"No, but some bad men are. We've talked to the police, and they're trying to catch these men."

"Why are they after her?"

Christopher hesitated, not wanting to get into the situation at that moment. "They think she owes them money. And it's more complicated than that. I'll tell you all about it once she's gone."

"Is she staying in my room? And is that one of my t-shirts she's wearing?"

Christopher winced. "She's only staying in your room for a few days. The other bedroom is filled with boxes. She didn't have any extra clothes, so I told her to borrow one of your t-shirts so she could wash and dry the clothes she was wearing. It's only for today. I'll wash it."

"She can keep the t-shirt. I'm never gonna wear it again." She wrinkled up her mouth and nose. "I didn't know she was here, and when I walked in and she was sitting on the couch, I was scared at first. I went back out, but Mom was driving off, so I couldn't run to the car." Amy flung her arms out. "I didn't want to bug Mom. I knew she was in a hurry. I didn't know what to do. I tried to call you. You didn't answer. I asked her why she was here. She said you were helping her."

"I'm sorry, sweetie. I would've told you if I'd known you were coming." Christopher touched her shoulder, wanting to hug her, but she seemed stiff, resistant. "You staying for dinner?"

"No. After I couldn't reach you, I called Bert. I didn't want to bug Mom because she said it was an important meeting. Bert said he would pick me up in a little while."

Christopher looked down and rubbed his head, at a loss for words. He felt like he'd failed his daughter, and Bert was again riding to the rescue. Bert, the successful businessman, the ex-army tough guy, his former best friend, and now stepfather to his daughter. They walked back into the house.

Kim watched from the couch, glancing back and forth between Christopher and Amy.

"Kim, this is Amy. She's my daughter. Amy, this is Kim," Christopher said.

Amy gave Kim a half-hearted wave. The exchange seemed to increase the feeling of awkwardness between all of them. Christopher tried to think about what to say next.

"I'll tell you about my trip to Dickson in a minute, Kim."

She nodded in reply.

He coaxed Amy into the kitchen, where he poured her some orange juice. "You want some crackers and cheese?"

"I'm not hungry." Amy took a sip of her drink. Christopher thought he should have more appropriate teenage food on hand.

"Listen, if you want to stay over, I'm sure Kim doesn't mind sleeping on the couch." He leaned against the kitchen counter with a glass of water, trying to salvage the situation. Amy sat at the kitchen table with her orange juice, rubbing Gracie's head. The dog's almost white muzzle rested on Amy's thigh.

Amy shook her head. "I was only going to stay until after dinner. Mom was coming to get me when her meeting was over."

"Well, she can stay on the couch tomorrow night and Saturday night when you come over," Christopher said, testing the waters for the weekend arrangements.

"No, I'll stay with Mom and Bert this weekend. I have a school dance on Saturday night, and I was going to ask you to take me, but it'll be a lot closer if I stay home." The guilt knife dug a little deeper into Christopher's side.

They struggled to find things to discuss, and Amy seemed relieved when the doorbell rang. "I'm going to get a book from my room," she said.

Christopher stepped out on the front porch, shutting the door behind him. Bert was three inches shorter but seemed to take up more space with his gym-toned arms and chest. At least he was dressed in civvies, not in his Solid Rock Security Services uniform and wearing his sidearm.

"Hey, C.J." Bert was friendly as if the past year's events had never happened.

"Bert." Christopher nodded slightly toward him.

"So, I hear you have a woman staying with you of the

Asian persuasion." Bert's familiar conspiratorial grin split his face. "Finally gettin' a little, huh?"

"She's only a friend I'm trying to help. We're *not* romantically involved." Christopher worked at not letting his irritation show in his voice.

"Hey man, that's the best arrangement. No romance, just gettin' it on." Bert made a thrusting motion with his hips.

"I think you know that's not the arrangement." Christopher pushed down a sudden urge to take a swing at Bert and bust him in the nose.

"Yeah, knowing you, I can buy it." Bert waggled his hand slightly. "Barbara, well, she may not buy it."

"It's none of her business," Christopher replied, putting a little heat into it.

"Only as it affects Amy."

"I talked to Amy, and I think she believes me. This person is not my girlfriend. I don't want Amy to feel uncomfortable about staying with me."

Amy opened the front door as if on cue and slid out with her book bag over her shoulder. Gracie slipped out with her. Usually, Amy hugged her dad, but this time she jumped down the steps as if in a hurry.

"Bye, Amy," Christopher said to her back.

She turned around on the sidewalk, gave a quick wave, and hurried through the gate and into the black SUV.

Bert looked at Amy and back at Christopher, raised one eyebrow, and shrugged. "I'll talk to her. Sometimes it's easier when you're not the real parent." He moved down the steps, stopped at the bottom, and looked back. "I know she doesn't show it much, but she worships you."

The relief Christopher felt made his knees weak. He watched them drive off. Gracie leaned against him as if to provide moral support.

■ ■ ■

Kim watched the conversation between Christopher, Bert, and Amy through the large picture window. Although she couldn't hear much of the conversation, she noticed the awkwardness between the two men. She moved back to the couch as Bert drove off.

When Christopher came back in, he dropped on the couch and gave Kim a synopsis of his Dickson trip. "The woman there said one of the men took Sukee to Atlanta."

Kim sighed. "She will not stay in Atlanta for many days. Girls who make trouble go to other cities and work for other men."

"Just like that, they get sent off, or maybe sold, to another spa owner?" Christopher asked, eyebrows raised.

Kim nodded.

"I'm sorry, Kim. I wish there was something else we could do to get her out. Do you want me to talk to the police about her? Maybe they could contact the police in Atlanta and get someone to go to the spa and look for her."

Kim shook her head. "No, no police. Someone will tell Boseu. He will make Sukee disappear tonight."

They were both silent, lost in thought. Kim turned to Christopher and said, "Thank you for trying to find Sukee. I am sorry your daughter was upset that I was here."

Christopher shrugged. "It's okay. I should have told her about you. I missed her phone call earlier, and I think it scared her at first, just not knowing who you were." He stared at the ceiling momentarily, then grabbed the TV remote and started flipping through channels with the sound turned low.

Kim could tell he was disturbed by the brief visit with Amy. She wasn't sure if he wanted to talk, but many men had shared their private thoughts with her at the spa. With just an indication from her that she would listen, customers seemed eager to tell her of their successes, and sometimes their failures.

She decided to give it a try.

"That is Amy's other dad?" she asked.

"Yes. Her stepdad." He continued to stare at the TV.

"Did your wife leave you? For him?" She kept her tone and her expression soft.

Christopher glanced at Kim but didn't seem offended by the direct question. He twisted around on the couch to face her.

"She left, but not for him. When I lost my job, I could no longer support my family, which meant Barbara had to find a job for the first time in fourteen years. I spent a lot of time here, taking care of my mother. She was not happy with me."

"Did she find job?"

"She's smart. She had no trouble finding a job at Chico's, a women's clothing store. Within three months, she was the assistant manager."

"You have job now?"

"Yes, I have job—have a job. I started a computer repair and support business."

"When did she meet Bert?" Kim asked.

"She knew him from college. He was my college roommate. We were jocks. That means we were athletes. I ran track in college, and Bert was on the football team." Kim nodded. She knew enough American slang to understand the jock label.

"Barbara and I started dating my senior year and married two years later. Bert never married. I mean, not until Barbara. He often came to the house, and I know they teased each other, but I don't think they did anything beyond that. Barbara used to fix him up with her girlfriends. Bert is... maybe because he is a successful businessman, Barbara found him attractive."

"Amy, she live with Bert and Barbara, and sometime she stay with you?"

"Yes."

Christopher sat silently for a moment; then he picked up the TV remote. Kim took that as a signal he'd said all he wanted to about Amy's living arrangements.

"I go cook dinner," she said.

▪ ▪ ▪

After Kim headed into the kitchen, Christopher didn't bother to turn up the sound on the TV. The conversation with Kim picked the scab off old wounds. He flashed back to the last year he and Barbara were together when his income was less than half of hers. They'd almost blown through what little savings they had. Christopher remembered the tension in the marriage, the arguments, and the demands. He shuddered, trying to throw off the humiliation as he relived that time as if playing a tape in his head, one he'd played many times.

A small measure of relief came when they were finally divorced. He was a free man. Barbara was a free woman. She got the house and the newer car, lost weight, and got a new hairstyle. She went out on dates or to dinner with girlfriends on the weekends, going to clubs and dancing, something she loved, and something he never wanted to do while they were married.

Having Amy only part time was the most challenging part of the divorce. He called and talked to her every day, but many days she seemed in a hurry to go. Most of all, he missed just hanging out with her, riding in the car, listening to the radio, listening to her talk to her friends on her phone. The absence of that leisure time together was eroding the close relationship they'd once had.

Christopher still had questions about how Barbara and Bert's romance and marriage happened so fast. It was now almost a year since their wedding. There were occasional uncomfortable moments as he negotiated the logistics of weekend visits, but there was not a lot of conversation with Bert. Not if he could avoid it.

CHAPTER SEVENTEEN

For dinner, Kim heated the soup she'd made earlier, pulled a block of Munster cheese from the refrigerator, and slapped mayonnaise, pickle, and cheese on wheat bread slices. The smell of bread and cheese toasting in a skillet with melted butter filled the kitchen, drawing Christopher in from the living room. They ate without much conversation. The emotion of the day seemed to leave them tired and hungry. Afterward, Christopher told Kim he needed to work on two customer computers. He moved to the table in the dining room.

Kim perused the books in front of the built-in bookshelves in the living room. She chose *A Short History of Nearly Everything* by Bill Bryson. Kim took it upstairs and read it in Amy's bed. The book seemed to be more about science than history, but she was also curious about science topics. Though English was her second language, Kim was almost as proficient in reading English as she was reading Korean, especially after four years of having no access to Korean books. Bryson explained complex topics such as the Big Bang theory in simple terms that she could understand, even if she had to translate the language in her mind.

A few hours later, she heard Christopher come up the stairs, go into the bathroom, and start the shower. She put the book down to think about him. After the day's events, especially watching him with Amy, she knew he was a nice man but seemed lonely. He didn't have to help her, and he certainly didn't need to try to find Sukee, but he did. How could she let him know she was grateful?

Her mind circled the obvious. At first, she rejected it because it was that part of her former life that she never wanted to go back to. Maybe he was different from the men she met at the spa. They only wanted to use her body and rarely showed any interest in who she was or her story. She'd been aware of his occasional glance at her figure, so she finally decided to offer the one thing that every man seemed to want from her, and that he seemed to want too. At least she could do that.

▪ ▪ ▪

Christopher stood in front of his dad's bureau and pulled open his underwear drawer. He was fresh out of the shower and in his bathrobe when he heard a soft rap on his bedroom door. He tightened his robe belt as he turned to open the door.

"Yes?" he said.

Kim had on the short white t-shirt she wore on Monday morning when he first saw her, but below that she only wore panties, actually a black thong, he couldn't help but notice with a glance. Her hands were laced together in front as if to hide her privates.

"You want massage?" Kim asked, her voice was pitched high and her face expressionless as she looked at him.

"What?" Christopher asked.

"You want me to give you massage? You have been good to me. I give you happy ending."

"I'm okay," Christopher said, momentarily confused. There was more to this offer than just a massage.

"You feel really good after massage and happy ending." She struck a seductive posture and pushed out her chest. It was as if she had become a different person.

"Look, Kim, I, uh," he stammered. "I don't; you don't have to give me, uh, happy ending." He put up a hand, stepping back, even as his groin responded to her offer.

Her face stayed expressionless. "You no have to pay. You help me. I do for you free."

"That's okay. I mean, thank you, but no." He put up both hands. He tried to not glance down again at her black thong. "Look, you're pretty, but I'm a lot older than you. And you don't have to do anything for me to stay here. It's okay. I only want to help you, that's all. Go read, get a good night's sleep."

Her eyes, void of expression before, warmed up. "Okay." Her voice returned to her normal tone, and she dropped the seductress act. She turned and went back to the other end of the hall.

Christopher watched her walk back to Amy's room, go in and shut the door.

He replayed the scene in his head as he got in bed, remembering her waif-like body, but more so the palpable sense of relief on her face when she accepted that he didn't want to have sex with her. She didn't expose her feelings easily, he was learning, but this time he read her correctly. He was sure of it. Turning down her offer was his initial response, but the right one. Even though he was aware of her body, and she was an attractive female, he couldn't take advantage of her.

For him, sex was more than the feel of a female body and the rush of a climax. The few times he'd settled for just a physical release, he'd felt listless and grubby. He knew the warm feelings of intimacy that came with sex in a healthy relationship. He suspected Kim had never experienced those emotions since she'd been used and sexually abused for most of her few adult years. Just a receptacle for a man's sexual desire. In their four days together, he'd seen fear, despair, and grief in her eyes, but he'd also seen a glimmer of hope, a longing for a different life. He wasn't about to chip away at that hope in exchange for a fleeting feel-good moment.

He couldn't sleep, so he lay in bed with his hands behind his head. He wondered what Bert would say about the incident. He could predict that Bert would probably say something like, "Dude, you haven't been laid in over a year, and you have a cute young thing come to your bedroom door and offer you sex, and you turn her down? Are you going for sainthood, or are you now batting from the other side of the plate?" Bert, not known for political correctness, would be all over his sorry ass, he knew. Asshole.

As he turned on his side and pulled up the covers on the bed, the bed his parents slept in for decades, he once more felt his dad's presence and his approval.

CHAPTER EIGHTEEN

FRIDAY

The lantern-shaped front porch light cast shadows as Christopher hurried to his car in the darkness to start his morning newspaper delivery routine. Gracie followed, her arthritic hips causing her to ease slowly down the steps. He waited at the gate, where he gave his usual goodbye pat on her graying head. It saddened him to think she could be a few months away from kidney failure.

"I'll be back in a little while and give you some breakfast, old girl."

Her tail wagged slowly at the mention of breakfast.

He drove a little faster since he was running about ten minutes behind his usual schedule. He was a good three miles down Ashland City Highway when a large black car from the other direction slowed at a mailbox, as if studying the address. Christopher wondered who they were visiting so early in the morning on this county road.

■ ■ ■

Kim had heard Christopher shut the door as he left. She decided to get up and fix a cup of tea. She'd not slept much, still too disturbed by Christopher's report of his visit to Dickson and learning that Sukee was probably in Atlanta. She pulled on her black tights and padded barefoot down the stairs to the kitchen, lifted the tea kettle from the stove and turned to the sink to fill it.

Gracie's fierce barking outside caused her to set the kettle on the counter and tiptoe through the darkness to the living room to check out the noise. She peeked out the window. Gracie stood at the gate and barked as two men got out of a large dark sedan parked in front. They stopped and looked at the dog for a moment, then one pulled a gun from the back of his waistline and slowly walked to the gate, holding the gun by his side.

Min-jun!

In the dim glow cast by the front porch light, Kim recognized his stocky frame and swept-back hair. She hurried to the back door in the kitchen.

As she opened the door, she heard a pistol crack and a yelp from Gracie. She pulled the door shut behind her and ran.

She ran across the back yard, ignoring the stubs of crabgrass and thistle weed prickling her feet. She stopped behind the storage shed to peek around the corner, her breath coming in panicked gasps. A few seconds later, the dark shape of a man crept to the back door of the house. When he found it unlocked, he pushed it open. He was silhouetted in the light from the kitchen. Kim thought the man looked like Kwan. He had a gun in his gloved hand.

Her heart pounded. She trembled, cold and scared. She squatted behind the shed and frantically looked around the back yard for the safest place to hide. In the shed? Under the camper? Both felt like a trap to her. She looked over her shoulder at the back fence, about twenty feet away, and decided her best chance was to get as far from the house as possible.

She ran across the wet grass to the fence.

She hardly noticed the pain as she stuck her toes in the four-foot, chain-link fence, climbed, and dropped to the other side. Her t-shirt hung on the top of the fence and then tore loose. She hurried through high stiff weeds to the orchard and dashed through the four rows of apple and pear trees. She ran as hard as she could in the low visibility of nighttime to the woods and stopped at the first large tree she could hide behind, turned, and watched again, her breath coming in gasps.

Kim was a good distance from the house but could make out the dark shapes of two men with flashlights walking out the kitchen door. She saw their lights slashing the darkness as they methodically searched the yard. They moved to the shed and searched inside, then around the back of the shed. They went to the Airstream, pulled open the door, and one of the men entered. She watched his flashlight glow through the windows of the camper. The other man walked to the back fence and moved his light back and forth across the high grass and through the orchard. Kim shrunk behind the tree, catching faint reflections of the light shining off nearby trees. She hoped she was far enough away and no part of her white t-shirt was visible. Several minutes after the moving beam disappeared, she risked a peek. No sign of any movement. She slid down to a sitting position at the base of the tree, hugged her knees, and huddled into a ball, shivering in the cool of the spring morning.

CHAPTER NINETEEN

As Christopher rolled to a stop in front of his house after his morning paper delivery, he first noticed that Gracie was not in her usual spot: on the porch at the top of the steps, sitting under the porch light in the dim morning light. As he stepped out of the car, he saw that the front gate was open. Dammit, did he forget to shut it? Then he noticed the front door was ajar.

Christopher hurried to the gate, then halted as he saw his dog lying still on the ground. He froze at first and then ran to check her. Her eyes were dull, half open, and her tongue hung from her mouth, her breathing labored. The fur on her back was matted with blood. My God, she's been shot! Christopher rubbed her head and whispered, "It's me, girl. I will get a blanket, and we'll get you to the animal hospital."

He straightened up and stared at the front door. Whoever had shot Gracie had broken into his house. Were they still inside? He looked around. No vehicle nearby, so probably not.

What about Kim? Was she shot, too? Or dead? The thought of what he might find inside socked him in the gut. Should he call the police? He should check on Kim. An ambulance might need to be the first call.

He approached the steps and tiptoed up—legs, arms quivering. The doorjamb was splintered. Someone had kicked in the door. He peered in. For the first time in his life, he wished he carried a gun.

"Kim?" He entered cautiously and moved across the living room to check the kitchen. He moved faster as he climbed the stairs. All the bedroom doors were open. The bed in Amy's room was sideways, and the mattress flipped up.

Christopher hurried down the hall to his open bedroom door. He stood inside the doorway and looked around. He realized that someone had rummaged around in the two small closets in the room. He peeked in the third bedroom. All the clothes boxes stashed against the wall were pulled away from the closet.

Christopher rushed back to Amy's room, stood in the middle, and pivoted around, unsure what he was looking for. Something he'd seen earlier that seemed out of place, not where it was supposed to be.

He picked up a picture frame lying face down on the floor. The frame was empty. He remembered it held a five-by-seven photo of Amy and her mom, taken just last year at Christmas. A close-up headshot of the two, smiling happily. He noticed a blank space on Amy's bulletin board where his favorite photo of her was usually thumbtacked. Did they grab the photos? And why would they want them?

He hurried back downstairs to the dining room. The three customer computers on the dining room table were thrown on the floor, and it appeared someone had stomped them. His anger rose at the malicious destruction.

Christopher pulled out his cell phone and started to dial 911 but hesitated. His hands shook so badly he could barely stop a finger on the nine. He'd call later. He needed to get Gracie to the vet, quickly, but he needed to be sure Kim was gone, not left somewhere injured or dead. This didn't feel like a random burglary since the TV and the computers weren't taken . . . since . . . Gracie was shot.

They had come for Kim.

What happened to Kim? Did they grab her? How did they know where she was? His mind spun with questions. If she was still here, where would she hide? He went to the basement door, opened it and switched on the light.

"Kim?" he called out as he ran down the stairs.

The basement was small, only one room with shelves of outdated canned vegetables on one side and his father's workbench on the other side. Old paint cans were stacked on the floor. No place to hide. He hurried back up the stairs.

As he stopped momentarily in the kitchen, he noticed the back door was open a few inches. Maybe Kim was hiding outside.

He ran out to the back yard, paused, and then hurried over to the shed. The doors to the shed were open. He looked in, but a quick glance told him Kim was not there. He saw that the Airstream camper door was open. He peeked inside. No sign of Kim or a struggle. He stood outside the camper and looked out beyond the fence across the yard.

As he focused on the high grass between the fence and the orchard, he saw bent grass and what looked like a small path cut through the tall, dew-wet green blades, barely visible in the early morning light. It appeared that someone had run through it toward the woods. Christopher put his hands on the top of the four-foot fence and vaulted over.

He followed the mashed-grass path left in the dew to the fruit trees and beyond. He saw movement, a flash of something white, perhaps ten feet into the woods.

"Kim?" he called. "Kim, it's me. No one else is here."

She slipped out from behind a large oak and stood with her arms crossed and shoulders hunched. Christopher rushed to her.

"Are you okay?" She nodded. He wrapped his arms around her shivering body, hugging her tightly. She hugged him back and started sobbing.

"It's all right. They're gone." He rocked her as if she were a child.

"They came after you left. Gracie, she bark. I went to front and saw them," Kim said between sobs. "I ran out back door. I hear gunshot. I hide behind the shed, and see a man come around to back of house, go in back door. He look like Kwan.

Other man was Min-jun." Her voice was shaky. "I run to fence and climb over, run to trees. I watch. They come out of house. They have flashlights. They go to shed, to trailer, back to house, then nothing. I was scared. I stay here till you come."

"They shot Gracie," Christopher said. "I need to get her to the animal hospital."

"She save me. Min-jun shot her. He would have shot me."

"I know. Let's hurry."

They ran back toward the house. Christopher boosted Kim over the fence, and then he vaulted over. He led the way to the back door and through the kitchen. He stopped at a closet in the hall next to the half bath, pulled a jacket off a hanger, draped it over Kim's shoulders, and then turned and grabbed a blanket from a high shelf.

"I want to wrap up Gracie and get her in the car. There's a pet emergency clinic that's open overnight."

Kim followed as he ran out the front door and threw the blanket on the ground beside Gracie. He gathered his dog, placed her on the blanket, and gently wrapped her in it after patting her head again. The fur on her back was blood-soaked, and she seemed unconscious. Her breathing was slow, with long pauses.

Kim got in the back seat with Gracie's head in her lap. Christopher slung gravel as he sped out of his driveway and onto the county road.

"I need to call the police and report this. I probably should have done that before I bundled up Gracie and took off, but I couldn't stand to leave her lying in the front yard another minute," Christopher said, looking in the rearview mirror at Kim. She still wore his jacket.

She shook her head. "Sukee say not talk to police. They tell Boseu."

He stared out the front windshield as he thought it through. "She may be right. These Korean guys knew you were here. Someone told them. If I'd been here, they would've shot me."

"The police will take me to some other place," Kim said.

"Yeah, probably," Christopher replied.

"Then someone at police tell Boseu. He send Kwan and Min-jun to get me there. I safer if I go someplace nobody know."

"Yeah. We need to get away from my house," Christopher said. "They might come back."

His mind raced as he thought over his options. Maybe the best place for now was a cheap hotel just off the interstate with an outside door. He wanted safety, and Kim needed anonymity. He sped down Ashland City Highway, got on Briley Parkway, went south to Interstate 40, and headed toward downtown.

"We'll be at the pet emergency clinic in about ten minutes," Christopher said as he looked at Kim in the rearview mirror. Her head was down. "How's she doing?"

Kim looked up at him. Tears were running down her face. "No more breaths. She is gone."

Christopher slowed down and got off the Interstate at the next exit. He pulled to the side of the road, unfastened his seatbelt, and twisted around. He touched his dog's head, still in Kim's lap. Her eyes were glazed, and her tongue hung out. Her stillness confirmed her death.

He hit the trunk button on his dashboard, got out, opened the back door, and gathered Gracie's blanket-wrapped body. As he laid her in the trunk, he patted her head one more time.

"Bye, sweet girl. You were brave till the end." Tears blurred his eyes as he tucked the blanket around her tightly.

He dug a roll of duct tape out of the side bin in the trunk. As he taped up the blanket, a rage descended on him like a red mist. This was his daughter's pet. His companion on many lonely nights over the past two years. He slammed the trunk lid and leaned over it, arms spread and hands on the trunk, head down. *Whoever did this will pay*, he vowed.

After he regained his composure, he got behind the steering wheel and turned to Kim.

"Okay," he said, voice still shaky, "we need to focus on finding a safe place to hide you." *And I need a place too,* he thought. *I'm no longer safe at my own house, but I want to bury Gracie there.*

CHAPTER TWENTY

Christopher got back on the interstate, driving west, away from the city, trying to focus on what to do next. He watched his rearview mirror for any suspicious car following them. He thought about the implications of the missing photos of Amy and her mom. Could they be in danger? He decided it was time to warn Bert. He picked up his cell phone.

"Bert, listen, I've got a huge problem."

"Yeah, 'bout time you realized that," Bert responded with a chuckle.

"This is no time for wise-cracking. I'm in trouble, and I'm going to need your help."

"Okay. Lay it on me, buddy." Bert's tone turned serious.

Christopher told him about the attack on his home and Kim's narrow escape from the men. "They shot Gracie!" His voice cracked. "She's dead in the trunk of my car."

"Why haven't you called the police?" Bert asked.

"Kim visited her friend at the jail yesterday, and her friend said that someone at the police station was talking to the Koreans. Kim says the men that came to my house were the Koreans who held her captive and made her work at the massage parlor. These guys knew she was staying with me, and that info must have come from within the police department."

"What? Hey, C.J., what else is going on here? This attack was by a Korean gang with informants within the police department?"

In a shaky voice, Christopher started filling Bert in on yesterday's events, beginning with the TV news about the raid on the spa in Green Hills.

"Wait, I think you need to start at the beginning." Bert didn't try to hide his incredulous tone. "You were at the jail yesterday, then a massage parlor? How did you meet this girl? Dude, what are you involved in?"

"This all started on Monday morning when I randomly met Kim and offered to help her." Christopher tried to be patient as he explained the past five days to Bert.

"Wow," was Bert's one-word response.

"But here's my biggest worry right now. The guys that broke into my house, I think they took two photos from Amy's room. One of Amy, and one of Amy and Barbara."

"Why would they do that?" Bert asked.

"I can only guess, but the Koreans may try to find Barbara or Amy and kidnap them. Maybe they would try to trade one or both for Kim."

"C.J., this is your daughter. And my wife." Christopher could hear the emotion in Bert's voice. "How could you—"

"Bert, believe me, I'm shook up by this. I had no idea it could go this way."

"So, what do we do?"

"I think we need to be prepared for the possibility they could be in danger. If these guys can figure out the connection between me, Amy, and Barbara, they can probably find where you all live."

"That wouldn't be too hard if they're internet savvy."

"I thought about going by Amy's school, but I have Kim with me, and Gracie is in the trunk." He knew if Amy saw the blood in his back seat and on Kim, she would want to know about it. He felt too rattled now to tell her about the Koreans breaking in and ransacking her bedroom. And about Gracie. "I need to find a place for Kim and then deal with Gracie, but I don't want to wait too long before getting Amy."

"Let me do it. Those Koreans could be on your tail. I'll get Amy from school, call Barbara, and get them someplace safe. Where are you now?"

"I'm on the I-40 near downtown. I think I'll head west. There's a Comfort Inn off the interstate, out beyond Bellevue. Maybe I should get a room there and hide Kim for three days until I can take her to Memphis to get her visa."

"Okay, I'm glad to help you, but let me take care of Barbara and Amy first. You sure you don't want to call the police about all this?"

"Bert, I called the police on Tuesday after I realized these men were looking for Kim. Since then, everything's gone to shit. I believe Kim. Someone tipped them off about her location. Only the police and that Assistant DA knew. These Koreans are nasty guys. They killed Gracie, and I think they'll use any means to get Kim, including kidnapping and possibly murder."

Bert was silent as he processed the information. "It's still early in the day. You should probably stay in a conspicuous place for a little while in case the Koreans find you. Find a coffee shop or a restaurant, some place where there are lots of people, and hang out there for a couple of hours. I'll call you. We need to think this through."

"Okay, thanks. And Bert, I may want to borrow a gun."

"I have several. You can take your pick."

Christopher ended the call and glanced over the seat at Kim to see if she understood the one-sided conversation. She was huddled in the back seat corner and staring out the side window.

As Christopher drove west, he thought again about his next steps. He realized that to check into a hotel, he would need to show ID and use a credit card. As Bert said, if the Koreans were savvy, they might have the resources to find out if he registered at a hotel.

Damn, he thought. If they grabbed up the stack of bills on the dining room table, they probably had a copy of his credit card statement and other information. With enough personal info, checking on credit card usage wouldn't be hard.

They would have the card number and billing address. They could call the credit card company, pretend it was lost, and ask about any recent charges. Maybe he should use cash. Do hotels still accept cash?

He needed a better plan for hiding Kim, but for now he'd go hang out in a public place until Bert called him back. Maybe Bert would use his credit card to check her into the hotel.

Christopher considered whether Bert would do that. He hated to ask him. He would rather find another option.

He looked at Kim in the rearview mirror. "I'll find a place for you to stay, maybe in a motel, but it needs to be where the Korean men can't find you. I'm working on how to do that."

She made eye contact, nodded, and then turned to look out the side window again.

"It only needs to be until Monday," he said, trying to sound reassuring. "We can still go to Memphis, get you a new visa and a bus ticket to San Francisco. We just need to hang out somewhere until Bert calls me back."

Christopher got off at the next exit and turned on a four-lane road, Harding Road, and headed west. There was a Starbucks a few miles away. They would wait there.

CHAPTER TWENTY-ONE

The detective was only two bites into his barbecue sandwich when the burner cell phone buzzed. He knew it was the Korean calling.

He and his partner sat at a picnic table in Centennial Park, across the street from The Heavenly Hog, a walk-up dive that served up what many considered the best pit barbeque in Nashville. It was one of their regular lunch stops.

"I have to take this," he said. His partner looked at him with eyebrows raised and mouth full. The detective wiped his hands on a napkin, reached for the cell phone in his suit coat inner pocket, got up, and left the picnic table.

"Yeah?"

"As you said it would happen, there was a raid at Dickson last night. We closed the spa and got our people out before police arrived," the raspy voice said.

"Good."

"But we did not get the girl at the house this morning."

"What happened?"

"You said the girl would be home alone after five this morning. We went to the house, but no girl."

The detective leaned against the rear fender of the unmarked patrol car and spoke in a low voice. "All I know is what this Christopher Jones guy told us. He said he would leave the house at 4:30 because he has a newspaper route. I didn't ask if she went with him. I just figured he went by himself since it was so early." He checked to be sure his partner was still at the picnic table.

"We need to get her. Today," the raspy voice said.

"I understand. He drives a Buick LeSabre, gold color, ten years old. You have his tag number. Have your guys look for his car. Drive by his house. If he's not home, he's probably around that neighborhood somewhere. Or maybe at a grocery store. Meanwhile, I'll think of something."

"I will send two cars to drive around and look for his car," the raspy voice said.

The detective turned to check on his partner again and chewed on a cuticle as he thought. "I can send a patrol car to the house to wait. I can have them call me if he comes back home. We can get him, take him in for questioning, maybe hold him a while, leave the girl behind, and your guys can get her." He thought about that plan, looking for problems.

"But if I do that," the detective continued, "you can't show up there right away and grab the girl. That would look too suspicious, as if someone tipped you off. You might not get away with it in daylight, anyhow. Probably should happen after dark." His partner stood up from the picnic table, gathered up the trash, and started toward the Mercury.

"Another thing. I'm in a car with my partner, so let me call you when I have something to report. Don't call me. It looks suspicious if I keep getting calls where I must ask him to pull over and let me out so I can talk in private. He's bound to know I'm into something shady with that kind of act."

"I will call you when I want." The voice was cold.

"Okay, okay. I'm just trying to keep him from wondering about these calls."

"Find a way for us to get the girl, even if we have to get rid of Christopher Jones."

His partner walked to the side of the unmarked car and stared at him as he ended the call. "What's going on?" he asked.

The detective momentarily considered telling him about the Koreans, the photos, and the blackmail, but he knew his partner was a by-the-book cop. No, he decided; he couldn't risk the exposure and potential fallout. It would mean the end of his career, his ambitions, and probably an indictment.

"It's personal stuff," he said as he walked to the driver's side.

"I think you're into something and probably in over your head," his partner replied as he shook his head. Then he opened the passenger door and got in.

They didn't speak as they drove away from the park.

▪ ▪ ▪

Cho hung up the cell phone and slid it into his jacket pocket. He swiveled in his chair, pointed at two of the three men sitting in front of his desk, and spoke to them in Korean.

"Take two cars and drive the roads on the west side of town near the house. Look for this man Christopher, who has Kim. He drives a gold Buick LeSabre, ten years old." He wrote numbers on Post-it Notes and handed them to the two men. "This is his tag number. Check parking lots at grocery stores. Maybe one of you will see his car. Call me if you do." He nodded at the third man. "Call Billy Lee. Tell him I want to meet in one hour."

Without a word, the three men left the office.

Cho studied them as they walked away. He leaned forward in his chair, placed his hands on the desk with his fingers interlaced, and, as he often did, worked through each of his employees, looking for any sign of disloyalty or threat to his network.

Sung-ho, the organizer, kept track of the income from all nine spa sites: the two in Louisville, Kentucky, the one off the interstate north of Bowling Green, Kentucky, the three in Tennessee, one in north Georgia near Chattanooga, the south Georgia one, and the Atlanta location. As young men, they served together in the Korean Army.

Kwan was a former elite soldier, well trained in the killing arts. He'd caught and tortured many North Korean spies in his military career. He was stoic, almost unfeeling, and when told to eliminate someone, he did so with no hesitation. His method often involved stomping them with his steel-toed shoes.

Kwan and Sung-ho had been with him for thirty years.

Min-jun signed on twelve years ago. Though not militarily trained, he was a natural-born killer. He was now in his early forties, at least two decades younger than the other two, and he seemed to enjoy cruelty. Cho did not trust him as much as Kwan or Sung-ho.

In addition to these three long-term confederates, there were three newer employees—one who traveled to the three sites in Georgia each week and two based in Louisville who handled the Kentucky sites. All were Korean men who had been in the States for several years. They seemed willing to do any task, but their loyalty hadn't been tested.

Kwan and Min-jun had lived in the house in West Meade, but since the raid at the spa and the house two days ago, they shared a bedroom at his Brentwood home, which now seemed crowded with their addition along with Sung-ho and a Korean housekeeper.

His business plan was simple. Four of the spas were in houses near truck stops off an interstate exit, and the girls lived where they worked. The places typically had kitchens and back rooms as their living quarters. The front rooms were converted into small massage rooms. Interstate billboards advertised the location for truckers and travelers.

Like Nashville, the Atlanta and Louisville spa operations were in urban strip malls. A small, rented apartment nearby served as living quarters for the working girls and the older female overseer at each location.

The most common problem for Cho involved the occasional girl who didn't work out. Some seemed to sink into depression and give up all hope. They would either quit eating or become so passive and uncaring about their appearance that they were no longer of interest to customers. He could sell or trade the girl through his American connections, but sometimes it was easier just to make them disappear. Kwan or Min-jun usually handled that.

All the men were under strict orders not to have sex with the working girls at any time. Experience had taught Cho that if the younger women did not feel some safe zone after servicing customers all day, they were quicker to sink into despair. Cho was not convinced Min-jun always followed that rule.

The system worked, and business was thriving. The men were paid well, and they were not hesitant to do any task.

His two Korean restaurants, one in Nashville and one in Atlanta, served as conduits for the tens of thousands of dollars he collected each week across his network of massage parlors. A highly paid accountant laundered a portion of the proceeds from the spas through his umbrella corporation, co-mingling the funds with the restaurant proceeds. His nephew, a college grad, managed the restaurants but stayed out of the spa business. He also served as his Internet guru. Cho occasionally called upon him to mine information about a customer. The boy's mother was a problem, though.

He sighed and pushed up from his desk chair. He needed Billy's help. He would deal with the coldness of the mother, Jung Lee.

CHAPTER TWENTY-TWO

Cho pushed through the restaurant door. It was mid-morning. There were no customers. Billy Lee and his mother sat at a table, waiting.

"Wae sam choon." His nephew stood and greeted him with a slight bow and the traditional Korean title, which meant "My mother's brother." He was fluent in Korean, though he spoke it with an American accent. His checked shirt, narrow maroon tie, and shiny black hair gave him a preppy look, but Cho knew behind the youthful appearance was a sharp business mind.

"I need your assistance, nephew," Cho said as he sat across the table. He nodded at his sister, but she didn't respond.

"How can I help you?" The young man continued to speak Korean in a respectful, almost formal manner.

"I need information on a customer. His name is Christopher Jones. He lives in Nashville, on Ashland City Highway. He is a problem to my business."

Billy opened a laptop computer on the table in front of him, booted it up, and started typing and clicking.

"I find several men by the name of Christopher Jones in Nashville," he said after a few minutes, "and more who are called Chris Jones, but none show a residence on Ashland City Highway. Do you have any information other than that address?"

"We know he delivers newspapers to houses near White Bridge Road," Cho said.

Billy focused on his computer screen for several minutes, ignoring his uncle as his fingers flew across the keyboard.

Cho watched him with feelings of pride and frustration. His nephew was his rightful heir, and he needed to be involved in all phases of the restaurant and spa businesses. There was much to teach him, including the dangers. There were aggressive customers, uncooperative girls, and the occasional takeover attempt from competitors. Men like Min-jun and Kwan were needed to be successful. Billy hardly knew them or their roles.

A few years ago, a local drug lord in Atlanta tried to take over his spa business in Georgia. He sent word to Cho that he wanted to buy his business and would burn him out if he refused to sell. Kwan and Min-jun located the man, and he and his bodyguard disappeared. His nephew needed to learn the importance of violence and intimidation as business tools.

He looked at his sister. She met his gaze with a look of disdain, and she was clearly not intimidated. Cho would not have tolerated the implied lack of respect from anyone else.

Jung Lee was only eight when Cho left home to join the Korean army, so he didn't know her well as a child. In her late teens, she escaped their family's poverty by marrying Gi, a bright young man in the nearby village. They moved to Seoul, and Gi found a good job at a factory. Jung worked at a restaurant, where she eventually became the manager. For many years, Cho only saw Jung at funerals and weddings.

A few years after he arrived in the States, Jung contacted him and asked for help. She and her husband had tried for many years to have a baby. Now in her mid-thirties, she was desperate and wanted to come to the United States. She had read of miracle treatments at a fertility clinic in Atlanta, where he lived then, and she hoped they could succeed with treatments at that clinic. Cho agreed to help them, stipulating that they relocate to Atlanta and operate a Korean restaurant for him. They reluctantly agreed.

Soon after the restaurant opened, a tall, stately man who seemed famous showed up for lunch. Even though he was at a table with other important men, he asked her name, how long she had lived in Atlanta, and why she came there. She found herself telling him about her hopes for a child. As he left, he said his name was Billy Graham and that he would say a prayer for her. She didn't know what that meant, but it left her feeling hopeful. When she told Cho about the encounter, he said her doctors would fix her problem, not a magic man with special connections to a god he didn't believe existed.

When her boy was born nine months later, she named him Billy Lee, after that magic man, not Gi, after her husband, or Cho, after the boy's uncle. That was the start of several decisions by his sister and her husband that angered Cho.

When Cho decided to move to Nashville a few years later, he ordered Jung and Gi to move there with him and open another restaurant. They refused. Atlanta was now their home, they said. Cho dispatched Kwan and Min-jun to the restaurant early one morning to confront Gi and convince him that his family needed to move to Nashville. If Gi refused to obey, their orders were to threaten him, perhaps rough him up. Gi was not easily intimidated. An argument broke out, followed by a physical struggle. Gi grabbed a knife, so Min-jun shot and killed him. The evidence pointed to a robbery, and the police bought into that scenario, but his sister didn't.

Jung and Billy, by then four years old, followed Cho to Nashville, but Jung wanted little to do with him. For the past twenty years, Jung ran the restaurant as Cho wanted. A bright boy, Billy excelled in school and earned a full scholarship to Vanderbilt University. He graduated with a degree in business two years ago.

"Okay, I eliminated a doctor and a lawyer named Christopher Jones," Billy said. "They are not going to be newspaper delivery guys."

He looked up briefly at his uncle. "I found a Christopher

Jones on LinkedIn. His profile says he is an IT consultant."

Cho nodded. "Yes, he has many computers in his house."

Billy looked back at his screen. "This is probably him. He graduated from Austin Peay University with a BA degree. It says he was employed in the IT department at HCA until four years ago. No employment has been listed since then. That's not good. He should have been able to secure a job in IT. He sounds like the kind of guy who might be delivering newspapers now."

Billy typed, clicked, and surfed some more. "I now have his middle initial, S, and that helps. I've confirmed his address. He lives alone, according to last year's census report. His mother owns the house on Ashland City Highway. Property tax records list the appraised value as three hundred and forty thousand. So, it's probably a modest place." Billy kept typing and clicking.

"I located an email address and found him on Craig's List. He advertises his business there and says he repairs computers and updates systems. He calls himself The Computer Doctor. The ad says he makes house calls." Billy frowned and muttered in English, "That's a lame marketing slogan."

Cho stared at his nephew and committed the information to memory.

Billy clicked more. "He's not on Facebook, Twitter, or any social media platform. He doesn't advertise his business except through Craig's List, so he's not a good marketer."

After another minute of searching, he said, "I'm in public records, looking for warrants and arrests. He looks clean except for a divorce a couple of years ago."

Cho considered asking his nephew to investigate the ex-wife to see if he could get an address. He glanced at his sister and decided not to go down that path at this time.

Billy put his elbows on the table, steepled his fingers in front of his face, and looked at his uncle. "Okay, we have a pretty good profile on this guy. He's a computer nerd, probably a loner, runs a home business, is not very successful, looks to be around forty years old, and is not active through the usual social media ways, so he chooses to remain relatively anonymous."

He glanced at his mother and then looked back at his uncle. "I don't know what he's done to you, and I don't need to know," he said softly, "but this guy sounds like someone you can easily handle, given your resources. He shouldn't be much of a problem."

CHAPTER TWENTY-THREE

Christopher went to the counter at Starbucks and purchased a coffee and a green tea. He handed the green tea to Kim and led the way to a seating area in the middle of the store where he could watch the front door.

Kim parked herself on a couch across a coffee table from him. She tucked her feet under her thighs, and her gaze became unfocused as she held her cup of tea.

Christopher mulled over his options. He was still shocked that the Korean men knew Kim was staying with him. That they would kill his dog and break into his house to get her made him angry and scared. Somehow, he'd exposed Barbara and Amy to danger, as well. His hands trembled as he sipped his coffee. How could this have happened to him? His life felt out of control. He only wanted to help a young woman get to the Greyhound station and catch a bus out of town, and on Monday morning, that seemed like a simple task, one that would take only an hour of his time at the most.

He breathed deeply and tried to relax, clear his mind, and give Bert time to report in. He picked up *The Nashville Scene*, a free weekly newspaper lying on the floor beside his chair, and flipped through it mindlessly as he waited for Bert's call.

An ad caught his eye near the back, where most of the advertisements were for gentlemen's clubs and dating services. It was in a small box, blue ink with a red border. It read, *Tired of stripping for a living? Are you looking for a way out? Need help? Call Gloria Jean at Stripper Ministry. No judgment, just help.*

Christopher remembered reading a newspaper article about this woman's mission. Who was this Gloria Jean? What kind of help did she offer strippers? He grabbed his cell phone and entered "*stripper ministry Nashville*" in the Google search box.

He found a *Tennessean* news article written last year. He read how Gloria Jean McNulty had started the ministry to help strippers after her husband died. She wanted to show God's love, with no strings attached, to women who worked in Nashville's adult clubs. The article said she visited strip clubs and talked to the young women, offering help if they wanted it. McNulty was doing this on her own, though she had a network of women friends who were involved by making donations, helping the strippers find better jobs, or assisting them with enrolling in school.

Christopher looked back at the advertisement. Could she help Kim find a place to stay till Monday? He debated whether to call the number, then decided, why not? He was sitting here with nothing to do while waiting on Bert.

An anonymous-sounding message said to leave your name and phone number after the message beep. He did and asked for a return call. A few minutes later, his phone rang.

"Is this Christopher?" The voice was mature, feminine, with a Southern accent.

"Yes."

"I'm Gloria Jean, returning your call. How can I help you?" she asked, her tone cautious.

"I'm trying to help someone. She's Korean and works in a spa, a massage parlor, doing some of the things that strippers do, I guess. She wants to get out of that life and start over. She's here with me now."

"I saw something on the news about some arrests at a spa. Was she part of that spa?"

"Yes, but she wasn't arrested. She left a few days before all the arrests."

"What does she need?"

"It's a little complicated. Her name is Kim, and she and the other women who worked at the spa lived in a house in

West Nashville. She ran away on Monday. Two men lived at the house, and she's scared of them. I'm not sure what kind of help you offer to strippers, but if you know of a place where she can stay for a few days, anonymously, that's her most immediate need."

"Where are you?"

"I'm sitting with her at a Starbucks on Harding Road near St. Thomas Hospital."

"How about I come there, and we can talk? I can be there in about twenty minutes."

"Okay. We're sitting near the middle."

"I bet I can spot you."

Exactly twenty minutes later by Christopher's watch, a woman with platinum blonde hair, a tight black skirt, red blazer, white blouse cut in a V, and spike heels walked through the door. She looked around, caught his eye, smiled, strode through the coffee shop, and sat across from him.

"Christopher?" She leaned across the coffee table to shake his hand, then sat back. Christopher thought a man with less moral fiber would have stolen a long look at her ample cleavage. He only took a brief appreciative glance.

"Thanks for coming so quickly to meet with us," he said.

She smiled. "That's what I do."

She turned to Kim, curled up at the other end of the couch. "And you must be the young woman he told me about. I'm Gloria Jean McNulty." She extended her hand. With a wary look, Kim gave her a limp handshake.

Gloria reached into her purse and pulled out a business card: Strip Club Ministry in red against a light blue background. The following line was smaller and said, *Bringing Christ's love with no judgment*, and below that line was her name, a website address, and a phone number.

Christopher examined the business card and wondered if

she was as strange as this card indicated she might be.

"I bet you're asking yourself, what is a Strip Club Ministry? And you're maybe a little wary. Am I right?" Gloria asked, sounding rational, not crazy.

"Well, yeah, maybe wondering what exactly you do?" Christopher asked as he laid the card on the coffee table.

"God called me to go to strip clubs where young women are involved in a lifestyle that's not healthy for them. Last year I started walking into these clubs and talking to the girls. The first few times I visited, I brought cookies or brownies," she said. "They liked that. They still do." She smiled.

"I introduce myself, chat a bit, maybe ask questions and get to know the girls. I tell them I don't judge. I understand why they are there, and with a few different choices, it could be me up there dancing on that runway."

Her eyes, blue like robins' eggs, examined his face as if to see if he believed her. He wasn't sure he did. He regretted his call to her for a moment, but he thought if she wasn't too pushy with her world view, maybe she could offer some options.

She turned and leaned toward Kim. "Honey, why don't you tell me about how you got to Nashville?"

Kim told her story, warming up to the woman as the words spilled out. Gloria leaned in to hear Kim's soft voice. She asked a few questions, but mostly she kept her expression sympathetic and allowed the young Korean woman to talk.

Christopher studied Gloria. He guessed she was in her early forties, was curvy in an attractive way, and overdressed for Starbucks.

"How'd you get involved in this, uh, ministry?" he asked when her conversation with Kim reached a lull.

"My husband was a minister at a Baptist church in Madison, and I was involved there, too. He had a stroke and died three years ago." She tightened her lips.

"Sorry—"

"My two boys were already out of the house, in college, when my husband died," Gloria continued. "They've both since graduated. One lives in Charlotte. The other one lives in Atlanta. At first, I felt lost without my husband and our work. We married when I was eighteen, and I became a mom at nineteen. I was alone and didn't know what to do."

Christopher propped an elbow against the couch's armrest and placed his hand under his chin. She was beginning to sound reasonable.

"The church was doing well with a new minister, so I needed to find my purpose." She spoke with conviction and appeared to enjoy telling her story. "Two years ago, I asked God to give me some direction. One night I had a dream, and God told me to find women in trouble, women on the wrong path, and minister to them. The next day I was driving near downtown Nashville and saw a billboard advertising a strip club. I immediately knew that's what I needed to do."

She stopped and looked at Christopher as if to see if he understood.

Christopher nodded. He'd grown up in a Baptist church, so the religious language was familiar.

"I took it to the women's group at church, and they've helped me ever since with fundraising," Gloria continued. "I don't need an income. My husband had good life insurance. All the money raised goes to help these girls see another way to live."

Gloria smiled a wide, red-lipstick smile. "So far, I've helped five leave the life. I found jobs for three, and two have returned to school."

Christopher watched her as she spoke. Her sincerity and joy in her work overcame his skepticism. He glanced over at Kim, and she seemed entranced as she stared at the woman. He felt some urgency to cut to the question: Can she help Kim find a place to stay for a few days? But, until Bert called, there was no hurry. He settled in to let her finish her story. If he established a rapport, that might encourage her to help Kim.

"So, you had to go to the clubs to meet the strippers. Do you still go there, or do you have another place where you meet with them?"

"I still go to the strip clubs. Usually, several nights a week. That's where these girls work, and where I can talk to them. It's been quite an education for a woman from Jackson, Tennessee, who'd never been to a nightclub or a bar." She leaned back and held her arms out. "I've always been a church-going girl, and I went from high school to married student housing at a Bible college, to being a mom twice, and a minister's wife, all in four years. That was my life until my husband died."

"You were sheltered," Christopher said.

She gave a little wave of her hand. "Not anymore. You wouldn't believe what I've seen in the last two years. I used to worry about showing too much leg if my skirt didn't cover my knees. Lord, I've seen more private parts, male and female, than a person sees at the monkey house in the zoo."

Christopher smiled, then asked, "The men who run these clubs let you come in and talk to the girls?"

"At first, they thought I might preach at the customers, so they kept an eye on me. They accepted me once they knew I wasn't going to chase away the paying customers." She smiled. "Now they just tease me or see if they can shock me. I've learned to ignore their jokes and suggestive language, or fire back at them. I've gotten comfortable with the glitz and the lack of clothes. And I kinda like the music."

Her look turned serious. "Occasionally, one of the bartenders will tell me I need to go talk to a certain girl who's having some trouble. Some of the men who work in the clubs care about the girls. They try to protect them from aggressive customers or from getting too involved with the life." She shook her head. "Hard to believe, I know. There is good and bad in almost all of us, and sometimes the good comes out in the worst situations."

Gloria looked at Kim, then back at Christopher. "I need to ask you something before we talk much further. Are you sexually involved with this young woman?"

"No, I'm not. And I was not a customer at the spa." Christopher said. He scooted up on the couch and leaned forward. "I need to tell you about how I met her, and even though it was only five days ago, a lot has transpired."

▪ ▪ ▪

"Boseu, I found them. They are at Starbucks. Harding Road and White Bridge Road. I see Kim sitting across from a man on a couch near the back." The Asian man in the driver seat lifted the binoculars and looked again at the interior of the coffee shop as he talked on the cell phone.

"Stay there and wait. If they leave, follow them. I will send Min-jun. Two cars will help us catch them."

CHAPTER TWENTY-FOUR

Christopher told the story of Kim's run from the house in West Meade, her near encounter at the bus station, the interview with the detectives, the raid on the Green Hills spa and the West Meade house, his visit to the massage parlor in Dickson, and the frightened woman who told him about the disappearance of Sukee, Kim's friend. Gloria's eyes widened as he filled her in on Kim's narrow escape from the Koreans this morning. He shared his suspicion that someone within the police department or the DA's office was working with the Korean men.

"On Monday, we have an appointment with an official at the Korean consulate in Memphis who can help Kim get a temporary visa," he said. "With a visa, she can take a bus to San Francisco. She's confident she can find people there, other Koreans, who can help her."

Gloria leaned over and patted Kim's hand. "You're a brave woman, and God has a plan for you. He's protected you till now and will continue to protect you."

She looked back at Christopher. "And you're a good man. It's no coincidence you were at the right place at the right time. I believe everything happens for a reason."

"I don't know about that," Christopher said. He fought the instinctive urge to roll his eyes at her religiosity. "But what I know for sure is that our paths crossed, and Kim needed my help. So here I am, and Kim is here, and I'm doing my best to help her get somewhere safe."

"So, you're pretty certain someone within law enforcement is connected to these Korean men and tipped them to where Kim was."

"It appears that way. I don't know how else they could've found out where I live. We're not going back to the police again. We can't take that risk." Christopher let out an audible sigh. "We need to find a place for Kim to stay, somewhere safe, until Monday. I thought about checking her into a hotel, but I don't want to use my name or credit card in case these guys are checking around or watching my credit card for charges. It's too easy to do that these days. I may see if a buddy will do it for me unless you know another option."

As Christopher waited to see if Gloria had any ideas, he glanced out the front window and scanned the parking lot. He stiffened as he noticed a man sitting inside a car nearby, using binoculars to look at the coffee shop.

"I have a better plan," Gloria said. "How about she stays with me until Monday?"

Christopher was distracted. Was the man in the car Asian, possibly one of the men chasing them? He focused back on Gloria. "I'm not sure that's a good idea. I don't know if these men could figure it out, but if they did, they might come after you."

"They don't scare me. I'm in a condo, and my neighbors know me and look out for me. It's just for three days. We'll stay in, watch TV, maybe go to church Sunday, but mostly stay out of sight. You can check in daily and make sure we're safe."

Gloria picked up her card in front of Christopher and flipped it over. She dug a pen from her purse, wrote something on the back, and handed it to him. "That's my private cell phone number and my address. You can call me or even stop by if you want to." She stood up and straightened her skirt.

"Wait," Christopher said. He looked out the front glass of the coffee shop again. "We may have a problem. "

Gloria sank back to the couch. "What's wrong? "

"I think we're being watched."

Kim immediately curled up, trying to make herself smaller, inconspicuous. Gloria reached for her hand.

"There's a guy in the parking lot. In a black sedan," Christopher said. "He's looking this way with binoculars. Don't turn around. Let's stay here and think about what we should do next."

"You think they followed you here?" Gloria asked.

"I don't think so. We left the house so fast. I kept watching to make sure no one was following us, and I didn't see anything suspicious. But that man looks like he may be one of the Koreans. I think somehow they found us."

Christopher snapped a finger as Kim started to pivot toward the parking lot. "Keep looking at me. I don't want him to know we're on to him."

Gloria looked around the coffee shop. "I'll check for a back door." She stood and walked down the corridor that led to the restrooms. She returned in a few seconds.

"There's a back door, and I can drive around to it. It's not locked, and the door alarm is deactivated." She stood near Christopher, facing away from the front of the store, talking in a low voice. "Looks like that's where the help goes to smoke on their break. You have to go through a door that says Employees Only and walk through their storage area."

She focused on Kim and pointed toward the back with her thumb. "Walk down that hall and act as if you know where you're going. Go out the back door. It's mostly teenagers working here, and they won't stop you. I just did it. I'm going to walk out and get in my car. You wait out back till I drive around."

Kim nodded that she understood.

Gloria looked at Christopher. "Why don't you wait for a few minutes after we're gone before you leave? That'll give us a head start."

She moved away from the seating area and stood behind a display at the front counter, slithered out of her red jacket, dropped it on a nearby table, put on oversized sunglasses from her purse, and then walked out the front door behind two other women, as though they'd all been together. Christopher was impressed with how quickly she got into the mindset of misleading tactics and crafted a plan. Not bad for a preacher's wife.

He looked at Kim. "We're going to be okay. Go with Gloria. I'll call you later. Be brave."

Kim nodded, then walked down the corridor and out of sight.

CHAPTER TWENTY-FIVE

Christopher planned to give Gloria and Kim a ten-minute head-start before he left, but as he watched out the plate-glass window of the coffee shop, a maroon minivan pulled up beside the black sedan. An Asian man got out of the van and leaned into the car's side window. Christopher decided the odds were not shifting in his favor. He dumped his coffee, left the store, and walked briskly to his Buick.

As he pulled out of the parking lot, he saw in his rear-view mirror that the black sedan followed him, maybe five car lengths back. His pulse picked up. Should he stay on Harding Road? It was a busy four-lane, so the person in the car could only follow him. But he needed to get rid of him eventually. He decided to deal with it now. His tires squealed as he turned off Harding Road onto a side street that wound through a familiar residential area.

The sedan was about thirty feet behind him but seemed to be gaining on him. There was only one person in the car that he could see. Would the guy try to run him off the road? Then what, shoot him? Christopher rechecked his mirror. This time the driver was holding a pistol out the window in his left hand and appeared to be pointing it at him. In the middle of the day, in a residential neighborhood!

Christopher hit his brakes, skidded around a corner, then stomped the gas pedal. This was the neighborhood where he delivered newspapers. He knew each house and yard, every street corner and ditch.

His phone rang, but he couldn't risk slowing down to dig it out of his pants pocket. He let it go to voice mail.

The streets were empty, and most had good sightlines at corners, so Christopher blew through two stop signs, leaving the sedan even further behind. He knew a residence around a corner a few streets away with a driveway that circled behind the house and out the other side. A hedge by the road hid the driveway entrance. After another turn, he was near the house and, with a good lead on the sedan, he turned the corner by the hedge, wheeled into the driveway, ducked behind the house, and slid to a stop, hoping no one was home. With his driver's window rolled down, he heard the black sedan roar around the corner and up the street. He briefly entertained the notion of following the sedan and ramming it from behind to strike back at the Koreans, but he decided that, since the driver had a gun, the chances of it ending badly for him were pretty good.

Christopher eased his Buick out the other end of the driveway, checked to be sure the black sedan was nowhere in sight, and then sped off. A few minutes later, he was out of the neighborhood and back on a busy four-lane road. Ditching the Korean made him feel elated momentarily, but his brow knitted again with worry about Barbara and Amy. He needed to reach Bert.

▪ ▪ ▪

The Asian man with the shiny pompadour stood inside the Starbucks, his gaze darting around as he checked every person in the store. After a minute, he walked to the back and down the hall. The bathrooms were empty. A door marked "Employees Only" was locked. As he walked back through the coffee shop, he checked out every couch and chair again. No sign of Kim.

▪ ▪ ▪

Christopher dug his phone out, checked the missed call, and then hit redial.

Bert said, "Barbara called her mother in Birmingham and said she needed to get away for the weekend and asked if she and Amy could visit. They're on the road."

"Good. I feel better knowing they are out of town."

"You won't feel good after Barbara gets hold of you. She's pissed. And Amy's not happy that she's missing the school dance."

"I'm sure I'll get an earful. Thanks for handling it so quickly. I found a safe place for Kim to stay until Monday."

Christopher told Bert about meeting Gloria Jean, handing off Kim, the Asian man showing up at Starbucks, and the car chase through the West Meade neighborhood.

"Damn! Those guys are serious. Wonder how they found you."

"Don't know, but I'm a little spooked."

"So, what about you?" Bert asked. "Where're you going to go?"

"I don't know yet. It's probably not a good idea to stay at my house, but I'm heading there to grab some clothes while these guys are still circling through West Meade looking for me. I still have Gracie's body in my trunk. I guess I'll go ahead and bury her in the back yard."

"You need some help? I'm at work, but I can leave and be at your house in thirty or forty minutes."

"No, I want to do this by myself. Maybe after that, I can think of what I need to do next. Probably should get a hotel room for a few days."

"Come stay with me. My neighborhood is a good distance away, so the Korean guys won't bump into you. Barbara and Amy are gone till Sunday. I'll be home in an hour. We'll hang out, have a beer, give each other shit just like we used to when we were roomies at Peay."

For a moment, the idea appealed to Christopher despite his ambivalence about renewing a friendship with Bert. He needed someone to help him think through his next moves, someone who had connections. He would love to confront these Korean guys but might need backup. Bert was the logical person. But then he thought about spending the night at his old house, now Bert's house. His hand tightened around the cell phone. No, that wouldn't work. He wasn't ready to rip the scab off that wound just yet. He realized Bert was still clueless about his hurt and anger. They needed to talk. But confrontation never came easy for Christopher.

"I need to think through what I do next," Christopher said, buying a little time.

"I'm serious, buddy. Come stay with me."

"I'll call you back within the hour."

▪ ▪ ▪

Gloria checked her rearview mirror and then glanced at Kim. "Your t-shirt has a little blood on it. Do you have any extra clothes?"

"I have one t-shirt and pants in Christopher's house. I cannot go back there," Kim replied.

"Well, a woman needs clothes and makeup. And shoes." Gloria switched lanes and headed toward an exit ramp that said Church Street. "I know a place where there's lots of clothes, nice clothes, all donated to help someone like you. It's part of Catholic Ministries, next to The Cathedral downtown."

They turned into the parking lot of the large, century-old church. Gloria wheeled around to the back and parked in front of a nondescript red-brick building. A sign by a propped-open metal door read LADIES OF CHARITY, DONATIONS ACCEPTED HERE. A woman unloaded boxes of clothes and shoes from a station wagon parked nearby.

"We'll help you carry all that," Gloria said. "Kim, grab one of those boxes, but watch for rocks on the pavement. Don't want to injure your bare feet."

They followed the woman inside and dropped the boxes on the counter. Kim looked around at the racks of clothes and shoes.

"Let's go see what they have that you might like." Gloria looked Kim up and down. "You look like a size two, maybe even a petite two. I don't think I was ever that small."

They found the right section, and Gloria pulled out a pair of light tan slacks. "What do you think about these?" She pawed through blouses and held one up. "This may fit you. It would work with those slacks."

As Kim took the clothes, Gloria pointed toward a dressing room. "Go back there and try them on. I'll get some more and bring them to you."

An hour later, they walked out of the building with a used roll-aboard suitcase filled with blouses, skirts, jeans, slacks, a hooded rain jacket, tennis shoes and ballet slippers, two pairs of flats, panties and bras.

Gloria had insisted that the clothes were practically free, but Kim saw her get a wad of bills from her purse and leave them on the counter after talking to the woman at the cash register in a low voice. Gloria seemed to fill the store as she chatted with all the women, including other customers and the staff. Her smile was warm, and she had a husky, infectious laugh.

"We'll stop at Walgreens next," Gloria said. "You need to get a toothbrush and other toiletries and some makeup. Then we'll stop at the grocery store. I want you to show me what you like to cook. I've never had Korean food, but I bet it's good." Gloria smiled as she cut her eyes toward Kim.

Kim smiled back and nodded. "You have chicken or beef?"

"I have chicken breasts in the fridge. What else do you need?"

"I fix you bi bim bap. It's easy to fix and delicious." Kim started ticking off the ingredients on her fingers. "I need rice, spinach, carrots, sprouts, mushrooms, and eggs. You have spices?

Sesame oil? I make special sauce, too."

Gloria nodded. "I have sesame oil and plenty of spices. I like to cook, and I like trying new dishes."

"You will like Korean dish. Healthy and spicy."

"Great! We'll stop by Kroger after Walgreens and get what you need. Cooking is always fun."

CHAPTER TWENTY-SIX

As Christopher neared his house on Ashland City Highway, he saw a police cruiser beside the road near his mailbox. He slowed to look and got a return stare from the officer.

His phone rang with a blocked call as he walked up to the broken front door of his home. He hesitated at first but decided he should answer.

A terse voice said, "This is Detective Simpson. Are you at your house?"

"Yes," Christopher answered.

"Stay there. O'Reilly and I will be there in about forty-five minutes."

After he hung up, Christopher grappled with how to handle the conversation with the detectives. Who was the leak, and what was his connection to the Koreans? O'Reilly seemed like a straight shooter. Simpson hung back, and with his furtive look, he appeared to be the most likely candidate. Of course, the leak could be inside the District Attorney's office.

He had always trusted law enforcement and the justice system. It was an isolating feeling to be dealing with a threat to his family and his safety and not be able to contact the police.

He walked into the dining room and looked at the strewn computers and broken parts on the floor. He stooped and gathered up the pieces. He needed to call the customers. He thought about the cost of losing two customers, plus the cost of replacing their computers, and his anger and frustration grew.

Christopher climbed the stairs to his bedroom and pulled

a worn duffle bag from his closet. He threw in his shaving kit and a few clothes, then returned to the living room and dropped the duffle bag on the couch. He went to his shed and grabbed a long-handled shovel and his work gloves.

The hole was easy to dig in the soft soil of the garden, near the scarecrow. Christopher returned to his car and gathered up the blanketed body of his dog. After he settled Gracie in the hole, he stood over her grave and tried to think of something to say.

"You were a good dog, and Amy and I were glad you were our dog for three years." His voice choked up. A tear ran down his cheek. "You saved Kim and didn't deserve to die for it. I swear I'll find who did this and make them pay." He rubbed the tears off his cheeks and shoveled dirt into the hole.

He had just put the shovel back in the shed when the unmarked car pulled into the drive and parked. The two detectives walked through the gate and met him in front of his house. Simpson dropped a cigarette on the sidewalk and rubbed it out with his shoe, which irritated Christopher.

"May we come in?" O'Reilly asked, taking the lead this time over Simpson, the older detective. Christopher shrugged, said, "Okay," and led the way up the steps to the front door.

"Why is your front door frame broken?" Simpson asked.

Christopher pushed the door open, stepped in, and turned to look at the detective with a skeptical eye. "Someone kicked it in this morning while I was delivering papers."

O'Reilly walked to the middle of the living room and looked around briefly. Simpson stayed near the door. Christopher felt as if they were trying to intimidate him.

"Where's the young lady, the Korean?" O'Reilly asked.

"She's not here."

"Where is she?"

"She's safe. I'm not saying anything more." Christopher said. He knew his tone was defiant, but he didn't care.

"Why not?" O'Reilly asked, his tone hardened.

Christopher hesitated but then decided it was time to put his cards on the table. "We had a home invasion this morning. It happened early, before dawn, while I was out delivering papers. Kim heard Gracie—my dog—barking. She saw two Korean men get out of a car in front. She ran out the back door and hid. They shot and killed my dog and ransacked my house. They threw my computers on the floor and stomped them before they left. I took Kim someplace where she's safe."

Christopher decided not to tell them about the missing photos and his feeling that his ex-wife Barbara and Amy might be in danger. They would probably blow it off as paranoia. His mistrust of the law enforcement system was growing.

Neither of the detectives reacted to the news that the Korean men shot Gracie. He could tell that she was just an old dog to them. No great loss.

"You didn't report the break-in?" O'Reilly asked.

"No." Christopher knew his one-word answer sounded curt.

O'Reilly stepped toward the dining room and looked around. "Looks like you've already started cleaning up. I can request the CI guys come and dust for fingerprints."

"Kim said they had on gloves," Christopher said.

O'Reilly glanced at Simpson and then crossed his arms as he faced Christopher.

"You should still make a police report. If you need protection, we can provide it. But we need to know where Kim is. We need to interview her again about this Korean, the Boss fellow. The DA's office wants us to bring her in today."

Christopher shook his head. "I'll check with her, see if she wants to talk again. For now, she's scared and wants to stay hidden."

O'Reilly stepped closer and pointed a finger in Christopher's face. "You can't hide her. That's obstructing our case against the spa owner. We need to know where she is."

Christopher stood his ground, crossing his arms and not hiding his defiance. "I don't think she trusts you guys. I know she doesn't want to go anywhere near the police station. One of the other girls you arrested at the spa told her someone there is telling the Korean, the boss man, everything that's happening. She feels threatened, and I think she's right. Somehow, they knew she was staying here."

O'Reilly stared at him for a minute. "Are you saying someone with law enforcement is tipping off the Koreans? You think there's a dirty cop doing this?"

"I'm saying I don't know how the Koreans found out where she was staying. They showed up here pretty fast." Christopher could feel his anger growing. His voice got louder. "Yeah, I think that girl from the spa you arrested may be right. Someone with the police or the DA's office is helping the Koreans."

O'Reilly's face flushed red with anger. "That's a serious accusation. And not telling us where Kim is staying is a mistake. I need to make a phone call. Stay here," he ordered. He walked out the front door, followed by Simpson.

Christopher watched them through the front picture window as they stood by their car. O'Reilly talked on his cell. Simpson fired up another cigarette as he stood nearby listening. O'Reilly hung up and spoke to Simpson for a few minutes. They appeared at first to disagree, but Simpson finally nodded. He turned to face the house again. O'Reilly made another call.

Christopher knew his raw emotions about burying his dog fueled his anger, and perhaps he shouldn't have yelled at the detectives. He considered apologizing for the heat in his remarks but decided he didn't regret the words.

The detectives stayed by their car, and within minutes a police cruiser pulled into the driveway. Two uniformed officers got out and talked briefly with O'Reilly. The four men walked back up the sidewalk and in the front door.

O'Reilly walked to within three feet of Christopher. "Mr. Jones, do you still refuse to tell us where the Korean girl is?" he asked.

Christopher nodded but took a half step back, a little less sure.

"Then you're under arrest for obstruction of justice. Put your hands behind your back. These officers will cuff you and take you to the Criminal Justice Center for processing."

Christopher froze and looked at the detectives in disbelief. "You're arresting me?" His voice rose. "My home is vandalized, my dog shot and killed, and you're going to arrest *me*?"

The two officers stepped toward him. "Sir, put your hands behind your back," said the one closest to him as he reached for the handcuffs on his belt. Christopher slowly complied.

CHAPTER TWENTY-SEVEN

The trip to the CJC and the processing took over two hours. After suffering the humiliation of mug shots and fingerprinting, he was allowed a phone call. He called the only person he knew who might be able to help him.

Luckily, Bert answered his cell. "Thought you were going to call me back in an hour."

"I'm in a bit of trouble." Christopher told him everything that had occurred since they had talked almost three hours ago.

"Damn, dude!" Bert said. "You have really..." but to Christopher's relief, he didn't say more. There was a long pause. "I have an attorney friend, Bruce Parsley. He's got juice within the court system, and I know a bail bondsman. I'll start working on getting you out. It may take a while, though."

After another pause, Bert added, "This is a bullshit charge. It's intimidation by the law at its worst. Parsley will get hold of a judge and explain what's going on. Don't worry. This crap will go no place."

"You think I'll have to stay overnight?"

"Cops love Friday afternoon arrests because that usually means you're in jail over the weekend. We'll have to hurry, but I bet Parsley can get you out today. If I see it's not happening, I'll get word to you."

Christopher thanked him. A few minutes later he was in a holding cell, sitting on the bench, head in his hands. This felt like a bad dream. How could he wind up in jail over trying to help a young woman? Couldn't they understand he was trying to protect her, not obstruct justice? How could he be arrested for that? This was the worst day of his life. His good deed may have put his family at risk, and his life was possibly in danger. Now he sat in a jail cell. How could it be any worse? He considered telling the detectives where Kim was staying but couldn't bring himself to do it. He knew she felt threatened, and she was scared. So far, the events seemed to indicate she was right.

"You okay?" Bert asked as they drove away from the Criminal Justice Center late that afternoon.

"Hell no, I'm not okay." Christopher slumped in the corner of Bert's Suburban. "First time I've been in jail, even if it was only a few hours. I'm humiliated, I'm pissed, and I feel lower than a flattened squirrel."

"You've been set up, that's for sure. Bruce Parsley swears he's never seen anything like how they railroaded you, and he's been around Criminal Court for over ten years."

Nothing else was said between them until they turned onto Ashland City Highway and headed toward Christopher's house. "What are you going to do now?" Bert asked.

"I've already packed a bag. I guess I'll go to your house for tonight, sleep on the couch if the offer still stands."

"Of course it does."

"I need to get my head together. I'm worried the Koreans may still be looking for me. Maybe we can talk about what I can do to shake them loose. And maybe talk about some other things."

Bert glanced over at him. "Hey, man, whatever's on your mind."

Christopher looked out the window as they pulled into his driveway. "I started to say I needed to lock up and feed Gracie, but my front door is kicked in, my customers' computers destroyed, and Gracie's dead and buried in the back yard. It's been a hell of a day."

"I have a six-pack of Sam Adams in the fridge, and I'll call in a pizza. Grab your bag. I'll wait here till you get in your car, just to be sure no one is watching your house."

CHAPTER TWENTY-EIGHT

The detective stood inside Daily's Market and held his phone to his ear, waiting. He glanced over his shoulder at his partner, sitting in the unmarked police car, and he pretended to look at bags of trail mix.

"Yes?" the man with the raspy voice said.

"Just so you know, we couldn't hold the guy, Jones, for very long. He had a good lawyer, and a judge ordered him released on his own recognizance."

The Korean grunted but said nothing.

"But I have a plan in the works." He waited for a response, but there was none. "I talked to a reporter, off the record. I gave him some background on the raid in Dickson, told him we had arrested Christopher Jones for obstruction of justice. This guy wrote the story about the Green Hills raid. I think he will do a follow-up story and mention Jones. That'll get Jones stirred up and probably make him willing to cooperate."

No response.

"I gotta go," the detective said. "I'll check in tomorrow sometime, maybe with the location of the girl you're after." He waited again, but no response.

The detective ended the call and slid the phone into his pocket. He strode to the cooler, grabbed two Cokes, and headed to the checkout counter.

▪ ▪ ▪

After a beer and pizza, Christopher felt somewhat human again, except for the rage still seething in his soul. He half reclined on the tweed sofa and looked around the familiar den. Same couch, different recliner, bigger TV. Bert leaned back in his leather chair and took a long swig from his second Sam.

"Barbara says I drink too much, says I need to quit the beer, or I'll develop a gut." He held the beer bottle up and tilted it toward Christopher, and grinned. "I tell her I'm not a quitter."

Christopher smiled faintly. "She had a rule about not having alcohol in the house after Amy was born. Her dad was an alcoholic, she would always say, and no way was she living with another man with a drinking problem. That was one of her many rules."

"She's a strong personality. Probably has something to do with her running a dysfunctional household since she was ten or eleven." Bert belched and changed the subject.

"You still worked up over the Koreans?"

"I'm mad as hell." Christopher could feel his face heat up. "I don't want to let those sons of bitches get away with busting into my house, destroying my computers, killing my dog, and stealing photos of my little girl and her mother."

"What do you want to do about it?"

"I want to fight back, make them pay."

"Okay, how?" Bert asked.

"I would love to mess with something they own. Maybe break into their house, bash out a few windows, steal something."

Bert drained the rest of his beer and looked away in contemplation. "We can do more than that. You think you can find out where this boss man lives?"

"The boss man?" Christopher thought about it for a minute, then sat forward in alert mode, both feet flat on the floor. "The Assistant DA made a comment about knowing that their top guy, the boss, lives around here, but they don't know where. He owns the spas and a Korean restaurant, maybe other businesses. One of the detectives said he was hiding behind a corporation. He said a Nashville law firm set it up."

"That means there's probably paperwork on file with the corporate address," Bert said.

"We might be able to find the boss's home address if we could somehow get access to the business license and corporate documents for that spa in Green Hills."

"I can't get access, but I know a guy who probably can." Christopher gave a half cough, half chuckle. "If we get their home address, then what?"

"I think we take it to these guys." Bert tilted his empty beer bottle at Christopher. "They may have resources in the police department they're using against us, but we have our own resources. You interested?"

"I don't know what you have in mind, but hell, yes, I'm interested. I'm tired of feeling helpless."

"I learned a few things over in Iraq, especially the second time around." Bert's smile had a touch of deviousness.

"Like what?" Christopher knew Bert was on the bomb squad on his tour during the first Iraq war. On his second tour, when his reserve unit was called up in 2008, Bert was in charge of the bomb squad. Bert hadn't told him much about his experiences over there, only that some of the squad guys were crazy. Had to be, just to stay sane, he'd said. Their job was to defuse live bombs, and the enemy continually improved their bomb-making capability. It made their already dangerous work riskier.

"We got tired of the Shittites trying to blow us up all the time, so we went on the offensive. We learned from them. They were masters of small but powerful bombs. Bomb-making materials were not a problem; most of the stuff you needed to make one was easily available. The same stuff's available over here, too. Hell, I have a storage unit with some devices ready to go. I say we find out where this boss guy lives, and we make a house call."

"Wait. You just happen to have a few bombs in a storage unit?"

"Maybe it's a bit of an odd hobby, but yes."

"Bert, that's crazy!"

Bert shrugged. "Lots of army guys who've served in Iraq or Afghanistan have skills and maybe a little paranoia that translates into collecting guns and other weaponry. Bombs just happen to be my thing. And I think this is the perfect opportunity to use one of these devices. These are evil dudes. Let's take it to this boss guy and blow his doors off. That'll give him something to worry about. What d'you think?"

"Pretty illegal."

Bert grinned. "Hey, we got the time, so let's do the crime."

"I don't want to kill anybody, but if you're just talking about messing up his house, doing a little damage, then I'm in," Christopher said.

"Atta boy. I knew you had a vindictive streak." Bert leaned forward and held up a palm for a high-five.

Christopher hesitated, then gave the high-five slap. They weren't buddies again, he thought, but at least they were united around this cause. He could put his mistrust toward Bert aside and have it out with him later.

"Tell me about your guy," Bert said. "The one you said could dig out the boss's address."

"Artie Samuels. He's a computer security consultant we hired at HCA to make sure hackers couldn't get into our systems. I headed up the project."

Christopher settled back on the couch as he told his story. "I'd heard of Artie, knew he lived somewhere around here, but when I finally reached him, he was reluctant to meet with us. Said he could check our systems from his home and email the results. Our chief tech officer insisted that Artie meet with us and tell us how he'd do it. Since we were going to pay big bucks for his skills, he agreed. I wasn't sure about him at first. Artie's a middle-aged fat guy with a smoker's cough. Thick glasses, chronic smoker, a loner, but computer savvy and smart as hell. I took a risk and vouched for him."

Christopher waved an arm. "Long story short, he found several vulnerabilities in our system. Our IT guys weren't happy, but they couldn't argue. They said his hacking skills were far superior to the typical hacker."

"Sounds like a guy I need to know. Did you stay in touch with him?"

Christopher hesitated, then said, "I guess you could say we became friends, sort of. We swapped emails regularly and occasionally talked by phone, especially after I left HCA. During one of those conversations a few months ago, I could tell he was short of breath and struggling for air. I told him he needed to go to the ER and get checked out. He refused, said he was too sick, and couldn't drive. Said he'd wait and see. I wound up taking him. So, I'm probably the only person who knows where he lives, except maybe a pizza delivery guy."

Christopher remembered the trip with Artie to the St. Thomas ER and the conversation with a pulmonologist. After a breathing treatment and more meds, Christopher took Artie back to his apartment west of downtown. He had slept on Artie's couch that night just to be sure he was okay.

"Artie wants to stay off the grid. He does some illegal hacking, and he's part of a network of guys who will take off-the-books projects for the right price."

"My kind of guy," Bert said. "You want to give him a call now?"

"He uses different phones to conduct his business; most are disposable. I'm one of a select few with his private number."

Christopher dug out his cell, located the number, and pressed it. "Wassup, my brother," a phlegmy voice said.

"Artie, I got a situation and need your special talents."

Christopher filled him in on the last few days and the need to locate the residence of the Korean boss.

Artie grunted. "This doesn't sound all that hard. I can access the Metro business license files and look for the application. There's probably a lawyer's name on it somewhere.

Law firms never have much security around their network systems. I should be able to find a legal contract with this Korean guy and get a name and address off it. I'll have this info for you in an hour, I bet."

"I'm willing to pay for it."

"Your money's no good with me."

Christopher could picture Artie's mammoth body sitting in his oversized leather desk chair, hunched over his bank of computers in the extra bedroom. He closed his phone and looked at Bert. "We'll have good intelligence in about an hour or two."

Bert slapped his palms on the arms of the recliner and stood up. "I need to run some errands. Be out a couple hours."

"No problem. I want to check on Kim, and I need to call Amy."

"I filled Barbara in on everything but told her not to tell Amy about Gracie. I said you wanted to be the one to tell her what happened."

"Thanks. It's not a conversation I want to have, but yes, I need to tell her."

CHAPTER TWENTY-NINE

Christopher texted Amy and told her to call him in the morning. He moved to the kitchen table and fired up his laptop to check his emails. Two customer inquiries asked about the status of their computer repair work. Christopher sent brief apologies saying he had a personal issue to deal with that would delay his promised delivery date till next week.

After Kim is gone next Monday, he might be able to salvage the hard drives out of the busted computers in his dining room, get replacement machines, and hopefully, deliver a satisfactory solution to his customers. He would explain about the break-in and the damage. Maybe he could keep them as satisfied customers. His homeowner's insurance would probably not cover the business loss. He should have purchased a separate policy, but it was an expense he couldn't afford until recently.

Christopher checked his calendar for appointments on Monday and sent two more emails to customers explaining he needed to reschedule their service from Monday till Thursday or Friday. He hoped they would accept the delay.

He shut down his computer and pulled out Gloria's blue business card from his billfold. He leaned against the kitchen counter as he called to check on Kim.

"She's doing fine," Gloria said in her soft drawl. "We've had a good talk, did a little shopping, and now we're watching TV. Given what she's been through, I already have a world of respect for her. There's a lot of toughness and smarts all wrapped up in this little package."

Christopher had to smile. He hesitated to tell her about his day but decided they shouldn't hold anything back from each other. There were a few gasps from Gloria as he laid out the saga of his arrest, his brief time in jail, and finally, where he was spending the night. He told her more than he intended.

"So, Bert was your roommate at Austin Peay, then after college, your best friend when he wasn't off fighting in the Iraq War, and now he's married to your ex-wife. That is a wild story. I bet things are a little awkward between you two after all of that."

"Yeah, a little awkward. I've hardly spoken to him since I heard about their engagement almost two years ago. We had to see each other occasionally, like when he picked up Amy, and he always tried to act as if everything was normal, but I couldn't buy it."

"And yet here you are today, calling on him when you're in trouble, and now staying with him." She chuckled. "God has a way of forcing us to face our demons."

"I wouldn't say he's a demon, but sometimes he does show some horns. And he doesn't always understand boundaries."

"What kind of business is he in?"

"Security. All kinds of security. For famous people, people in trouble, even big events."

"That's got to be a rough business. Maybe he's the right person to have on our side for what we're dealing with."

Christopher was glad she included herself. He liked this woman, even if she was too religious and mystical for his taste.

His phone beeped, and he saw it was Artie calling.

"I gotta grab this call. I'll check in again tomorrow sometime."

"No worries," she responded. "We're staying in."

Christopher pressed the button on his phone to end his call with Gloria and accept the incoming call.

"The guy's name is Cho Lee, and I have his address for you." Artie's short-of-breath voice was animated.

"Great! How'd you do that?"

"Didn't take long. I found the spa's address, then chased down that rabbit hole for incorporation papers. You don't want to know the firewall I broke through. From there, I got the lawyer's name who created the shell corporation, went into their office network, and found notes with a name and mailing address in Brentwood."

"That's some good detective work. We'll figure out a way to confirm it's the right house," Christopher said.

"Yeah, I got that handled, too. I called one of my drone buddies. He lives not far from the house and liked the idea of a flyover mission. We looked on Google maps, confirmed the location, and saw that Brentwood High School is a few blocks away from the house. He drove to the field behind the high school and launched his drone to get aerial shots. I think you'll be pleased when you see them."

"Wow, Artie. You did a lot in a short time."

"Timing and luck were on our side. I think we hit the jackpot. A maroon van pulled in as he flew his drone over the house. He circled overhead and watched the video feed on his computer. He took a few photos and got a great shot of this Asian guy getting out of the van and looking up at the drone. I emailed the photos to you. Check 'em out."

Christopher booted up his laptop as they talked and scrolled through over a dozen photos of a two-story brick home. The next-to-last photo showed a maroon van pulling into the driveway beside a black sedan. The last one had the upturned face of the Korean man that Christopher now knew as Kwan.

Bert walked in the kitchen door, and Christopher waved him over as he finished the conversation with Artie.

"It's the right house and the right man. Artie, you and your drone buddy outdid yourselves. I owe you both big time."

Artie laughed, then coughed. "I'll apply it against the debt I already owe you. We are far from even."

Christopher ended the call and picked up his laptop. He placed it on the kitchen counter and tilted it toward Bert.

"Artie found the Korean boss man's house. His name is Cho Lee, and he lives in Brentwood. I have his address, and I've got a picture of one of the Korean guys. I remember him from the bus station on Monday. Look at these photos." He paged down through the pictures.

"How'd you get all that?" Bert squinted as he leaned forward to peer at the computer screen.

"Like I said, my computer genius friend loves these riddles. He tore into this like a beagle after a rabbit." He filled Bert in on how Artie had tracked down the address where the Korean boss lived, and how he'd enlisted a buddy to do a drone flyover.

"This is the one that seals the deal." He pointed at the photo of the maroon van with the man looking up at the sky. "I've seen this van. Kim says this guy's name is Kwan. He's the enforcer."

Bert looked around the kitchen, then grabbed reading glasses off the counter nearby. "I need to look at these again with my peepers on."

Christopher stepped back and watched Bert as he paged through the images and studied the streets and the views of a big, two-story brick house with front columns.

"Typical Brentwood McMansion," Bert said. "Probably over five thousand square feet."

"So, now that we know where he lives, what's next?"

Bert twisted his head and looked at Christopher over his readers. "Let's take the fight to them. To quote the wise philosopher, Mike Tyson, 'Everyone has a plan until they get punched in the mouth.' Let's punch back, give them something else to worry about, and maybe they'll forget about Kim and you."

"What do you have in mind?" Christopher asked.

"I have a couple of backpacks I rigged up a while back in my storage unit. We wait till midnight, go to Brentwood, and leave a present on their doorstep." Bert wiggled his eyebrows. His eyes were wide and bright.

CHAPTER THIRTY

They decided to take Christopher's car since Bert said he needed to be the one to leave the present on the porch step.

It was after eleven when they arrived at a large storage complex tucked in behind a U-Haul rental store. Bert entered the code, the mechanical gate swung open, and he directed Christopher to drive down several rows of buildings and stop in front of unit 56. Bert pulled a ring of keys from his pocket, unlocked the padlock, and raised the door. "Pop your trunk," he said as he hurried inside.

Christopher saw a long narrow space with shelf units on one side and a metal workbench on the other. There was a gun safe and stacks of plastic bins in the back, all organized and anonymous. It looked like an excellent place to stash the detritus collected from two stints on the battlefield and almost twenty years of bachelorhood. Stuff Christopher knew Barbara would never let a man drag into her house or her marriage.

Bert pulled a storage trunk out from under the workbench, opened it, and removed two black backpacks—a small one like a kid would use to carry a few schoolbooks and a slightly larger one the size of an adult daypack. He dropped them on the bench, unzipped one, fiddled with something inside, and then zipped it shut. Bert went through the same drill with the other backpack, grabbed both, slid the door down, and padlocked it. He dropped the backpacks in the trunk of the Buick and slammed the lid. Then he slipped inside the car.

"There's a disposable phone in each backpack. I just turned them on. I'll call from another phone, and that's the ignition for the Semtex." Bert had explained this briefly while they were making plans earlier, but he went over it again as they drove to Brentwood. "I'm careful to use untraceable phones since pieces may survive the blast."

"Why two backpacks?" Christopher asked.

"I call them Big Boom and Bigger Boom. I want to assess the situation and decide which is the right one for what we want to do."

"You said our plan is only to scare them, not kill anyone. What if one of the Korean guys hears the phone ringing and comes to the door?" Christopher asked.

"The ringer is turned off. But even if it weren't, it would only ring once, only a half ring, then boom. And I may not leave it on the porch. Just somewhere near the front of the house. I'll decide where we'll leave it once we get there."

Bert wore black jeans and a black hooded sweatshirt. Christopher had on his light gray hoody, the one he wore every morning delivering papers. Another reason for him to stay in the car, Bert said.

Christopher thought a moment about their plan. Could they get away with it? What would happen if they were caught? He bit a fingernail and worried a bit but didn't say anything to Bert.

They drove slowly down the street in front of the Brentwood house. The yard was wide and deep, with a long driveway flanked by brick columns topped with gaslight fixtures that shed a faint light. Two cars were parked in the driveway, side by side, in front of the double garage. Christopher recognized the maroon minivan he'd seen at the bus station.

"Drive by again, this time with your lights off," Bert said. "Go slow so I can look for security cameras." He twisted around as they drove by. "Looks like cameras at the front door and the corners of the house. The front door camera may reach out about fifty feet. I need to sneak up from the side, let the cars shield me." He twisted around again and checked out the houses nearby. "Probably most of these houses have cameras at their front door and above their garage, but their lawns are huge. Their front door cameras aren't reaching this road."

They kept going and approached the next intersection. "Stop here," Bert ordered. He reached up and flipped off the interior light so it wouldn't flash on when a door opened.

"Pop the trunk." He got out and went to the back of the car, raised the trunk lid, then shut it carefully and slid into the front passenger seat.

Christopher eyed the backpack in Bert's lap. "Remember, let's not kill anyone. I want to scare them. Make them think someone is after them."

"This one has a smaller damage radius. Here's how we're doing it. Drive back to the house, lights off, and stop across the street from their driveway. I'll jump out and drop this backpack between the two cars, get back in, and we cruise on down the road." Bert had a crooked grin.

Christopher did not grin back, but he did complete the U-turn and drove slowly up the street to the house, car lights still off. He stopped at the driveway and watched Bert open the car door and scuttle to the rear of the cars, carrying the backpack in both hands. He left it leaning against the back wheel of the black sedan.

"Okay, let's go," Bert said as he jumped in the Buick and shut the door.

Christopher kept his car lights off, and as he punched the gas, momentarily fishtailing in the grass on the side of the street, he clipped a mailbox.

"Dammit! That probably messed up my right front headlight."

"And also left evidence. Maybe paint, maybe tire treads," Bert added grimly.

Christopher turned on the main drive leading out of the upscale subdivision as Bert dug out his wallet, pulled a slip of paper from it, retrieved his reading glasses from his sweatshirt pocket, and reached for a cell phone in the console between them.

"That's the phone number?" Christopher asked.

"There are three phone numbers. Pull off over there." Bert pointed at a wide spot on the street, in a dark area away from streetlights. He switched the interior light on and focused on the paper.

"Three numbers?" Christopher asked as he slowed to a stop about a half-mile from the Korean's house.

"Yeah, the first one is this phone." Bert held it up. "The second one is Big Boom, the phone in the backpack I just dropped off." He entered the number and twisted around to look out the rear window.

"Boom," he said softly. Almost immediately, there was a dull boom a few blocks behind them, then another crack and a flash of fire.

"That was probably one or both of the car gas tanks. Let's boogie."

Christopher hit the gas, and the Buick lurched. They sped down the neighborhood street, turning first on a connector street. He switched on the car headlights as they turned out to the main road. Bert kept looking back at the red glow, now over a mile away.

They were quiet as they stopped at a traffic light on an almost deserted four-lane road in the commercial area near the ramp leading to Interstate 65. Then Bert pointed at a police officer in a patrol car waiting at the corner, even though his traffic light was green.

"Let's hope that cop is not staring at the front of your car. Can you tell if you knocked out a headlight?"

"Can't tell," Christopher muttered. As their traffic light turned green and they started through the intersection, the patrol car's emergency lights and siren switched on. Christopher's stomach lurched as he prepared to pull over. Bert wheeled around to stare out the back window. The patrol car turned away from them and sped off in the opposite direction.

"He must have got a call about the explosion and fire," Bert said.

Christopher drove slowly to the next intersection and stopped at a red light before he glanced over at Bert and let out a long slow breath. "I was preparing myself for another arrest. This time for blowing up two cars."

Bert shook his head. "I was too." He glanced down at the paper in his hand. "I briefly considered if I should just go ahead and dial this third number."

"What was the third phone number?" Christopher asked.

Bert looked down at the paper in his hand. He handed it to Christopher. "See the third number labeled Bigger Boom? That's for the backpack still in your trunk."

Christopher studied the numbers written on the notebook paper. "How did you know you were calling the right one the first time?"

"Well, I figured that was important, so I double-checked the numbers on the cells," Bert said.

"How could you be sure you had the right backpack?" Christopher asked. "You were grabbing it in the dark."

"I made sure. Bigger Boom is a lot heavier. It packs a big enough wallop to bring that house down if we felt we needed to do that."

Christopher looked at him, his eyes wide. "You have a bomb still in my trunk that can knock down a house?"

Bert nodded. "Yeah. If I'd put it in the yard, a short way from the front of the house, it would've knocked the front columns down, broken out all the windows, and probably knocked loose most of the brick on the front. But we just wanted to scare them, so I went with Big Boom, not Bigger Boom."

"And the numbers to each are on this strip of paper, labeled correctly, hopefully," Christopher said, staring at the paper in his hand, then glancing at Bert.

Bert grinned his maniacal grin, familiar to Christopher from their wilder, single days. "If I'd mixed up the numbers, then we would've joined all the martyrs in paradise." He looked out the front window and pointed at the traffic light. "And that's as green as this light gets."

Christopher looked up at the light and stepped on the gas as he stuffed the paper with the numbers in the front pocket of his hooded sweatshirt.

CHAPTER THIRTY-ONE

SATURDAY

The talking head on Channel 4 led the five AM local newscast with the story of a mysterious explosion in front of a house in Brentwood. No one was hurt, but the blast destroyed two automobiles. Police klieg lights shined on the front of the house as the camera panned across to show the hulks of two cars still smoldering in the morning darkness, and damaged garage doors bent and pushed in. Pieces of cars decorated the driveway and the front yard. The front of the house didn't appear to be damaged, though a few windows looked broken.

A TV reporter stood near the house and held a microphone as she breathlessly informed her audience that police were investigating, but it did appear to be an intentional act. The owner of the house was unavailable for comment, and she could not get his name, the reporter added.

Christopher turned off the TV, slipped out the front door, and walked to his car. He knew the story would not make the morning newspaper since it happened after midnight. He moved sluggishly, not feeling fully awake. The adrenaline rush from the late-night caper had kept him and Bert up till after two, and between them they polished off a six-pack of Sam Adams dark. Even after they went to bed, Christopher found it impossible to sleep. Bits and pieces of the late-night conversation drifted around his mind.

"You learned to make bombs by dismantling them?" he'd asked Bert as they sat in the den. ESPN's SportsCenter was on the TV, sound turned down. Neither of them paid attention to it.

"Yeah. The bad-boy bomb makers were always working on their art, packing more punch in smaller packages, fine-tuning the ignition device, and we had to stay at least even with them or get blown up."

Bert tipped back his beer, drained it, and continued. "We began to make our own bombs, at first from their supplies we discovered during raids. When our guys received intelligence about where the bad boys were hanging out at night, we'd go with a patrol during daylight and hide one of our bombs nearby, rigged with a disposable phone. At night we could get up on the roof of a safe house, a good distance away, or fly a drone over if we couldn't watch from a rooftop. If we saw a group of guys go in the house, or hang out in front, then we'd make the call. Ring ring, boom boom."

"How could you be sure they were the bad guys?" Christopher had asked.

"That's the trouble over there. You couldn't be sure unless you saw them shooting at you, and of course, if you waited till then, you might wake up dead."

"So, based on suspicion, you would blow these guys up."

"We went with the best intelligence we could get, but yeah, sometimes there were mistakes. I'm not gonna lie."

That's when Bert had tightened his lips, and his back seemed to curl a little as he leaned forward.

"If civilians were killed, especially a woman or a kid, a local delegation would show up at our post, accusing us of planting the bomb. The good news for us was it was easy to deny involvement. After all, we were nowhere near the scene. There were lots of accidental explosions caused by fumble-fingered bomb makers in these neighborhoods."

Bert had then brushed his hands together in an unconscious washing motion.

"You couldn't trust anybody. Even the kids. They were

used as couriers to drop packages in front of our Humvees, and then they'd run to keep from getting killed when the package blew up. Chances were good the same young boys would be carrying AK-47s a few years later, looking to kill an American. Any American. So, take out a bomb delivery kid and save an American."

Bert had smiled at his joke, but Christopher could tell he was covering up.

"Somehow, I think y'all weren't quite so cavalier about civilian casualties, especially a kid," he said.

"We all have demons in our heads from that time," Bert said with a shrug. "Most of us don't talk about the shit that went down over there. The deaths, the destruction, the mindset. I've tried to put it behind me as best I can."

Christopher kept playing the conversation in his head as he drove the dark streets in the suburban neighborhood, windows rolled down on his Buick, tossing rolled-up newspapers out one side, then the other, watching them land on long driveways in front of brick ranch-style houses.

He found it hard to believe, even harder to accept, that Bert had made bombs that killed civilians, including women and children, in Iraq. He knew his buddy often rationalized his questionable acts, but how do you justify killing innocents, even if unintentionally?

Of course, he'd helped set off a bomb last night that blew up two cars and damaged a house. His world had been turned upside down in five days. He'd harbored a sex worker, been chased by bad guys, lied to cops, been arrested, and yes, set off a bomb. He'd committed crimes far beyond anything he could have imagined. He could go to jail for a long time just for planting that bomb.

Strangely, he didn't feel a sense of regret. Those Korean mobsters had shot and killed Gracie, ransacked his house, and destroyed his customers' computers. They'd probably kill Kim if they found her. Blowing up their cars served them right. No one was killed or injured. At least not yet.

It would all end in two days. On Monday, Kim would get her passport, get on a bus to San Francisco, and his life would return to normal.

CHAPTER THIRTY-TWO

The morning sky grew lighter with the promise of dawn. Christopher parked in front of Brueggers Bagels and grabbed the stack of newspapers from the seat beside him.

"Morning, Christopher. What's going on in your world?" Stella asked him as she held out his morning coffee.

The store was empty, typical for an early Saturday morning.

"You don't want to know," Christopher said as he dropped the *Tennesseans* on the counter, reached for the cardboard cup, and then got a sugar packet and stir stick.

"Okay, if you do not want to talk about it, let me check the morning headlines." Stella unfolded the top newspaper, laying it across the glass counter in front of her.

"Ah, it's not that I don't want to talk," he said as he stirred in the sugar. "A whole lot is going on."

When Stella didn't respond, he turned to see what she was doing. Her head was down as she read the news. She slowly looked up at him.

"Man, you do have some troubles. I can read all about 'em here on the front page."

Christopher hurried over and looked at her newspaper. Even upside down, he recognized his face. He set his cup down and pulled the front section from another *Tennessean* in the stack. The other newspaper sections dropped to the floor as Christopher backed up to a table and eased down in a chair to read the article. The mug shot of his arrest yesterday was below the fold and small, but still prominent. His blank stare, uncombed hair, and hoody sweatshirt made him look like a homeless person. The headline said, "Local man questioned in the disappearance of a Korean woman." The story stated that Christopher Jones of Ashland City Highway in Nashville was arrested for obstruction of justice and questioned regarding the disappearance of Soon Yee Kim, an employee at The Orchid, the massage parlor recently raided by police in connection with prostitution. The police were searching for Kim as a possible witness. Mr. Jones admitted she'd stayed with him, but he would not tell police of her whereabouts and was uncooperative. He was known as a frequent visitor to massage parlors but had no previous arrests. He was released on bond yesterday and scheduled to appear before a judge next week.

Christopher sat paralyzed. A frequent visitor at massage parlors? He'd only been once, in search of Sukee. How did his arrest yesterday afternoon make the news this morning? Who gave this information to the press?

He looked up at Stella, who was staring at him with her mouth open.

"This is not true." His voice cracked. "Yes, I was arrested because I was trying to protect this woman. I found her here on Monday, a few doors down, hiding, scared. I never go, I mean, I went to a spa to try to help another woman, her friend, but...." His voice trailed off as he pushed away from the table and walked out the door, leaving his coffee cooling on the counter.

...

"Bert?" Christopher called out as he walked through the front door of his old house that was Bert's home now.

"In here," came the reply from the kitchen.

Christopher slammed down the newspaper on the counter. "Take a look at this." He pointed to his photo on the front page.

Bert reached for his reading glasses and picked up the newspaper. After reading the article, he shot a glance at Christopher.

"What's this about frequenting massage parlors?"

"I told you. I went to the one in Dickson. I went on Thursday afternoon because Kim thought her friend Sukee might be there. She wasn't there. I've never been to one before. I want to sue these bastards for saying I'm a frequent visitor."

Christopher beat his fist on the counter. "This will ruin my business."

Bert shrugged. "They must've had surveillance going on at that parlor. It probably means they have photos of you going in and coming out. Not good. This article is not libelous if they have hard evidence you were there."

"How did this make the morning paper? And why is it important enough to make the front page?"

"The police and the DA's office are messing with you. It's payback for not cooperating. It's dirty tricks. Luckily, most people under fifty don't read the newspaper." Bert picked up his coffee mug and took a drink.

"Yeah, well, most of my customers are over fifty." Christopher hit his forehead with his palm. "This pisses me off. What the hell will people think? Just when I thought it couldn't get any worse, my life slides further into the shitter."

"People who know you will not believe this story."

"No, most folks know I've been a little messed up these past two years. They'll think I'm into some weird shit."

Bert's cell phone rang. He checked the caller ID and answered.

"Hi, Barbara." Bert winced as he listened. "Yeah, he told me everything. The article gives the wrong impression. He's standing here. Talk to him." Bert handed the phone to Christopher.

"Christopher, what have you done to us? How did you get into this massage parlor world? And who are these guys after you?" his ex-wife yelled without any greeting; her voice pitched high. "You have a daughter to think about!"

"I was only trying to help someone. I'm sorry this has impacted you and Amy."

"Where did you meet her, this Chinese hooker?" Her accusatory tone was all too familiar.

"She's Korean, her name is Kim, and she's not a hooker. I saw her near the bagel store on White Bridge Road early Monday morning as I was delivering papers. She looked like she needed help, and I offered. I thought it was just a lift to the bus station downtown, but it turned into much more, as you now know."

"Amy said she met her, and she's staying in your house, in her room. It upset Amy to know a woman was living with you. She didn't know you were involved with another woman. When she learns this woman is a prostitute, she'll be embarrassed."

"Barbara, if I'd known Amy was coming over, I would've been there to explain. I only got involved, as you say, because I tried to help this woman. She's not my girlfriend, in any sense of that word."

Christopher looked over at Bert, still thumbing through the newspaper, but Christopher knew he was following the conversation.

"You went to the massage parlor where she worked?"

"I went there at Kim's request to look for her friend. The two young women wanted to get away from the Korean men holding them there, making them work in the sex trade against their will. And that's the only time I've ever been. I think you know the kind of man I am. It's not something I would do."

There was silence on the other end. Christopher resisted the urge to keep explaining. He decided she would either believe him or not.

"These Koreans broke into your house yesterday looking for this girl, Kim?" Barbara asked.

"Yes, it's the same guys she's running from. She wants to get to San Francisco and get help from the Korean community there. I need to get her to an appointment in Memphis on Monday so she can get a replacement visa, which is required to get a bus ticket so she can go. This will all be over, one way or another, on Monday."

"Bert says we should stay here until Sunday evening." There was another pause. "Do you want to talk to Amy?"

"Yes, put her on," Christopher said.

He heard some whispering, then Amy's voice.

"Dad, Mom said somebody broke into your house. Did they steal anything? Did they take any of my stuff?"

"No, they didn't take any of your stuff. The men were looking for Kim. They broke a few things but didn't steal anything. I don't think they went into your room," Christopher lied.

He hesitated, then said, "Gracie saved Kim, Amy. She started barking when the men pulled up to the house, and Kim saw them and ran out the back door. Gracie kept barking and made the men wait at the front gate until Kim got away. But they shot Gracie."

"What?" Amy shrieked. "Did they kill her?"

"Yes, they did. I'm sorry, Amy. She was a sweet dog, and brave. She's the reason the bad men didn't get Kim. They would've hurt her."

Amy started sobbing. "I loved her. She's my all-time favorite dog."

"I loved her, too. I buried her in the back yard. We will always know she's there and remember her bravery." Christopher gripped the phone hard, trying to keep his composure as he felt his child's pain.

"I hate these men. They didn't have to kill Gracie. I hope the police catch them." She cried some more. "I need to go, Daddy."

"I love you, and I'm so sorry about Gracie."

"I love you, too. Do you want to talk to Mom?"

"No, I think we said everything that needs to be said. I'll see you next week." Christopher hung up the phone, handed it back to Bert, and leaned against the kitchen counter, head down.

"I know that was tough." Bert put down the newspaper, folded his arms, and looked at Christopher.

Christopher said, "I guess it's true. No good deed goes unpunished."

"Amy took Gracie's death a little hard, huh?"

"She was upset. Gracie was her dog, even though she stayed with me. And you heard my answers to Barbara's questions. I'm not sure what she'll say to Amy about the news article. She's mad about how all this is impacting her life."

"That woman can be a ball buster," Bert said, shaking his head. "She's a small package, but she walks around like she's ready to take on people twice her size. If she were a man, I would say she has a Napoleon complex."

Christopher shot a quizzical look at Bert.

Bert continued. "And man, is she competitive. It doesn't matter if it's a card game or comparing herself with other women. She wants to be the winner, the best. Lord help any innocent woman who doesn't realize the game is on."

Christopher pointed his finger at Bert. "You are about as competitive as anyone I know. And bull-headed, just like her."

"Yeah. It makes for some terrific fights. We've got a few issues."

Christopher hesitated and then plowed on with the questions he needed to ask. "You had to know all this about her. You were around her, us, for more than ten years. Why did you get involved with her after we divorced?"

Bert scratched his chin. "You know I'm competitive. Too much so. And I've always envied you. You were the good-looking one, the natural athlete, the intellectual. All the girls adored you. I know it was stupid, but when you and Barbara broke up, I wanted to see if I could satisfy her."

Christopher's eyebrows shot up. "I never picked up on any envy. I thought we were buds. It bothered the hell out of me for you to go out with her so soon after we split."

"I know. I'm sorry. I was thinking with my little head, not

my big one. Even though I knew it might hurt you, I wanted to ask her out. I always thought she was sexy as hell. She brings heat to anything she does. Dammit, I was turned on by her fire." He looked at Christopher to see if he'd stepped over a line.

Christopher looked away for a moment as he processed Bert's comments. "Okay, that explains why you went for her. But I still don't see why you married her. In college, and ever since, you've always been a catch-and-release guy regarding women."

Bert winced a little at Christopher's label. "Aw, I've lived with a couple of women and liked it. But Barbara, she wouldn't cohabitate because of Amy. Not even overnighters. So, in a moment of passion, I said we should get married." He toggled his head. "I knew it was a mistake at the altar, but I went ahead. Now the fire is just about out. I've been pretending everything is okay in my marriage, just as I've been pretending our friendship was still solid."

Christopher's phone rang. He peeked at the caller ID. "It's my sister. I'll let it go to voice mail. Somebody's probably called her about the news article."

"Don't blame you," Bert answered. His head was down for a moment, and then he looked at Christopher. "I really am sorry for hurting you."

Christopher hesitated, looked away, then said, "Okay. I accept your apology." He knew he wasn't over it, and Bert could still be selfish and impulsive, but they did have a long-term friendship. He'd give it another try.

Christopher extended his hand. Bert pulled him into an awkward, back-slapping hug.

Bert looked at his watch. "I have a pal in the police department. I will call him, complain about this article, see if he knows about the bombing in Brentwood, and make sure we aren't on their radar."

"I'm going to grab a short nap. Then I'll call Gloria, maybe drive over to her house, check in with Kim and make sure she's okay there until Monday. Not that I have an alternative plan to offer," Christopher said.

"I'll go with you," Bert said. "We can take the Suburban. The Koreans may be looking for your Buick, but they don't know I'm connected to you. At least not yet. I got nothing better to do this afternoon."

CHAPTER THIRTY-THREE

The detective was in his den, still in his bathrobe, half watching ESPN on TV and reading the sports section of *The Tennessean* when his cell phone rang. He dug it out of his robe pocket, looked at the number, and then glanced at his wife across the room. "I have to take this call. It's work-related."

He knew she was observing him as he hurried toward the kitchen. He hit the receive button on the phone, said, "Wait a moment," and stepped out the back door. "I wish you wouldn't call me on this phone."

"I called the phone I gave you, but you did not answer," the raspy voice said.

"I left it in the car," the detective answered.

"Someone blew up my cars last night. Two cars."

"What? I saw something on the news about a bombing in Brentwood. That was your house?"

"Yes." The tone was terse.

"You know who did it?"

"Yes. We have a security camera in a tree out front by the road. A car drove by slowly, then came back and parked across from the driveway. The man who has the girl, Kim, it was his Buick. We see another man get out, not the driver, leave something next to my car, and get back in the Buick. They drive away, and then the explosion. My two cars blew up."

"So, you think it's the same man, Christopher Jones, we're trying to find?"

"Yes, we are sure. We were going to our other house in West Meade early today. You say he delivers newspapers on that street. We planned to wait for the Buick to drive by early when he delivers papers. We block his car, grab Christopher Jones, and make him tell us where the girl Kim is. This bomb stopped us. We have other cars in the garage but could not use them until the burned cars were towed off. Police were here till one hour ago."

There was silence. The detective started to fill it, but then the Korean spoke again. "We underestimated Christopher Jones and his resources. We will not make that mistake again."

The detective said, "I'll call the office and see what they know about this bomb incident. Do you want to show police the security camera footage? With that evidence, we can arrest Christopher Jones."

"No. We tried the police. They did not hold Christopher. Now we will take care of him. I do not want any more connection to me. Too many know my name now. Someone may get suspicious if there are questions. We will find Christopher Jones tomorrow. Then we will find Kim and get rid of her. After that, I will move to Atlanta. My house needs repairs. I will live in Atlanta for a while. I will check with you often to make sure no one is after me."

The detective liked that plan. If the Korean moved operations to Atlanta, then he wouldn't be calling him and demanding information. That would decrease the likelihood of someone figuring out the connection. They just needed to find Jones and get rid of him and the girl.

"When you find Christopher Jones, what do you plan to do with him?" the detective asked.

"We will go to his house. No one will hear us question him there. We get the information we need, and then we burn his house down with him in it. I want you there in case we need help to find the girl once he tells us where she is."

The detective did not want that, but he knew he had to do it. "Okay. Call me when you get him. I'll meet you at his house."

CHAPTER THIRTY-FOUR

Christopher called Gloria and asked if it was okay if he and Bert dropped by. She was friendly, so he guessed she hadn't seen the newspaper article.

Bert's Suburban was a big SUV with second- and third-row bench seats and tinted windows. Christopher watched his side rearview mirror for any suspicious cars following them as they sped down the interstate.

"This car feels heavier than I expected," Christopher said.

"Yeah, the company tricked it out with reinforced side panels and heavier glass windows as a security measure for the VIP customers since they like feeling bulletproof. But my favorite thing is the set of blue lights in the front grill." He reached under the dashboard and flipped a switch. Immediately, the cars in front of them moved over, opening a clear lane. Bert switched off the blue lights after a couple of minutes.

"Are they legal?" Christopher said.

"If they're like fog lights, I'm okay. But if I have them flashing on wig-wag, like I just did, then no, it's not legal since that's considered impersonating a police car. Still, I like to use them in that mode when I need to move someone out of my way. There's a speaker behind the front grill. Just like police cruisers have." He pointed at a small microphone and cord hanging under the dash. "If I need to yell at someone to move over, it's pretty effective."

■ ■ ■

Gloria's condo was in a small complex in East Nashville. Each unit had a large picture window facing the drive and parking area. Gloria was right—not many opportunities for someone to break into her house without being noticed by neighbors.

She opened her front door with a welcoming smile for Christopher, then looked appraisingly at Bert.

"You must be Bert." She stuck out her hand. "I'm Gloria Jean McNulty. Come in. We're in the den." As Gloria led the way to the back part of the condo, Christopher didn't look Bert's way, but he knew Bert was admiring her fitted beige slacks and nice shape.

Kim smiled at him and said hello. She was sitting barefoot on one end of a couch, feet tucked under her. Christopher was glad to see she was okay and seemed comfortable with Gloria.

They made small talk for a few minutes. Christopher decided to deal with the newspaper story. He didn't want Gloria to hear it from another source.

"I guess you've not seen the morning paper."

Gloria raised her eyebrows and nodded her head slightly. "A friend called and told me about it."

Christopher could feel his face flush. "It was an awful story. Very misleading."

"I knew some of it was true based on what you told me yesterday." Gloria's expression stayed pleasant.

"What did your friend say about the story?" He cocked his head, curious to know.

"That you weren't willing to tell the police where Kim was staying, and they arrested you. They claimed you were a frequent visitor to massage parlors, but I didn't believe that. You told me you went to one a couple of days ago to look for Kim's friend, but I didn't think you went often."

Bert snorted as he laughed. "You're right. Christopher is too straight-arrow to visit a strip club, much less a massage parlor."

Gloria gave Bert a direct look. "I gather you would have no issue with either."

"Whoops. I forgot you help strippers get out of that business." Bert hunched his shoulders. "Didn't mean to offend."

"No offense taken. But I'm still curious. You have no problem going to a strip club?"

Bert shrugged. "I see no problem with strip clubs as long as you're not participating in anything illegal. It's just men looking at women—something that's gone on since men and women were created, except in this instance, men pay to look, and women get paid for letting them look. It's men having fun and women doing business."

"There are so many ways I can go with that reply, starting with the purpose of why God created men and women. I'll focus on the most obvious. The business, as you put it." Gloria settled on the couch and leaned forward to address Bert.

"You're right. Men have been looking at women since creation. That's normal male curiosity, and most women don't mind a man noticing they're attractive. But there's a line between noticing and ogling, between appreciation and objectifying."

She held out one hand, palm up, then the other, representing the two faces of the issue. "In a strip club, the problem goes beyond guys viewing women as objects. We're a product you buy."

"But aren't the women there willingly? Don't they want to be bought?"

"They like to think they're there willingly, but once you get past the wall they've built to protect themselves, most have a story of abuse or coercion that led them to this point—selling their bodies to men." Gloria's voice was intense as she leaned in closer. "For many, it's an easy slide into hooking. So, as you say, it's not just men having fun and women doing business. It's early-stage prostitution."

Bert was silent. Christopher watched his reaction and enjoyed his loss of words.

"Well, hell," Bert finally replied. "I think you robbed me of any future enjoyment in a strip club. But I've never been to a massage parlor, and we know Christopher wasn't there last Thursday for the reason most men go to a massage parlor."

"I know why he went there," Kim said. Her voice was soft, and she drew everyone's attention. "He went to find my friend Sukee. But she not there."

"The massage parlor he went to in Dickson was under surveillance because it was raided and closed the next day. A buddy of mine in the police department told me," Bert said.

"And they probably have photos of me from when I visited there," Christopher said. "They're using this story to pressure me, but I won't tell them where Kim is staying. It's just two more days. At this point, I don't trust the police or the DA's office with Kim's safety. I'll get her to Memphis and on her way to San Francisco, and then I'll deal with this."

"When's your preliminary hearing?" Gloria asked.

"It's supposed to happen on Monday, but I'll be on the road to Memphis. I'll get it rescheduled, probably for Tuesday. My attorney swears he can make this go away."

"I have a better plan," Gloria said. "How about I take Kim to Memphis on Monday? I've talked with a friend of mine who was a social worker for many years, and her job was to help immigrants get the papers they needed to stay here. She's been to this office in Memphis and met with immigration officials. She's offered to go with us. She's already downloaded and printed the forms so we can fill them out before we travel."

"That's too much to ask of you," Christopher responded almost automatically, yet feeling relieved at the option.

"No, it's not." Gloria smiled and nodded at Kim. "This young lady is something special. I'm not ready to say goodbye. Traveling with her on Monday will give us almost one more day together."

Kim smiled back at Gloria, then looked at Christopher and shrugged as if to indicate it was out of her hands.

"I guess I won't argue," he said. "You've got it all planned out."

Kim clapped once, and Gloria chuckled at her excitement. "We plan to leave early Monday at six-thirty so we can make the eleven o'clock appointment at the federal building in Memphis. We'll go to the Greyhound station and get Kim off to San Francisco. I'm working on a plan for when she gets there," Gloria said.

"What plan? What do you mean?" Christopher asked. "How can you work on something in San Francisco on such short notice?"

"There's a network of crazy women like me who are committed to helping girls like Kim get out of the sex trade. We talk and email each other. One of the better programs is in San Francisco. They arrange housing for women and offer job training. I emailed their Executive Director, and she'll call me tomorrow." Gloria smiled at him.

"Wow," Christopher said as he turned to Kim. "Finding Gloria was a real piece of good luck for you."

"No, it's more than that. It's meant to be," Gloria said. Christopher didn't know how to respond, and he thought it could be true, so he just nodded.

"We better head across town," Bert said as he pushed himself out of the overstuffed chair. He led the way to the front door and stepped out on the porch. Christopher stopped before exiting, turned toward Gloria, and stuck out his hand. "I appreciate everything you're doing for Kim."

She ignored his hand and reached out her arms for a hug. "I'm just continuing the work you started." Christopher was not much of a hugger, but with Gloria, it didn't feel awkward.

Kim stood next to him, waiting for a hug.

"You're a special young lady, Kim, and I'm glad I had the opportunity to meet you," Christopher said as he squeezed her. She fit under his chin, almost like his daughter did.

Kim didn't reply, but she held onto him for what felt like a long time, then turned and went back into the condo.

Gloria put her hand on Christopher's arm. "She's doing remarkably well, considering all she's been through over the last four years. I think she's still worried about her friend

Sukee and wonders where she is and if she's okay."

"I wish I could've rescued her."

■ ■ ■

The two men drove in silence for a few minutes. Christopher yawned, thinking the less-than-four hours of sleep last night were not enough. He could use a nap.

Bert said, "I guess I stepped in it with my strip club comments to McChesty."

Christopher ignored the name twist. "Yes, she's pretty passionate about what she does."

"She's passionate, and she's pretty." Bert looked over. "I think she's sexy, in a maternal sort of way."

Christopher shook his head. "That is wrong in so many ways."

"What? You didn't notice?"

"I'm not dead," Christopher responded, giving Bert a side glance. "Of course I noticed she's attractive."

"I saw the hug. I think she also noticed you're not hard to look at either."

"Bert, don't go making this something it's not. She's trying to help a young lady who's been trafficked. I'm trying to help Kim get to San Francisco. We're focused on the task at hand."

"Not saying you aren't focused on that task, just saying you can multitask if you desire. And I'm thinking you so desire. And by the way, nice ta-tas, as I'm sure you also noticed."

"I never looked past her mind," Christopher responded, looking straight ahead.

Bert's head snapped around. When he saw a faint grin on Christopher's face, he said, "Okay, I'm calling bullshit on that comment."

Christopher's phone rang as they pulled into Bert's driveway. He glanced at the caller ID. It was Gloria calling. He answered as they walked into the house.

"Christopher, Kim and I have been talking, and we've decided to drive to Atlanta tonight. Kim thinks Sukee is staying at the spa this Boseu guy owns. Kim was there for several days a couple of years ago. She remembers it was called The Royal Spa, and once the spa closed at night, she and the other girls were locked up in a back room. Kim thinks Sukee is there in—"

"Okay, wait, but how can you know for sure, and what will you do?"

"We don't know for sure, but she could be there in the back room. Kim wants to find the spa and try to get her. Kim thinks it's Sukee's last chance to escape and go with her to San Francisco. In a few days, the Koreans will ship her to another spa or trade her to another trafficker."

"Gloria, do you know where this spa is in Atlanta? And how are you getting in? Are you just going to knock if you find it? If you wait till after it closes, I bet it's locked up."

"We're still figuring all that out. It closes at one o'clock. We'll probably wait until after it closes and see what we find. I felt like I needed to let someone know where we're going, you know, in case something happens."

"You need a plan before you hit the road to Atlanta." Christopher looked at his watch. "It's only four o'clock. No need to leave until about seven or eight o'clock. There's time to get better organized. I'll go with you. We need to confirm the name and address. I'll start working on that now and call you back when I have more details."

There was silence for a second. "Thank you," Gloria said. "I was hoping you might consider going with us."

Christopher ended the call and turned to Bert. "Okay, there's been a development since we left Gloria's."

"Yeah, I gathered that." Bert shook his head as he heard the women's plan. "So, they are going to drive to Atlanta by themselves and try to find this spa, then devise a scheme to break into the place and, hopefully, rescue Kim's friend."

"That's the plan. It's not a good plan. I think Gloria knew it, but she wanted to do something since Kim is desperate to find Sukee," Christopher said. "I'm going with them. My car is bigger, and we may have more than one woman to rescue."

"I'm in, too. We'll take the Suburban. It's even bigger and a better road car than your crappy old Buick."

"Bert, you don't need to get involved," Christopher protested. "You have a lot to lose if it goes sideways."

"So do you. Besides, I want to go. Hell, it's got the makings of a real caper." Bert wiggled his eyebrows and grinned at him. "No way I'm missing out on this road trip."

CHAPTER THIRTY-FIVE

Christopher googled the name of the spa in Atlanta and located the address, while Bert went into his garage and threw a few tools in the back of his Suburban.

They stopped for dinner at Edley's, a favorite barbecue joint near Belmont University, then drove to East Nashville again. Christopher suggested that Bert call Barbara and tell her their plan to go to Atlanta.

Bert said, "No way. She will be mad and forbid me to go, and it will escalate from there. There is no need for her to know. We'll be back by early tomorrow morning. If we're not, then we'll have bigger problems."

At eight that evening, they left Gloria's condo. Clouds to the south and the scent of rain indicated they might catch some spring showers as they drove to Atlanta.

"According to Google Maps, this spa is in a small strip mall a few blocks off Peachtree Avenue, near Midtown," Christopher said as he looked at his phone. "Interesting that it's near downtown and in the high-rent district, not in some sketchy part of town."

"I've been to Atlanta many times," Bert said, glancing at Christopher. "Some of the side streets near Midtown are a little dicey. The upscale shopping area is a little farther north of Midtown. In Buckhead."

He twisted around from the driver's seat. "Kim, tell us what you remember about the security system at the spa."

"I do not remember much. They have a glass door they lock at night. We stay in back room."

"Did they have cameras or a security system?" Christopher asked.

Kim shrugged. "I do not know."

Bert said, "We'll figure it out when we get there."

They were silent for a while, listening to the metronome beat of the windshield wipers as they drove southeast on Interstate 24 through light rain. Bert, not one to stay quiet for long, said, "I know a good blonde joke if it won't offend anyone."

Gloria spoke up from the second-row seat. "Since I'm the only blonde in the car, I guess you're asking me. I'm not easily offended, so go ahead."

"A cowboy walks into a lesbian bar and says to the bartender, 'Want to hear a good blonde joke?' She glares at the cowboy and says, 'You can see I'm blonde, but what you don't know is that I keep a ball bat behind the bar, and see that woman on the stool at the door? She's blonde and a professional wrestler. And the blonde woman standing next to her? She's the owner, and she carries a pistol in her purse. Are you sure you want to tell us your blonde joke?' The cowboy looks at the bartender, at the door bouncer, and the owner, all staring at him. He turns back to the bartender and says, 'Well, I guess not if I'm going to have to explain it three times.'"

Christopher groaned. Gloria said, "Not bad. I think you managed to insult blondes, lesbians, and even cowboys. I guess that counts as a good joke."

Bert rubbed his chin. "Didn't mean to insult cowboys. I'll have to rethink that one."

Gloria was silent for a moment, then said, "I can only think of one joke, and it's a religious one."

Christopher said, "I don't think any of us will be offended on religious grounds."

Gloria leaned forward and laid a hand on the armrest between the front seats. "The disciples and Jesus walk into an upper room for dinner on Passover. Peter steps forward and asks the proprietor for a table for twenty-four. The proprietor hesitates, then says, 'I'm only counting twelve, maybe thirteen.

Why do you need a table for twenty-four?' Peter responds, 'Because we all like to sit on the same side of the table.'"

Christopher laughed. "That's a clever one."

"I don't get it," Bert said.

"Probably have to be a Christian to understand it," Gloria responded.

"And maybe know famous artists like da Vinci," Christopher added.

"I think you both just insulted me," Bert said.

"Didn't mean to offend," Gloria replied, but with a small laugh.

"No offense taken," Bert said.

Once they were past Murfreesboro, an hour out of Nashville, traffic was light, and the interstate took on the monotony of nighttime travel on any interstate in rural areas between cities. Christopher thought the SUV felt enclosed, as if it was an encapsulated ship flying through an unknown world.

"This reminds me of nights in Iraq," Bert said. "We would get a tip the bad guys were gathered at some house, and we'd head out around midnight. All of us crammed in a bomb-proof truck. We'd pound on the door, and some old lady would tell us just women and children were inside. We'd bust in and find the men, who would protest they were only visiting."

Bert nodded as he talked, as if he was reliving one of the nights. "If we found weapons or bomb-making supplies, we'd cuff the men, call for another vehicle, get them back to camp, and lock 'em up. Sometimes bad things happened on the way back."

"Like what?" Gloria asked.

"Like an ambush, or one of the guys would start a ruckus. We'd have to shoot 'em. The danger started the minute we left our camp and continued till we got back."

"This isn't Iraq. If it appears dangerous, we bail," Christopher said, looking at Bert.

Bert glanced at him. "Plans often go sideways in the heat of the moment."

Gloria leaned forward in the back seat, her brow knitted. "When you were standing outside the house in Iraq, not knowing what you would face inside, weren't you guys scared? How did you decide who went through the door first?"

Bert toggled one hand off the steering wheel. "Shit yeah, we were scared. But every time, someone would volunteer to lead the charge through the door."

"So, were the guys who led the charge just being macho? It sounds like they either had a death wish or thought they were invincible."

"I don't think it was a death wish," Bert said. "Some guys like the adrenaline rush. Many believed if they died, it was just their time."

"That's what I believe," Gloria said. "God is in control."

Bert looked over at Christopher. "You were a philosophy major in college. What do you think?"

Christopher drew in a breath. "I guess I'm somewhere between nihilism and evangelicalism."

"That's a wide swath," Gloria said. "You're somewhere between Nietzsche's 'God is dead' view and the evangelical claim that God guides our steps?"

Christopher's eyes widened as he turned to respond to her. "I like the message of the Gospels, but I'm not sure all things that happen are controlled by God. Life feels too random." He put up a hand. "But I have a question. *You* know Nietzsche's philosophy?"

"I've read Nietzsche. I have a degree in Religious Studies." Her face glowed in the dashboard lights as she arched an eyebrow at him. "I wonder if it's my blonde hair or my Southern drawl that makes it hard for you to believe I know something about Friedrich Nietzsche."

Christopher smiled. "Sorry if I sounded incredulous."

"Okay, you like the message of the Gospels, but what do you believe?" she asked.

Christopher measured his thoughts before answering. "I

believe in God. I'm not a nihilist. I believe the world is not an abyss, but a God-given preserve. We can find a higher purpose, a calling, if we tune in to our spiritual side."

"I think this trip to Atlanta is led by that higher purpose," Gloria said.

Bert slapped the steering wheel. "I thought there was a higher purpose for us to go to war with Iraq. You know, fight for God and country. But I saw a lot of people die over there. Good people, like the soldiers I served with. There were many times when I questioned the purpose of that war."

"And lots of innocent people, even children, died in that war," Gloria said.

Bert nodded. "That's true. What we called collateral damage was just a rationalization for our mistakes and poor judgment. If you're a decent human being, you don't shake that off."

"As a Christian, I can't justify taking another life. Even in war," Gloria replied.

"I knew good Christian men in the Army who believed they were called to protect our country, which sometimes required killing." Bert glanced at Christopher. "What's your stand on taking a life to protect those you love?"

Christopher thought for a moment, then said, "I'm not sure I could kill someone, and I hope I don't have to find out. But if I had a shot at that Min-jun guy who killed Gracie..." he shook his head and didn't finish his thought.

"I could kill to protect someone I love," Kim said, her voice soft, her features hidden in darkness as she sat, almost forgotten, in the corner of the back seat.

CHAPTER THIRTY-SIX

It was almost two in the morning when Bert drove his Suburban into a strip mall parking lot near mid-town Atlanta. He stopped about twenty feet from the spa storefront. No cars were in front of the businesses; they were all dark.

The front of the spa looked to be about twenty-four feet wide, with three large storefront glass panels painted solid blue up to about five feet. ROYAL SPA was painted in large, red letters on the clear part of the glass.

"Is this the place?" Christopher twisted around to check with Kim.

Kim nodded. "Yes. Blue on window."

The neon OPEN sign on the door was dark. Bert switched off his car lights and rolled down his window. A recent rain shower glistened the blacktop and left a wet pavement smell.

Bert eased past the spa and parked in front of the neighboring business. He looked over at Christopher. "My pry bar should get us in the front door."

"So, Kim," Christopher said. "There's no light on, but if the Nashville girls are here, they're in a room in the back, right?"

"That is where I stayed for three nights. The door was locked."

"The other girls who work here and the old lady who runs the place all leave every night and go to their apartment? No one else stays here?"

"The girls said they stay in one bedroom at apartment," Kim answered. "Kwan or Min-jun come each week, stay in other bedroom at apartment."

"City codes don't allow people to live in their businesses,"

Bert said as he studied the front of the spa. "Could be there's no one here tonight. They may all be at the apartment, even the Nashville girls."

Christopher nodded. "Yeah, but we need to break in to find out." He pointed at Kim. "If they are, you get Sukee, bring her out, and we leave."

"Wait," Gloria said. "We need to see if the other girls want to leave, too. What are their names?" she asked Kim.

"June and Ji-hu. June will come with us. Ji-hu, she probably stay. She never talk about leaving."

"That poses a problem," Christopher said. "She'll identify us."

Gloria said, "Maybe just Kim and I should go in and see if the girls are here."

Christopher shook his head. "I'm going in too."

"The real danger is if someone drives by, sees us, and calls 9-1-1," Bert said. "Or if the place is wired into an alarm system and the Koreans show up while we're inside."

He looked at Christopher, then Gloria and Kim. "I have a Glock under my seat. Let's get in, but then I'll stay in the car while y'all look around. If I beep twice, get the hell out. Someone has shown up. Most likely the police."

"If they do," Christopher said, "we'll tell them we're trying to rescue Sukee. Kim's story might convince them. They could decide to help us."

"Nah, all they'll see is a clear-cut case of breaking and entering. Another problem is my Glock," Bert said. "The police will be all over me for having a loaded weapon while we're breaking into a business."

"You're saying that we could all land in jail."

"Yep. But a gun might come in handy if the Koreans show up."

"So, we could get in a shoot-out." Christopher looked at Bert with raised eyebrows. "I can't believe we're talking about jail or a gunfight." He shook his head, then reached for the car door. "Let's do it and get out of here."

"Wait." Bert held up a hand. "There's a security camera

above the door. I have a can of spray paint."

Bert punched a button on the dash, and the tailgate lifted with a creak. He went to the back of the SUV, pulled on a hat and sunglasses, shook a can of black paint, walked to the door, and sprayed the camera. He hurried back and threw the can, hat, and sunglasses in the back of the SUV, grabbed a pry bar, returned to the driver's seat, and backed the car up to the front of the spa. He turned off the ignition, leaving his window down.

"Wait here while Christopher and I work on the door," Bert said to Gloria and Kim as he got out of the car. He reached under the driver seat, pulled out his Glock, raised his shirt in the back, and stuck the gun in the waistband of his pants.

Bert wedged the pry bar between the door and the frame above the door lock while Christopher watched the street for approaching traffic. Bert leaned on the pry bar. The aluminum frame bent with a pop and a screech, and in less than a minute, the gap around the door lock was wide enough to slide the bolt past the frame. The door swung open.

The two men stepped inside and closed the door. Bert held his Glock by his side as they checked out the lobby and listened for noise or movement.

Across the lobby was a wall with a door in the middle. The only furniture in the lobby was two folding chairs with a small table between them.

"They don't have a monitored alarm system, and I didn't expect they would," Bert said in a low voice. "That would give police an excuse to enter the spa. They don't want law enforcement to show up if the alarm goes off." He pointed at the camera above the door across the lobby. "That's an old security camera, so I don't think they monitor it remotely on a computer. Probably have an internal tape system in a closet or under the counter somewhere. We can take it with us."

"Let's see if the girls are here before we look for the tape," Christopher said.

Bert handed the pry bar to Christopher and pointed to the door in the wall. "Check that door. I'll get Gloria and Kim. I'll wait outside while y'all look around."

Christopher checked the door. It wasn't locked. He slid the pry bar behind his belt at his side and halfway into his front pocket, turned the doorknob, pushed the door open, and peered down a narrow, dark hall. Faint light from the parking lot let him see three closed doors on each side. The hallway ended at another door.

Kim and Gloria slipped in behind him.

"I see some light under the door at the end. Is that where you stayed overnight?" Christopher whispered to Kim.

"Yes," Kim whispered back. She led them, tiptoeing, down the dark hall. Gloria grabbed Christopher's arm and squeezed as they followed.

The doors on either side of the hall were alternately numbered 1 to 5. Christopher remembered from his visit to the Dickson spa that the rooms probably held only a chair, a small side table, and a massage table for customers.

Kim reached the door at the end of the hall. Without hesitating, she turned the bolt lock and opened the door. Christopher and Gloria followed her into a large room.

A woman, Asian, sat on a mattress, huddled in fear of the intruders. The blankets and pillows on the bed seemed to indicate she had just settled in for the night. Christopher glanced around the room. A counter with a lamp, sink, microwave, and refrigerator was at one end, and two open suitcases with scattered clothes were on the floor near two mattresses.

"Ji-hu. Where are June and Sukee?" Kim said as she hurried to the woman. Christopher and Gloria followed. The woman answered back in Korean, her voice trembling. Kim responded with what sounded like a question. The woman nodded, then her eyes shifted to Christopher and Gloria and then to the open door behind them.

Kim wheeled around and gasped. Christopher pivoted toward

the door. A man walked in, pushing a naked young woman in front of him. He was Asian, with shiny hair slicked back in a pompadour. He smiled as he pointed a revolver at them.

CHAPTER THIRTY-SEVEN

"Kim, we have been looking for you." The man walked to the center of the room, pointing his gun at Kim first, then Gloria and Christopher. They both raised their hands. He said something in Korean, and the naked woman with him ran to the mattresses. She wrapped a blanket around herself and crouched next to Ji-hu.

"Min-jun," Kim said, almost in a whisper.

"Surprised I am here?" Min-jun said.

She nodded.

"I decided to stay, sleep here, not go to the apartment. Good thing because I hear voices, open door a crack, and I see you." His wide grin showed his delight with the chance meeting.

Min-jun turned to face Gloria and Christopher and pointed the gun at them. "And your friends. Boseu will be happy I have you."

Christopher looked at the barrel of the large revolver a few feet away. His anger flared as he realized this was the guy who killed Gracie. He thought about lunging at the man, then considered the probability that he would be shot against some hope of wrestling the gun away. The odds were not in his favor.

"Why did you come to Atlanta?" Min-jun focused on Kim as he took a step toward her.

"I come to get Sukee."

The Korean man smiled and said some words in Korean.

Kim slapped her hands over her mouth. Her eyes filled with tears, and then her shoulders shook with her sobs. Min-jun continued talking, appearing to enjoy her horror.

Gloria moved to Kim and wrapped her arms around the young woman, as if to provide a shield from the man's assault of words.

"I don't know what you're saying, but I won't let you hurt Kim."

"I tell her I killed Sukee." He replaced his smile with a brutal look. "Get away from her." He gestured at Gloria with the gun.

"No!"

"Then you both die." Min-jun stepped closer.

Christopher slowly lowered his left hand as the Korean focused on Gloria and Kim. He reached for the pry bar tucked in his pants and slid it out.

The Korean noticed the movement and turned toward Christopher. Before he could point the gun and shoot, Christopher lunged at him and swung the pry bar, hitting Min-jun's wrist with a solid whack. The gun flew out of the Korean's hand and landed five feet away. Min-jun grabbed his wrist as pain and anger flashed across his face. He took a quick step, bent over and reached for the revolver. Christopher slashed down hard with the pry bar on the back of the Korean's head.

The Korean froze in motion, his eyes rolled up, and then he collapsed to his knees, teetered, leaned forward, and fell, his face smashing against the floor.

"That's for shooting Gracie," Christopher muttered. He gripped the pry bar tightly as he crouched over him. He felt an urge to hit the man again, but he controlled the adrenaline rush and rage.

He stepped over the Korean's legs and grabbed the revolver. He pointed it at the man sprawled on the floor, unsure what to do next. Did he kill him with the blow to the head? As he studied the Korean's face, he saw him blink twice. No, he was not dead but probably concussed.

He turned to Gloria and Kim. Gloria's arms slid off Kim. She put both hands in front of her mouth. The two girls on the mattress behind them were curled into each other, eyes wide.

Christopher said, "I need to go tell Bert. We've got to figure out what we do now." He reversed the revolver, stepped toward Gloria, and extended it. "I think I've knocked him out, but keep this gun pointed at him, just in case. Make him stay on the floor."

"I don't want that gun. I couldn't shoot the man if he did come at me." Gloria held up both palms as if to block the weapon.

"I will hold it." Kim leaned forward and took the revolver from Christopher's hand. She fit her fingers around the grip and slid one finger over the trigger. The gun seemed even larger in her small hands. She pointed it at Min-jun and held it firmly. "Go tell Bert."

There was no fear—only determination in her eyes.

▪ ▪ ▪

Christopher charged out the front of the spa and to the driver's side of the Suburban. Bert jerked his head into the open window, eyes wide and eyebrows up. Christopher gripped the car doorframe, mouth open, trying to catch his breath.

"What's going on?" Bert asked as he looked back at the front of the spa. "Where're the girls?"

"Two girls here, but not Sukee. We . . . we have a big problem." Christopher hurriedly told Bert what happened with Min-jun. "He's probably knocked out, and Kim's got the gun pointed at him, just in case he tries something. What do we do now?"

"Holy shit. You saved Kim. And probably all of us." Bert said as he pushed the car door open, jumped out, and hitched up his pants.

"Should we call the police?" Christopher asked. They both instinctively looked out at the street as if expecting a car with flashing lights to arrive any second.

Bert rubbed the side of his face, then shook his head. "I don't know how we'd explain it to them. This guy can claim he caught us breaking into his business. He tried to stop us, and we beat him with a crowbar. Which, of course, happens to be the truth."

"Then let's tie him up and get out of here. Someone will be here in the morning. They can cut him loose. We'll have to take our chances that they don't call the police."

"I got a roll of duct tape." Bert leaned inside the car and pushed a button on the dash. The tailgate slowly lifted.

Bert started toward the back of the car, then stopped and wheeled around. "He'll tell the boss and the other Koreans in Nashville, and they'll know you were here with Kim. These guys will come after you hard. They don't know me or Gloria yet, but they know you and where you live."

"Yeah, but what else can we do? I don't think it's a good idea to take him with us and hold him hostage. If we get caught, it will add kidnapping to the list of charges. If we don't want the police involved, then I guess we take our chances with the Koreans."

"Okay," Bert said as he dug under the front seat. "Let me grab my gun and get the tape. We need to get in there before this guy comes around."

CHAPTER THIRTY-EIGHT

The Korean man on the floor opened his eyes and blinked, then rolled over and slowly pushed up on his hands and knees. Min-jun rocked back on his haunches and shook his head slowly. He leaned on one propped arm and rubbed the back of his head with his other hand as he turned slightly to look around the room.

He moved into a position where he could stand. Kim didn't back up. She remained in front of Min-jun, her hands extended with the pistol pointing at the man.

"You stay there," she yelled. "Do not stand up. Do what I say, or I shoot."

Min-jun focused on her. He frowned and squinted as he examined her posture and the barrel of the gun. His eyes met hers, and a smile broke across his face. He leaned forward on both hands, gathered his feet underneath him, rose partway up, and placed his hands on his knees as he prepared to jump at her. He struck at her first with words.

"You are maechunbu. You will do what *I* say."

He lunged forward.

Kim shut her eyes and pulled the trigger twice.

▪ ▪ ▪

Bert reached for the button on the dash to close the tailgate on the Suburban. The sound of two rapid pistol shots from within the spa caused both him and Christopher to freeze. Bert grabbed his Glock, and they scrambled to the spa door. Christopher feared the worst.

Two shots. Kim. Gloria.

The two men quietly entered. Bert pointed his pistol in front of him as they moved across the lobby and stopped on either side of the open door in the interior wall. They heard the panicked voices of the women from the room at the end of the hall.

The two men took a few steps down the hall, stopped, and listened. They heard Gloria's voice but couldn't make out the words.

"Gloria?" Christopher called out.

"Christopher, come here. We need you," she said in a shaky voice.

They hurried into the large room.

The Korean man was sprawled face-first on the floor. Blood oozed from his mouth, his face, and the top of his head. Kim was a few feet in front of him, hand over her mouth, the revolver still in her other hand, pointed at the floor. Gloria clung to her arm. The two Korean women stood behind them, holding onto each other.

Gloria pointed at the Korean man. "He rolled over and got up, jumped at Kim, so she shot him."

"It's okay, it's okay, she didn't have a choice," Christopher said, holding his hands up in a soothing manner. "He would've killed you both."

Gloria turned to Kim. "He called you something. What was it he said?"

Kim looked up at Gloria, her expression filled with the horror of the dead man before her. "He called me maechunbu. Whore. He said I must do what he says."

Gloria wrapped her arms around Kim from the side, staying away from the gun. "You warned him. He didn't believe you."

Bert stooped over the Korean, hands on his knees, still holding his Glock. "Looks like you shot him in between the eyes first and then in the top of his head, probably as he fell toward you."

He stood up and looked at Christopher. "One thing for sure, he's dead."

The revolver fell from Kim's hand, landing with a loud clang on the floor.

"Whoa, be careful with that thing," Bert said. He stuck his Glock in his pants and stooped to pick up the revolver.

"Colt 45," he said, examining it, turning the barrel to look at the ammunition. "This is the kind of gun a killer would carry, with a soft load, a killer load."

He looked back at Christopher, then at Kim. "This guy meant to kill anyone he shot, but his own gun killed him, so I say that's justice in a way."

"Min-jun told me he killed Sukee," Kim said, starting to sob. "He ran over her with car, then Kwan stomp on her, break her neck. They put her in trunk, take her to dumpster, like, like she was trash." She buried her face in Gloria's shoulder and cried. "She died alone. No one knows where she is now."

"Sukee knew you loved her, and God loves her, too," Gloria said, her voice quavering as she patted Kim's head and held her tightly.

The two men turned to look at each other.

"We need to focus on our situation," Bert said. "We need to figure out what we do next."

"We need to call the police, don't we?" Gloria asked.

"I'm not sure we want to do that," Bert said, shaking his head. "We'll all be arrested and in jail here in Atlanta, probably for several days, while the police sort this out. For sure, Kim would be charged with murder. We'll be charged with breaking and entering, at the least, if not accessory to murder. They won't be in any hurry to release us or set a bond hearing. We would need outstanding lawyers to avoid serious jail time."

"What else can we do?" Gloria asked. No one said anything as they stood around the body, watching the pool of blood slowly expand.

"I think we leave him here, just as he is," Christopher finally said. "Someone will come here this morning, probably the other women who work here. They'll find him and call the boss in Nashville. He'll either report it to the police or he won't."

Bert nodded his agreement. "I'm betting he won't. These guys don't want law enforcement scrutinizing them or their business. I bet they'll clean everything up and start looking for who did this. They're probably used to taking care of their own problems."

"With this guy dead, they won't know it's us that broke in," Christopher added.

"We need to get moving," Bert said. "We'll get the surveillance tape and leave no evidence." He looked at the revolver in his hand. "I'll get rid of this pistol somewhere on our way back. But for now, Christopher, you take it. Let's check the rest of the rooms."

He pulled his gun out of his waistband. "I'll start at the front. Look in every closet." He turned to Gloria and Kim. "Wipe down anything we've touched in here, just in case the police get involved." Bert held his gun by his side as he walked to the hall.

"Gloria, you don't have to go along with this plan if you don't want to," Christopher said as he moved closer and squeezed her shoulder. "If all this comes out later, the consequences will be higher than if we call the police now."

Gloria held his look for a moment. "We dragged you guys into this mess."

"No, you didn't drag us. We volunteered. In fact, we insisted. And you volunteered on Friday when I called you. That's how I got you in this mess."

Gloria smiled faintly, then her worried look returned. "But if you hadn't come with us, this guy would have caught us and probably killed us if we'd managed to get inside the spa. Nothing can happen to us worse than that."

"What about these two?" Christopher asked, looking at the two young women huddled in front of the mattresses.

Kim glanced at them and then said to Christopher, "They go with us. They do not want to be here with Min-jun dead. Kwan will come here, be very angry."

"They can go with us back to Nashville," Gloria said, "and maybe we can get them on the same bus to San Francisco with Kim on Monday if they're willing to go. My friend there will be glad to help them, too."

"Maybe I should drive them to San Francisco," Christopher said.

Gloria answered, "Maybe." They both thought for a moment. Christopher said, "I have a court date. Might need to check with my attorney about rescheduling, make sure I don't get in more trouble by being out of state with Kim."

"And Kim, probably the others, have to go to Memphis on Monday to get new visas," Gloria added.

"It's a complicated situation," Christopher said, shaking his head. "We need to think it through."

Christopher checked with Kim. "You okay with us returning to Nashville and then deciding the next moves?" When she nodded, he pointed at June and said, "Find some clothes for that girl and help them get their clothes packed. I'll go see what I can do to help Bert."

Bert was in the hall, holding two electronic components. "I found their surveillance tape system in a closet near the front. I'll load them into the Suburban and grab a rag to wipe down all the doorknobs."

Christopher said, "Gloria and Kim are helping the other girls get their clothes. I'll check the rest of the rooms."

He used his shirttail to open doors so he wouldn't leave fingerprints. In one of the massage rooms, he found a suitcase and a small canvas duffle bag that he assumed belonged to Min-jun. Christopher placed the suitcase on the massage table, opened it, and found only clothes. He shut the suitcase and opened the duffle bag. It was half-filled with rubber-banded packets of money. He pulled out a few packets and spread them on the table. At the bottom of the duffle bag, he found June and Ji-hu's visas and passports, but no documents for Kim.

Bert walked in, stared at the money, and picked up a rubber-banded packet. He whistled low as he thumbed through the half-inch thick bundle. "Looks like mostly twenties, with a few hundreds thrown in. How many bundles did you say?"

"Don't know. It's about full." Christopher held up the duffle bag by the handles. Bert looked at the money bundle in his hand and then pointed at the bag. "I want to take a look."

Christopher opened the canvas bag wide, and Bert stepped closer. He stuck his hand in, pulled out a stack of the bundled bills, held them up, and looked in the bag again. He counted the packets on the table and then added the others from the bag.

"I'm counting forty-eight packets. I might have missed one or two. If these bundles are mostly twenties, each one is probably a thousand." He grinned at Christopher. "We can divide this however you want. Not a bad day's work between us, bro."

"I'm not taking it. We're not taking it."

Bert stared at him. "Why not?"

Gloria walked in, followed by Kim. "What's going on?" she asked.

Christopher turned to her. "I found this bag." He held it up. "It's filled with bundled money, maybe fifty thousand. I think we should leave it here. It's not ours."

"I say we take it," Bert said. "The Koreans will think this is a burglary, and Min-jun was killed because he happened to be here during the break-in."

"It's money that men paid to have sex with the women. It feels dirty," Christopher said.

"Yeah, so what?" Bert said. "We can use some of it to pay

for these girls to get to San Francisco. Maybe give half to Gloria to help her cause if it'll make you feel better."

"Bert, it still feels like dirty money. I say we take June and Ji-hu's passports and visas, but the money stays here. Otherwise, we're just thieves." Christopher's tone was adamant.

"If you take the passports and leave the money, the Koreans will know someone came for the girls. It's a dead giveaway." Bert jutted his jaw and glared at Christopher.

Kim stepped around Gloria and stuck out her hand. "I take the bag. I earned it. June and Ji-hu earned it. We use it to help us in San Francisco."

"I think she's right about earning it," Gloria said.

Christopher turned to Bert, saying, "That makes sense to me." Bert glared at him, then rolled his eyes, shrugged and started stuffing the bundles in the bag.

Christopher handed the bag to Kim.

Two minutes later, they snuck out the spa's front door, piled into the Suburban, and were on their way back to Nashville.

CHAPTER THIRTY-NINE

SUNDAY

Not much was said for the first hour of the drive as they headed north out of Atlanta. The city lights faded in the rear-view mirror, and Interstate 75 was almost empty of traffic. A truck stop at a remote exit ahead appeared to be an oasis in the dark of the night.

Bert pulled off the interstate and parked at the gas pump that was the furthest away from the store. It was nearly three in the morning, and the other pumps were deserted. A couple of eighteen-wheelers idled near the diesel pumps on the commercial truck side of the main building.

"I don't see any security cameras on the pump islands, but they'll have them at the front door and inside." Bert leaned around in his seat as he talked to the women. "I don't think we should go in as a group. Kim, you and June and Ji-hu go in first."

He looked at Gloria. "Give them a minute, then you walk in, but make it seem as if you have no connection to the Korean women if you see them."

After the women left the car, Bert pointed out the front window of the SUV. "That trash can will have something I can use to wrap up the revolver. There's another gas station, a smaller one, over there." He waved a hand at the other side of the road. "We'll go there next, and I'll circle around to the back and throw the gun in their dumpster."

Within ten minutes, they were back on the road to Nashville.

Christopher noticed it wasn't long after that before June and Ji-hu were asleep in the third row of the Suburban. He felt almost delirious due to lack of sleep. The night before, Friday night, he had been too keyed up after they bombed the Korean boss's house. Now, even though he was exhausted, he was not sleepy.

"Gloria, you okay?" Christopher asked, glancing at her over his shoulder. Gloria's crossed leg jiggled. Her eyes seemed sunken and dark in the shadowed interior of the car, lit only be the glow of the dashboard lights. She took a moment to respond.

"I can't get rid of the image of the dead man back at the spa," she said. "We just left him there, lying in his blood."

Christopher twisted around and studied her. "I think we're all trying to get our minds around what happened, but I can't come up with a better path than the one we took."

"I know," she replied. "I've tried to figure a way we could have done it differently, then I think about what Bert said would happen if we called the police." After a long pause, she continued. "I witnessed a man get shot and killed, and then I left. How can that be the right thing to do?"

"I'm shook up about it," Christopher said. "First time I've seen a dead guy. First time I've been involved in anything like this. But we rescued two young women from a life of abuse. That was the right thing to do."

"Yep. Given the circumstances, we made the right choice," Bert chimed in. "But we still don't know what lies ahead. We've got to hope the police don't get involved and somehow track us down. If they do, the consequences will be worse than if we'd called them. And if the police aren't notified, that means the Koreans are covering it up, but they will try to figure out who shot Min-jun, and they will try to find the two women in the back seat."

"Kim, do you think they'll go with you to San Francisco?" Christopher asked.

"June, she will go. Ji-hu, I don't know what she will do." Kim leaned forward and spoke in a quiet voice. "June, she always say how much she hates Min-jun. She youngest, only nineteen. When Kwan not around, Min-jun make her go to his room. When she return, she always cry. He calls her his little maechunbu. His whore."

Gloria blew out a breath. "What a bastard. He deserved to be shot for what he did to June."

Kim nodded. "Two years ago, he try with me, but I say no. He beat me. I still say no. But June, she is from traditional Korean family, so she obeys men like Min-jun. That is why last night he stay at spa, not go to apartment. When other women leave, he make June take her clothes off, go to room with him."

Christopher saw Gloria lean over and pat Kim's leg. "You were the strong one."

Kim's face changed into an expression somewhere between a smile and a grimace. "But now June no longer have to obey Min-jun."

She checked to see if either girl was awake. "Ji-hu, she not mind work at spa, different men each day. She work for Min-jun and Kwan ten years, maybe more. She not know anything else. They give her key to basement, sometime she in charge at spa. She think they like her. She think Kwan and Boseu take care of her when she is old, but they will not."

Identifying with her captors. The Stockholm syndrome at work, Christopher thought.

"If she doesn't want to go to San Francisco, then what do we do with her?" Bert asked.

"Let's not jump to conclusions until we've given her time to process everything that's happened tonight. We'll talk about it with her," Gloria responded. "If she chooses not to go, then we'll deal with it."

Bert toggled his head. "Yeah, but we can't let her get back to the Koreans. She'll tell them all they need to know to find us."

--

They drove into Nashville on Interstate 24 and veered around on the east side of downtown. The early morning sun lit up Nissan Stadium, home of the Titans. The light stanchions shone brilliant red as they reached into the sky like giant cranes standing guard over the football field. They exited the interstate near the stadium and drove a short distance east before entering a residential neighborhood.

"We all need to rest," Gloria said as the women climbed out of the SUV in front of Gloria's condo. "I'm thinking showers, food if anyone is hungry, and we all take a long nap. Why don't y'all head home and do the same?"

"Sounds like a good plan," Bert said. "We'll check in with you this afternoon."

Christopher looked at his watch as they drove away. "It's seven o'clock. I'm not going to make the eight o'clock deadline for the Sunday paper delivery, which means lots of complaints." He drummed his fingers on the door armrest as he looked out the window. "Some of the retirees on my route aren't happy if I don't have their Sunday newspaper in their driveway by six thirty."

Bert glanced at Christopher. "It's a paper route, for crying out loud. Your computer business is working pretty well. Why don't you dump this newspaper delivery job? Can't be much income."

"You're right. Not much income. But folks count on me delivering their paper and doing it on time." He yawned, fighting the fatigue.

"You've always been Mister Reliable," Bert said, grinning at him. "You pick up the papers downtown, right? Let's swing by there now and get them. I'll drive while you sling papers, and we'll get 'er done in no time, maybe under the wire. Then we go home and catch some Z's."

"Okay, I appreciate it." Christopher looked at Bert and

nodded. "We need to transfer that other backpack out of my trunk and into your car."

Bert looked at Christopher with eyebrows raised. "You have an issue driving around with a bomb in your trunk?"

Before Christopher could reply, Bert put up a hand. "Just jerking your chain. We can transfer it later. I'll run it over to my storage unit this afternoon."

CHAPTER FORTY

The Korean man answered his phone as he waited in the black sedan in the driveway of the house on Cedar Street.

"Kwan!" A frantic female voice called his name.

"Yes," the man replied in Korean.

"Min-jun is dead! I am at the spa. Somebody broke the front door, and no one answered when I called out. I walked in and found Min-jun dead on the floor. He is shot. His blood is all over." Her voice rose, fed by hysteria.

"What about June and Ji-hu?" Kwan asked.

"They are gone." In panicked tones, the Korean woman continued to answer Kwan's questions.

The other Korean man in the black car watched as Kwan asked questions. He noticed how still and expressionless Kwan had become as he talked on the cell phone. He had worked for Kwan for four years now, and he'd seen him kill with that same stillness and lack of expression.

"Leave the OPEN sign turned off," Kwan instructed. "Stay away from the back. Wait in the lobby. Do not turn on any lights. Do not let anyone in. I will take care of everything."

He directed her to the closet, where the security tape machine sat on a shelf. She reported back that the shelf was empty.

Kwan hung up and quickly dialed another number. A raspy voice answered the phone and asked a question in Korean without any preamble.

"You have found Christopher Jones?"

"No, Boseu, he has not delivered newspapers this morning. Now it is too late. The sun is up. People are out walking the streets. They already see our car and stare." Kwan took a deep breath and continued. "I must drive to Atlanta. Min-jun is dead. Shot last night. The old woman in Atlanta found him this morning and called me." Kwan shared all the information he had gleaned from the earlier phone call.

"You must get the security tapes for the camera at the front door."

"It is missing, Boseu. I had the woman look in the closet for the taping machine, and she said the shelf was empty. I asked her to look for his leather bag in one of the rooms, but don't open it. She said there is no leather bag, but there is a suitcase in a room. She thinks it belongs to Min-jun."

The Korean man named Cho was silent for a moment. "This could be the Chinese trying to take over our territory. If it is them, I should have been warned." There was more silence, then more speculation. "The blacks, the Mexicans, the Guatemalans, they all run women in Atlanta, but they use the Internet and outcalls; they do not operate spas. We stay away from the Internet business, and they leave us alone."

His voice turned cold. "We need to find out who did this."

"I will get rid of Min-jun's body," Kwan said. "If I see anything that tells us more, I will call you."

"Go there and clean everything up, then drive back. We must take care of our problem here in Nashville tomorrow. We must find Christopher Jones and Kim. Then we will go to Atlanta, take care of that problem."

Kwan hung up and accelerated out of the driveway. As he approached White Bridge Road, a large black Suburban turned in front of them. Kwan slowed only briefly to confirm the SUV was turning, then he punched the gas pedal and roared through the intersection and onto the four-lane city street, heading east.

▪ ▪ ▪

Cho sat in silence at his desk as he pondered the events in Atlanta and Nashville. For the first time in more than thirty years in the United States, he felt as if he might not be able to deal with the threats to his business interests. If this was the Chinese or even a black gang in Atlanta, they might have more men and better weapons. Christopher Jones was a problem, but the Atlanta threat could be much bigger.

He needed information and more resources. He leaned forward, picked up his phone, and called Billy Lee, his nephew. It was time to get him involved.

"Wae sam choon." The voice of his nephew spoke the traditional Korean greeting. Cho always spoke Korean when talking to his sister or her son. The native tongue seemed to him to be the language of family, even when one's family did not often communicate.

"We have a problem, nephew."

"Of what nature?"

"Our spa in Atlanta was attacked last night, and Min-jun killed. We don't know who did this, or why." Cho told his nephew all he knew about the situation.

"Did the police have any leads? Did they find fingerprints?"

"We did not call the police. Kwan is going to Atlanta. He will take care of Min-jun and clean up the blood."

There was silence on the other end.

"Two girls were staying there," Cho continued. "They were from the spa here in Nashville. They are gone. I don't know what happened to them. I have heard of chat rooms where men talk about the women at spas. There may be something about new Korean girls in Atlanta. You must look for this information so that we can find them."

"Why were the girls in Atlanta?"

"They were arrested here four days ago. It was in the news." Cho let a little impatience creep into his voice. "We had to move them away. Atlanta was a good place to send them, at least for a few days."

"Do you plan for them to return and appear in court?"

"No. They will stay in Georgia or maybe go to another state."

"Where do *they* want to go?"

Cho's voice turned hard at the impertinence of the question. "They do not decide where they go. I decide."

"My mother's brother, I do not know your spa business very well, but I do know a little about American law. If the girls do not show up for court and they are arrested later and charged, they will go to jail. If they choose to help the police in order to reduce their sentence, they can say that you would not let them go to court."

His nephew cleared his throat and continued with a cautious tone. "It's possible you could be arrested for kidnapping and human trafficking. If they testify that a man was killed in the spa in Atlanta, and you did not notify the police, you could also be arrested as an accessory to murder. That could be very bad for you and anyone else associated with the spa business."

Cho decided to end the call rather than continue to get a lecture from his twenty-five-year-old nephew. Billy Lee didn't want to be involved. He did not offer to help with protecting his uncle's business interests, even though these interests would eventually become his.

Cho said, "Doo ro ga"—Korean for "I'm hanging up."

The Korean punched the off button and slammed the cell phone down on the top of his desk. He leaned back, frustrated with his nephew's lack of interest or concern with Min-jun's killing. Once again, Cho considered whether he was worthy of inheriting his business. The traditional Korean way was businesses stayed within families, but Billy did not show proper respect. He had killed men for less.

Cho shook his head. Must focus on the attack in Atlanta. He needed answers. Who broke into his spa in Atlanta and killed Min-jun? What did they want? Until he knew this, he couldn't make a plan to deal with the threat.

CHAPTER FORTY-ONE

Christopher woke up around noon after less than four hours of fitful sleep. He made a pot of coffee and sat at the kitchen table with a cup, trying to fight off the grogginess. Bert's bedroom door was still closed, so he grabbed his duffle bag and left the house, leaving a note to say thanks for the bed. Barbara and Amy were due back from Alabama this evening, and he didn't want to be at their home and deal with that awkwardness. He'd sleep in his own house, even though the front-door lock was still broken.

On Sundays, he always ate lunch with his mom at Abraham and Sarah's Place. Lunch was served between eleven and one, followed by a brief church service in the sunroom. The staff would wonder why he missed lunch today, but his mother would not. Her ability to remember anything was almost gone, and usually, if she acknowledged him at all, she would call him Bud and tell anyone else at her table that he was her husband.

It was after one o'clock when Christopher walked into the lobby. The sound of a piano and a few quavering voices singing a hymn came from the sunroom, so he headed in that direction.

There were about forty residents gathered near the piano, sitting in wheelchairs or in chairs with their walkers nearby. He spotted his mother near the back of the group, slumped in her wheelchair. He found an empty folding chair and moved it beside her. An elderly woman banged out the gospel tune on the piano, missing about as many notes as she hit. A white-haired man was sitting at the front near a podium, his thumb in his Bible, bellowing out the words to the gospel hymn.

His mother mouthed the words. She loved gospel music and played the piano at her church when she was younger. She often sat on their front porch on pleasant evenings and played hymns on her accordion. She taught Christopher and his sister how to harmonize with her. Christopher learned chords on a beat-up guitar his mother got him so he could strum along. Even now, when the evenings were nice, he would spend an hour or two on his front porch, strumming his old Martin guitar and singing. Just because it made him feel happy and sad.

He'd just settled in to endure the sermon from the visiting preacher when his phone vibrated. He slid it out of his pocket and took a peek. The text was from Gloria saying to call ASAP. He leaned over, kissed the top of his mom's head, and tiptoed out of the room.

"Ji-hu is gone," Gloria said. Her voice sounded panicky.

"What? Where has she gone?" Christopher stood outside the main entrance of the assisted-living facility as he talked on his phone.

"I don't know. I was asleep in my room, and June and Kim went to the other bedroom. Ji-hu said she would sleep on the couch. We were all exhausted. I don't think any of us thought of this possibility. Kim got up just a few minutes ago and found her missing. She came and woke me up."

"I'll head your way now," Christopher said. As he walked to his car, he called Bert's phone. It went straight to his voice mail, so he left a message.

. . .

Gloria looked through the peephole, then opened the front door a crack, her eyes wide as she looked up and down the residential street. She pulled the door back, and Christopher slipped in.

She repeated the story of finding Ji-hu missing, along with her suitcase. Bert called and Christopher told him everything he knew to that point.

"I can be there within the hour," Bert said. "I might take a drive down Gallatin Road, see if I spot her."

An hour later, the five of them gathered at Gloria's kitchen table to hash out the likely path that Ji-hu took once she left the house. "I didn't see her on Gallatin. I counted three turns and eight or nine blocks to get from there to here," Bert reported. "Think she found her way there?"

"She's probably resourceful enough to follow the traffic noise and get to a busy street," Christopher said. He looked at Kim. "You said she knows Kwan's cell number?"

"Yes," Kim said. "Sometimes they leave her in charge at spa. She knows how to call Kwan and Min-jun if something happens. She knows their phone number, but she has no phone. None of us have hand phone. The only phone was on wall at spa."

"She couldn't call anyone from here," Gloria said. "I don't have a landline, and my cell phone was in my bedroom."

"So, assuming she found her way to Gallatin Road, she probably either caught a ride with someone or found a way to make a call to Kwan." Christopher looked around the table to see if anyone wanted to add more thoughts.

"She's probably already called him. If so, she's identified us," Bert said. His tone was grim. "The Koreans may be looking for this house right now."

Gloria said, "All the condos in this complex look similar. Ji-hu won't remember it, even if they get to our street. They'll have trouble finding this one."

"They know my car, and she'll describe your car," Christopher said.

"Right." Bert crossed his arms and looked at the ceiling as he thought through the situation. Then he checked the door to the garage, the sliding door off the den, and the front door. "This place is pretty secure. It's open in the back off your patio. Someone in the condos behind you would likely spot someone sneaking up to your sliding door. The other doors are steel and have good deadbolts."

"My neighbors can be nosy, but we look out for each other," Gloria volunteered.

Bert slapped the counter. "Okay, here's what we need to do. Gloria, back your car out of the garage and let Christopher pull in there. You can park on the street. Take that wreath off your front door, and let's move the flowerpot off the porch and into the garage. She may remember those things, so hopefully, it will throw her off."

Gloria put her hands against the kitchen table as if to push herself up.

Bert nodded at Kim. "You and June and I will stay in here, out of sight, just in case they drive by." He laid his Glock on the kitchen table.

"Let's get that done now," Christopher said as he stood up.

It only took a few minutes to make the changes. The air felt heavy as they gathered back in the kitchen. Christopher pulled out a chair, then dropped into it. Bert leaned against the counter and rubbed his chin. "Can you think of anything else we need to do?" Christopher and Gloria looked at each other and then shook their heads.

They discussed Christopher's idea of driving Kim and June to San Francisco. "I would need to spend most of Monday rearranging my customer appointments, lining up someone to take my newspaper route, and, of course, show up for my hearing. If I left early Tuesday and drove straight through with only a few hours of rest, I could get there and back in six days."

"That would leave Gloria and Kim and June here for an extra day, which worries me a bit," Bert said. "Depending on how aggressive the DA wants to be, you might be back in jail Monday afternoon for not revealing where Kim is."

Gloria said, "You would miss the appointment in Memphis, and who knows how long it would take to get an appointment with the Korean Consulate in San Francisco."

After more talk back and forth, they decided to stick with the original plan of Gloria leaving early Monday to drive to Memphis, and then the two young women would ride the bus to San Francisco. That felt like the safest choice. Christopher could keep his court date, and by telling them of Gloria's involvement, hopefully not risk the wrath of law enforcement. Her excellent reputation in the community of working with women who were trafficked would probably shield her from any punitive action from the DA's office.

"Okay, I think we're prepared," Bert said. He pointed at Christopher. "I'll leave my Glock here with you. I'm going to line up one of my guys for this evening and overnight. Are you planning to stay here tonight?"

Christopher looked across the table at Gloria. "You okay with me staying here?"

She nodded. "I hoped you would consider that." She looked at Bert. "I have no problem with a gun here as long as I don't have to shoot it."

"I can shoot," Kim said.

They looked at her. "We know," Bert and Christopher said almost simultaneously.

Bert said, "I'll get another guy here by nine tonight, and I'm sure he'll have more than one gun."

"I'll tag team with him," Christopher said. "One of us can stay awake. That way, if they find this condo and make a move, we'll be waiting. I need to leave around five in the morning to take care of my newspaper route, but I can be back here around seven."

"Now is not the time to worry about a damn paper route," Bert said, exasperated.

"I got customers who count on me. It'll take less than two hours. If you have a guy here, Bert, everything should be okay."

Bert shook his head. "Okay, Mister Responsibility, or should I say Mister Compulsive."

Gloria said, "My friend is coming by at six thirty in the morning. We're riding with her to Memphis. Can you be back by then?"

Christopher said, "I'll try. If I'm running late, I'll call you."

"I'll come back over early tomorrow, around six," Bert said. "I'll park down the street and watch for any approaching car or other activity. That way, we have someone outside and someone inside."

"How can we get your gun back to you?" Gloria asked.

"I have other guns," Bert said. He looked at his watch and slapped his hands together. "I need to boogie. Got to be home tonight around five. That's when Barbara and Amy get back in town."

CHAPTER FORTY-TWO

"Boseu, I just talked with Ji-hu." Kwan's voice was low, but Cho knew him well enough to know he was excited.

"She is at a restaurant called Shoney's on Main Street, near the big stadium. I have much to tell you."

"Huh. Go on."

"She said Kim was the one who shot Min-jun. Kim was with Christopher Jones and another man named Bert. Also, a woman named Gloria. They drove to Atlanta." Kwan told Cho how Ji-hu said they broke into the spa, killed Min-jun and took the money. "They made her and June go back to Nashville, but she left the condo this morning after everyone was asleep." He told Boseu that a man stopped and gave Ji-hu a ride. She borrowed his cell phone.

"I am driving back from Atlanta now but must go the speed limit because Min-jun's body is in a bag in the trunk. Ji-hu is waiting at Shoney's."

Cho understood his caution. "I will send Sung-ho to pick up Ji-hu. She can come to my house and wait till you get here. You must find a place for the body first. Do not bring it here."

"I know a dumpster behind a restaurant that is closed today," Kwan said. "The dumpster is probably full of boxes and rotting food, so it will stink. I will place the body where no one will see it."

"Does Ji-hu know how to find the house where Kim is?" Cho asked.

"She does not know the name of the street where the woman lives and where Kim is staying. She says the houses are close together, and they all look alike. We will drive around tonight."

"If she does not remember the street name, you will probably not find it. It will be dark by the time you return," Cho said. "I will have Sung-ho drive her around to look for the house." He paused for a moment. "It is good to know our enemy. We will find them. They will be punished."

Cho ended the call and sat motionless at his desk. It was a relief to know that Christopher Jones caused his problems in Atlanta, not another cartel trying to put him out of business. Jones and his friend Bert were his focus now. They will pay with their lives for their interference with his business.

▪ ▪ ▪

The detective and his wife had just ordered dinner at the Outback Steakhouse, her favorite restaurant, when the burner cell phone buzzed in his pocket.

"I need to take this call," he said as he dug out the phone. "Believe me, I wish I didn't," he muttered as he slid out of the booth. His wife did not reply as she sipped her Martini, barely acknowledging his comment with a head tilt.

This was their routine—Sunday night dinner out, the one night he was almost guaranteed to have off each week. They would go to a restaurant, order drinks, sit in silence, study the menu, then study the crowd, but not talk to each other.

"I have more problems with Christopher Jones. You must help us find him," the familiar raspy voice said.

"I'm doing what I can," the detective said. He tried to not let a whine enter his tone as he walked out to the parking lot.

"He broke into my spa in Atlanta last night. Another man was with him. Min-jun was there. They killed Min-jun," Cho said.

"What?" The detective's tone was incredulous. "Does the Atlanta police know they killed your man?"

"We do not call the police. I sent Kwan to Atlanta this morning to clean up everything."

"What happened to Jones and this other guy? Where are they?"

"They are all back in Nashville." The Korean told the detective of Ji-hu's call and the information she'd shared with Kwan.

"One of my men drove Ji-hu through streets to look for the house where they are staying, but she could not find it again. We know this other man drives a big black SUV. He is Christopher Jones's friend. Ji-hu said his name is Bert. I need to know his full name and where he lives. We must find Kim, and we must find this other man. They cause me many problems."

"I-I need to think about this." The detective stuttered, trying to process this new information. Suddenly, he thought of an idea, a trail to follow, perhaps.

"Jones made a call from the jail when we held him those few hours," he said. "I remember seeing a record of that call. I can get it and trace it. It might be this guy, Bert."

"Go do it," the raspy voice said.

"I can't go in tonight. It'll look suspicious if I go in on my night off and get on the computer and look for information on Jones. If something happens to him and this other guy, someone might notice I was looking up information on them and start asking questions."

He instinctively looked at his watch and glanced around the parking lot, making sure no one was close enough to overhear any of the conversation.

"My shift starts at seven in the morning. I'll go in early and get on this. I can get a name and address in a few minutes once I'm on my computer."

"Go in at six o'clock," the raspy voice said. "I will have two cars waiting for Christopher Jones early tomorrow morning. If he delivers newspapers, we will grab him. I may need you, so be available." The Korean ended the call.

The detective slowly slid the phone into his pocket. He stood in the parking lot for a few minutes, staring into the distance. He had no desire for the steak he'd ordered, or to sit across from his wife. The only solace was that she would not ask him about the call, so he wouldn't have to lie. He'd been caught in many lies through the years, and now she didn't even bother asking questions.

Once again, he wished that he'd never visited the spa in Dickson. The Korean had owned him ever since. The photos taken there could cost him his marriage and his job. Most importantly, the Korean had threatened to kill him if he didn't continue to cooperate, and the detective believed him. He couldn't think of a good way out of this bondage.

CHAPTER FORTY-THREE

"Can you think of anything else we should do to protect ourselves?" Gloria asked. She stood in her living room with Christopher and Kim and looked out the front window at the street.

"I think we've done everything we can do for now," Christopher said. "Bert's guy will be here this evening before dark."

Gloria shivered. "It's scary, needing an armed guard for protection. Lord, the things I've been a part of in just forty-eight hours." She shivered again.

"I am sorry. You are in danger because of me." Kim almost whispered as she shrank into herself.

Christopher put his hand on Kim's shoulder. "You didn't ask for my help. I offered."

Gloria nodded her agreement. "I volunteered, too." She squeezed Kim's hand. "Now, let's get busy with other things. It'll help calm our spirits. Y'all hungry? I can whip something up." Christopher and Kim followed her into the kitchen.

Kim said, "I not hungry. I just have tea."

She filled a cup with water, microwaved it, and dropped in a tea bag. "June is in the den watching TV. I go sit with her."

Gloria watched as Kim headed toward the den with her cup and some crackers and cheese. "She's torn up over Sukee. That part of her escape plan is gone, and she's feeling alone."

"Just think how alone she would be without your help and the help you've arranged for her in San Francisco."

Gloria nodded. "She's strong and determined, but she still needs to go through her time of grief."

Christopher turned to look at Gloria. "How are you handling what happened in Atlanta?"

"I think okay," she replied, rubbing her forehead. "I prayed about it last night."

"Did you get any peace from your prayers?"

"Maybe," she replied, nodding and looking up at him. "What about you?"

"I talked to God too. And I talked to my dad."

Gloria cocked her head and studied him. "Do you talk to your dad often?"

"Yeah, about as much as I talk to God."

"Does your dad answer you back?"

"No, but then, neither does God. I usually do feel better though talking to God or my dad, even if I don't get answers."

"Sounds like you're getting the two confused. Maybe you should talk to someone."

Christopher gave her a quizzical look. "I thought that was what I was doing."

Gloria smiled faintly. "Yes, and I'll have to do, for now." She led the way to the kitchen. "How about shrimp and pasta? I have frozen shrimp and the makings for a salad."

"I haven't eaten in twenty-four hours, so just your words have my mouth watering."

Gloria set a wedge of Brie cheese and a few crackers on a wooden cutting board on the counter. She struggled to pull the cork from a bottle of red wine. Christopher reached to take it away, wrapping his hand around hers briefly. She glanced at him and smiled.

After a lot of pan rattling and trips between the counter and refrigerator, Gloria had water heating in a pot on the stove for the pasta, and she had filled the counter with lettuce, scallions, mushrooms, an avocado, and cherry tomatoes. Christopher snacked on crackers and cheese, sipped wine, and watched her work. He decided that a good-looking woman bustling around in the kitchen was a turn-on.

Gloria went to work on the vegetables. "You can unwrap the shrimp." She touched his arm and pointed at a package of slightly thawed large shrimp. "Rinse them in lukewarm water."

She talked about her life while they worked: about growing up in a religious, middle-class family in Jackson, Tennessee. Getting married young and becoming a mother left little room for her to explore other options or consider any lifestyle other than that of a mom and preacher's wife.

"Did you ever wish your life was different? Did you want more?" Christopher asked.

Gloria stirred the shrimp into the butter and garlic sauce in the skillet. "Not really. I loved my husband, and I adored being a mom. I guess I'm a caregiver by nature. But now I'm in a different calling, and I love this life too."

She poured the angel hair pasta and boiling water into a colander in the kitchen sink. Christopher liked how the steam moistened her face and dampened her hair. She grabbed tongs and lifted out a healthy portion of pasta onto plates.

"The first forty years of my life were spent in a bubble." She spooned shrimp and sauce over the pasta and added fresh chopped parsley as garnish. "Hanging out in strip clubs the last two years has been a quick baptism into the seamier side of life."

Gloria smiled at Christopher. "I'm more open-minded now than I was before. I've found I can enjoy a few things about a club atmosphere, such as the music. And I appreciate a good glass of wine." She held up her empty wine glass.

Christopher poured them more wine and raised his glass. Gloria smiled, leaned toward him, and clinked her glass against his. He picked up the salad bowl and followed her to the kitchen table.

"What about you?" Her blue eyes searched his eyes. "How did you grow up?"

"Not a lot different from you." He told her about growing up in a blue-collar family with good parents but not as many friends and not as much church involvement.

"My sister and I went to church on Sunday with my mom.

My dad went fishing or hiking. He said the outdoors was his church." He smiled as he talked about his dad.

"When I turned thirteen, I decided I wanted to go with my dad. He negotiated a deal with my mom where, if I went with him on Sunday, he had to tell a Bible story or scene and explain it to me. I think that was when I fell in love with philosophical wisdom. My dad was a reader and a thinker. He just wasn't much of a joiner. We had great discussions, and as I got older, great debates."

Finally, there was a lull in the conversation. The momentary silence felt comfortable to Christopher.

"I haven't had a conversation like this with a man in over four years," Gloria said, her face flushed with the effects of the wine. "Not since my husband died."

"Nor I, with a woman, in the last three years."

"I knew when I heard your name you would be someone I could relate to. You know Christopher means 'Christ-bearer,' right?"

"Yeah, I've been told that," he said with a smile. "But my goal is to *not* get crucified by these Korean bastards."

Before either of them could say more, his cell phone rang. It was Bert's friend, their guard for the night. He was parked out front and would be at the door in a minute.

Holding Bert's gun down by his leg, Christopher looked through the front door peephole to study the guy on the front porch. He cautiously turned the knob and pulled.

A big guy, thick chest and arms, buzz cut, wearing jeans and a polo shirt, stood on the front porch holding a small duffle bag.

"I'm Greg." He stuck out his hand. His grip was tight but not bone-crushing. Christopher was glad he didn't go for that alpha male trick of establishing dominance with a hard handshake.

Greg walked through the condominium, studying the doors and windows. He joined them in the kitchen to discuss logistics for the evening. Kim joined them, too.

"The nice thing about condos like this is there's only the sliding glass door out back and the front door to worry about. The front window is double-paned plate glass and visible from the road and other condos. All the other windows are upstairs," Greg said, sweeping his arm at all the entrances and windows. "The garage door is steel and can't be easily opened."

Gloria and Christopher nodded, following his gestures. He went on, examining the premises and assuring them.

"Your back yard is open. Some of the homeowners probably have surveillance cameras with automatic lights that flash on with motion, so that'll alert us if anyone approaches from the back." He looked at Gloria. "Do you have a broom stick or anything to block the sliding glass door?"

"I have a rod made expressly to block that door. My older son got it for me after I moved in," Gloria said. "And the front door deadbolt is reinforced."

"I noticed it," Greg said. "I don't think anyone can kick that door in. Of course, someone could throw something, like a cinder block, through the plate-glass window or the sliding glass door, but that would make a lot of noise, and then they would have to climb through it. We would have time to react."

He looked around as he continued to talk. "I'll station myself in the hall, near the front. I can see the front door and out the front window, and when I lean back, I can see the sliding glass door in the den." He moved in position in the hall and demonstrated as he talked. "I'll place a chair where I want to be, and I'll move around some, but mostly I'll just keep an eye out."

"Have you had dinner?" Gloria asked. "We have a little salad left, and pasta."

"No thanks, I ate earlier," Greg said.

"I may go to bed soon, since I didn't get much sleep this morning," Christopher said. "I'll take over for you around one. Sound all right to you?"

Greg shook his head. "I'm fine until morning. You get a good night's sleep."

Christopher started to protest, but Greg held up his hand. "You can get up whenever you want, but I'm not going to sleep. I'm on duty here till morning."

"I stay on couch tonight." Kim looked at Greg, then at Christopher. "I sleep many hours this morning. I won't sleep tonight. I watch TV."

She pointed at Bert's Glock on the kitchen counter. "Show me how to shoot this gun."

Christopher knitted his brow. "I was planning on keeping that with me."

Greg said, "I have another revolver in my bag here, plus more ammunition." He held up the duffle bag. "Bert told me you've already shot a revolver," he said to Kim, "so I brought a smaller one I think you can handle."

They finished talking through the logistics of the evening. Kim settled again on the couch in the den in front of the TV. Christopher went to get his duffle bag from his car in the garage. When he came back in, Gloria was at the sink rinsing the last of the dishes. She called his name and waved him over.

"Are you going to bed now?" she asked as she turned around and leaned against the counter, still holding a dish-towel. She glanced to be sure that Greg was parked in the hall near the front.

Christopher nodded as he looked at his watch. "It's after nine, so probably in the next hour. I feel like I could sleep for a week. Which one of the upstairs bedrooms shall I take?"

"I thought you could sleep in my room." Her face turned red. "I'm not proposing that I sleep with you," she hastily added. "I'll go upstairs and sleep in the bed where Kim slept, since she's staying down here on the couch. My room has its own bathroom, and you need to get up early."

Christopher studied her face and then nodded. "Okay, I think I understand. I'm to sleep in your bed, but not with you."

Gloria turned red again and looked away. "I meant..."

Christopher waited her out.

"I sometimes talk, and things come out before I've thought them through." She wrinkled up her nose.

He grinned. "We have plenty of time to think things through." He leaned over and gently grabbed her chin, turned her face toward him, and kissed her. She dropped the dish towel, put her hands on either side of his face, and kissed him back.

"I know it's too soon, but I'm gonna say it. I'm attracted to you." Christopher slid his hands down around her waist.

Gloria smiled up at him. She put a hand on his chest. "I better go say good night to Kim." She turned and walked away but said over her shoulder, "To be continued."

Christopher watched her walk out of the kitchen. He'd not felt this stirring in a long time. He hoped he could calm down enough to get to sleep in the next hour. Four-thirty in the morning would come soon enough.

CHAPTER FORTY-FOUR

MONDAY

The cell phone alarm woke Christopher from a dead sleep. After two nights of little sleep, his body wanted to stay in bed, and his mind seemed in a fog. He turned the water in the shower to almost cold to get fully awake. He pulled on cargo shorts and a t-shirt, slipped his feet into his OluKais, and grabbed his duffle bag. It was probably a little cool outside, but he could throw on his hoodie sweatshirt once he got in the car.

Kim sat on the couch in the dim light from the TV as he walked through the den.

"I may not be back by six thirty when y'all leave for Memphis," Christopher said to her. "So, I'll say goodbye now. Tell Gloria I'll call her later if I'm not back."

She stood up, put her arms around him, and hugged him close. "You save me," she whispered.

Christopher felt awkward as she clung to him. He patted her on the back. "I helped you, and Bert helped you, and Gloria and Gracie."

"Gracie. Yes, poor Gracie. She save me, too." Kim's voice broke, and she swiped at tears.

"But mostly, you saved yourself." Christopher grabbed her shoulders and leaned back to look into her eyes. "It's a three-day journey by Greyhound; then you'll be in San Francisco. Your new life will start. Promise me you'll call. I want to know what happens once you get settled out there."

They finally separated and Kim wiped her eyes again. Greg leaned in from the hall.

"I'll follow you out the garage door," he said to Christopher, then looked at Kim. "Kim, lock this kitchen door behind me. Wait until I say it's all clear before you unlock it to let me back in. Don't open unless I say those words: all clear."

Greg stood in the open garage with his pistol in his hand as Christopher backed out of the driveway. No sign of men in a dark sedan. Bert had said he'd be back around five thirty or six, but there was no sign of his black Suburban yet. Christopher headed to the *Tennessean* depot to pick up the newspapers and then to his delivery route.

▪ ▪ ▪

Christopher's radio was tuned to Fisk University's jazz station, his default music source for those mornings when all was quiet and peaceful. Even though darkness still ruled, there was a faint hint of morning light. His front windows were down as he drove the streets in the Nashville suburban neighborhood, tossing newspapers in familiar driveways. Usually a bagel, coffee, and Stella awaited him at Bruegger's Bagels after one more street, but this morning he would call Gloria and hurry back to her condo if they were—

A large sedan, headlights not on, surged in front of his Buick. He slammed on his brakes. "What the hell!" Then he was rocked by a solid thump on his back bumper. He looked in the rearview mirror and realized another sedan had boxed him in. As he twisted to look, doors popped open on the car behind him, and two men exited, arms extended, pistols pointed at him.

Christopher looked around wildly. Another man with a gun was in front of his car. He recognized the wiry Asian man he'd seen at the bus station. Someone opened his car door.

"Turn off the ignition and get out," an accented voice commanded.

Christopher obeyed. "Is this a robbery? I don't have much cash, but you can have it."

The wiry Asian man slammed his pistol barrel into Christopher's forehead, causing a gash. Christopher yelled and grabbed his head. The man punched him in the gut, then raised his knee as he jerked Christopher's head down, smashing it, sending blood gushing out of his nose. The Asian man kicked Christopher's lower right leg, striking the bone with the steel toe of his lace-up boot. The bone broke with a distinct crack that sounded like someone had stepped on a stick.

Christopher fell to the ground as pain seared through his leg. Another kick, this time in his side, and he felt his ribs crack. He struggled to breathe. He moaned and rolled from one side to the other. The blood in his eyes blinded him.

Christopher heard words he didn't understand. Two men snatched him up by the arms, dragged him to a car, and shoved him in the rear seat. One of the men dug his wallet out of the back pocket of his cargo shorts and then wrapped duct tape around his ankles. The other man leaned in from the other side of the car, jerked his arms and hands together, and wrapped duct tape around his wrists. Car doors slammed, and the vehicles accelerated, picking up speed as they exited the neighborhood.

"We have Christopher Jones and his car," the wiry man said into his cell phone.

"I will meet you at his house," the raspy voice responded.

CHAPTER FORTY-FIVE

Christopher lay on his back on the kitchen table in his house. His bound hands extended over his head, his duct-taped legs were flat on the table, and his feet hung off the end. A man stood at the end of the table and held his feet. Two men were near his head, one holding his arms flat while the other man lit a cigarette. He bit his lip and squinted in the overhead light. He fought the urge to scream from the pain of his broken leg. His forehead was no longer bleeding, but the dried blood in and around his eyes limited his vision. He couldn't wipe it away. His nose was swollen, so he breathed ragged gasps through his mouth.

A man leaned over and looked into his eyes. He was older than the other men. His face was lined and looked like worn leather. He took a drag on his cigarette and blew the smoke in Christopher's face.

"You have caused me much trouble. Now you tell me where to find Kim." His voice was raspy and had little inflection.

Christopher didn't respond. He knew this man was Cho, the boss of the Korean mafia, the man whose house he and Bert had bombed. He also knew he would not survive long after telling them how to find Kim.

Cho leaned back and nodded at another man standing nearby. "Pull up his shirt."

The man grabbed Christopher's sweatshirt and t-shirt and roughly pulled them up under his armpits, baring his chest.

Cho took a drag on his cigarette and stuck the lit end of it on Christopher's right nipple, causing a sizzle and the pungent odor of burned flesh.

Christopher screamed with the pain and rolled his head from side to side. He arched his back and bucked on the table, straining against the hands of the men holding him down.

"I think I shall burn you again, so you know we are serious." Cho took another drag, then pushed the lit cigarette into the left nipple, twisting it to maximize the burn.

Christopher screamed again and flailed against the hands as his flesh sizzled.

"Do you have anything to say to us?" Cho leaned over him.

"Kim . . . staying with a woman . . . I don't know the address," Christopher said through gritted teeth.

Cho stared into Christopher's eyes. "You are lying."

He lit another cigarette, took two puffs, and ground it into Christopher's navel. Christopher twisted his torso and bucked, trying to throw off the lighted cigarette. He clenched his face and moaned as he tried to keep from yelling. His burned flesh twitched and quivered.

A cell phone rang. Cho pulled it out of his pocket, looked at the screen, hit the speaker button, and put the phone on the table so all the Koreans could listen.

"What did you find?" he asked.

"I tracked down the other guy." The voice sounded familiar to Christopher. "I got the number Jones called from jail, and I think I know who this is. The phone is registered to Albert Hawkins. He runs a company called Solid Rock Security. I know about him. They sometimes hire off-duty cops. I went on their website, and it looks like they use several black SUVs in their work. He's listed as Executive Vice President and Managing Partner. I suspect he drives one of the SUVs."

Cho turned back to Christopher and leaned over him, his face near Christopher's as he stared into his eyes. "The man who helped you in Atlanta was Albert Hawkins."

"Don't know . . . anybody named Albert."

Cho's eyes narrowed. "You are lying."

He spoke into the phone. "This Albert Hawkins; you have his address?"

"Yes. It's west of downtown. I'm driving that way now. I'll do a drive-by and look for the black SUV."

"No. You come to Christopher Jones's house. We have him. I will send other men after Albert Hawkins."

"I-I'm on duty. I'm supposed to report my whereabouts. My partner is coming in late today, so I'm alone now. If I drive out there, I can't stay long."

"What we are doing will not take long. I will send two men after Albert Hawkins. I will need one more man here."

"Okay, I'm on my way. Be there in ten minutes."

Christopher squinted his eyes and tried to focus through the shroud of pain as the Korean man with the raspy voice talked into his cell phone. He thought about what he had overheard. Bert was probably still parked in front of Gloria's condominium. That meant Barbara and Amy were home alone.

The Korean men huddled near the sink and talked in low voices. Christopher raised his head and looked at the clock on the wall. It said six fifteen. He stared at the eyes in the face of Jesus on the clock. They seemed alive.

He lowered his head, shut his eyes, and prayed for strength, praying to function over the pain. He needed to hang on for another fifteen minutes. It was at least a thirty-minute drive to Gloria's house in East Nashville. Even if the women were slow to leave the house, they would be gone by seven. And, if there was a little more daylight, the Koreans searching for Bert might not break in and grab Barbara and Amy.

He thought about Amy. He'd brought this danger into her life. He prayed no harm would come to her.

A few minutes later, he heard the front door creak open, followed by the tap of leather heels across hardwood floors. Christopher turned his head. Detective O'Reilly. He was the voice on the phone, the mole in the police department. The detective stood in the kitchen doorway, his eyes wide as he looked at Christopher and the Koreans.

"What are y'all doing to him?" he asked.

"Christopher Jones will soon tell us where we can find Kim. We will get her and the woman that helped her," Cho said, his voice flat, uninflected, as if he guaranteed that outcome.

"Sung-ho and Kyung will go find the man called Albert Hawkins. Give them his address. If he is home, they will kill him."

O'Reilly reached into his suit coat pocket and pulled out a folded paper. He looked at it, then slowly walked across the room to hand it to Sung-ho. "Wait until you can catch him by himself. I think he's married. He may have a family at home with him."

"No. We must get him now. This morning." Cho lit another cigarette. He blew out smoke and leveled a deadeye stare at O'Reilly. "Once we deal with Christopher and the woman named Gloria, he will know we are coming for him. We won't be able to surprise him. If he has family, it is too bad."

O'Reilly, his face flushed, stared back at Cho. He shook his head as if he disagreed.

Cho turned to Sung-ho. "You go now. We will get our business done here soon."

▪ ▪ ▪

Christopher had ceased to scream each time the Korean ground the lighted cigarette tip into his chest and stomach. He gritted his teeth against the pain, but he didn't faint. He called upon the mantra he used when he ran in a marathon. He would count his steps, muttering them out loud, and when he reached one hundred, he started a new hundred, counting "one hundred and one, one hundred and two." The hundreds would pile up with the miles as he focused on numbers, not the pain in his lungs and legs. Now he willed the time to pass as he walled off the pain. His flesh twitched with each new burn, but his lips muttered numbers.

The smell of burning flesh permeated the air. O'Reilly had

shed his suit coat and loosened his tie. Sweat beaded his forehead as he stood at the end of the table, holding Christopher's legs.

"Jesus, I don't know how he's standing this. I can hardly watch." O'Reilly looked at the Korean man. "You need to bring this to an end."

"Soon." He drew on his cigarette and let the smoke filter out his nose as he stared at Christopher. "He is tough, but not too tough."

"Boseu, maybe we cut off his fingers," Kwan said, holding onto Christopher's arm.

Cho shook his head and replied in Korean. "No, he will tell us soon where Kim is. After that, we will burn his house down. He will burn up with it. His flesh will be gone." He took another drag of his cigarette. "The firemen and police will believe it is an accident. They will think he fell down his stairs, broke his leg, and could not get out of his house. But if he has fingers missing, they will know he was tortured."

He switched back to English as he pointed at the gas range. "Turn on the stove and get the tea kettle hot. We will press that on his chest."

Kwan moved toward the stove and clicked on a burner.

Even with his mind in a fog, Christopher feared this burn. He felt his breaths coming faster and shallower. He didn't know if he could bear that pain.

He heard a voice.

His rational mind realized this was probably a hallucination, but it sounded like his dad's voice. It seemed real, as if his dad stood next to him, whispering in his ear. "Save yourself. You have the power. Find a way. Think. It's in your pocket."

His mind raced. He had no power. His hands and feet were taped. All he had in the pocket of his shorts was his cell phone. There was nothing else. He was sure of it. His hoody had a pocket, but it only had—

The paper. Phone numbers. The plan formed in his mind,

but many things would have to fall into place for it to work.

"Stop!"

Kwan drew his hand back from the kettle on the stove burner.

Christopher groaned, his breath coming in gasps now. "I'll tell what I know."

Cho leaned over him. "Where is Kim?"

"I have a backpack . . . in the trunk." Christopher panted. "There's a card in the front pocket. It's blue and red. Has a name on it. Gloria Jean McNulty." He groaned. "Her address is on the back."

Cho studied his face, drew on his cigarette, and nodded. "This time, he tells the truth." He looked at Kwan. "Who drove his car here?"

Kwan pointed at the Korean man holding Christopher's left arm. The man pulled the car keys from his pants pocket.

"First, we will get everything ready," Cho said to Kwan.

"Do I kill him now?" Kwan asked.

"No. I want him alive when he burns. Find something to make a torch."

Kwan opened the door off the kitchen and went down to the basement. He returned with a can of paint thinner and a broom, picked up a kitchen towel, and liberally sprinkled paint thinner on it. Then he tied it around the broom and handed it to Cho.

Cho leaned over Christopher. "You pay now for the trouble you caused me. You will burn in your kitchen, and nothing will remain of you but bones." He turned to O'Reilly and pointed at the roll of duct tape on the counter. "You wrap more duct tape around his arms and his body so he can't move."

The Koreans walked out of the house as Kwan moved quickly through the downstairs rooms, pouring paint thinner. He emptied the rest of the can on the floor near the front door.

O'Reilly didn't pick up the duct tape. "I wish it didn't have to end this way, but I can't think of a way out," he muttered as he waited near the kitchen door. He shifted from one foot to the other and avoided eye contact with Christopher.

Christopher didn't respond.

"We all leave now," Kwan called from the front door. The detective left the kitchen with one final glance back at Christopher.

As they left the house, Cho stopped on the porch and pointed at the Korean man with Christopher's car keys. "Get the backpack out of the car trunk and find the blue and red card," he instructed in Korean.

The man went to the rear of Christopher's Buick. He fumbled with the car keys, found the trunk key, and inserted it. The trunk lid opened. He lifted out a black backpack. It was heavy and solid, so he used both hands to place it on the ground next to the car. O'Reilly and Kwan stood near the back of the car and watched as the man unzipped the front pocket of the large backpack and rummaged around for the blue card.

Cho waited on the front porch by the open front door. He dug a lighter out of his pants pocket and lit the cloth tied around the broom. He watched the men gathered around the backpack.

▪ ▪ ▪

After the men went outside, Christopher rolled on his side and struggled to sit up. He groaned at the pain from his broken leg and the multiple burns on his torso. He brought his hands to his mouth and chewed on the duct tape wrapped around his wrists, starting a small tear. He raised his arms over his head, swung them down and pushed out against the duct tape around his wrists, wincing as his cracked ribs sent a fresh wave of pain through his body. The tape yielded, almost tearing loose. He raised his hands, bit his lip, and swung down again. He put every ounce of remaining strength into the motion, yelling through the pain.

The tape gave way.

He peeled the duct tape off his wrists, reached a hand into the side pocket of his cargo shorts, and extracted his cell phone. He slid his other hand into the front pouch of his sweatshirt and pulled out a wrinkled piece of paper. There were three phone numbers on it, in Bert's handwriting. He remembered Bert saying the last number was for Bigger Boom.

With trembling fingers, he dialed the phone number. He hit send, dropped the piece of paper, slid off the table, and collapsed on the floor.

The house shook from the force of the blast. Shrapnel pockmarked the front and knocked out the living room picture window. Pieces of glass blew into the interior room walls like small sharp knives.

Cho fell in the front door, still clutching a flaming broom. He landed in the puddle of paint thinner and was swallowed by the flame. He writhed briefly on the floor and then became motionless. A second explosion followed the first by only a moment as the Buick's gas tank blew up, catching the car on fire.

Christopher felt the whump from the explosion outside as he half scooted, half rolled to the back door, still clutching his cell phone. He leaned against the door to catch his breath, shoved his phone in his pocket, and reached up to turn the knob. He pulled the door open and fell through it onto the back porch.

It took several minutes, but he managed to scoot off the porch. He used his hands and elbows and moved his taped-together legs in a caterpillar motion as he crawled away from the house, ignoring the pain he felt. He rolled on his back and pulled out his cell phone again.

"Siri . . . call Bert," he said as he held the phone in front of his face.

"Calling Bert Hawkins," the soft female voice said.

"Yo, bro. Where are you?" Bert asked when he answered his phone.

"I'm lying in my back yard." Christopher was breathless, and he couldn't move another inch. Talking was an effort. "Where are you?" He lifted his head to look at his house. He saw the orange glow of flames through the kitchen window. Black smoke was billowing up from the front of the house.

"I'm at my storage unit. Greg and I swung by here to pick up a couple things. Gloria and the girls got on the road to Memphis about fifteen minutes ago. Why are you in your back yard?" Bert's tone turned serious. "And bro, you don't sound good."

"Listen to me," Christopher said, forcing scratchy syllables out. "Two men, Koreans, are on their way to your house." He breathed out shallow puffs and moaned. "In a black sedan. Looking for you." He paused and struggled for air. Adrenaline helped him not succumb to the pain. "Get home fast. They'll be there soon, maybe already." He blew two pants. "They could be holding Amy and Barbara hostage."

"I'll go there now," Bert said, the words terse. "What's *your* condition?"

"I'm messed up. My leg is broken, but I'll make it." Christopher took a couple of ragged breaths. The words seemed surreal. "The Koreans brought me here, tortured me, and set my house on fire, but I got out." He panted again. "My car blew up from your bomb in the trunk. I dialed the number. I think they were near it. I'm hearing sirens. Help is coming. Go home! Take care of Barbara and Amy."

"Okay. I'll call you back once I get Barbara and Amy safe."

"No, don't call me . . . I need to get rid of my phone. Don't want a call traced to you. Erase this call from your end."

"I'll do it. I'll track you down later."

Christopher ended the call and turned his cell phone off. He threw it over his head and out in the yard, away from the house, as far as he could while lying on his back. He winced at the pain in his ribs caused by the motion.

CHAPTER FORTY-SIX

Two men sat in the black sedan and studied the house across the tree-lined street in the early morning light. The other houses nearby were dark and set deep in large lots.

"There is no garage, only the carport. No black SUV, so he is not home, or we have the wrong house," the driver said in Korean.

"It is early, not seven o'clock," the other man said as he looked at his watch. "It is odd that his car is gone. Maybe he does not live here. What do we do now?"

Before the first man could respond, a large SUV with flashing blue lights behind the front grill pulled in behind them. The spotlight on the driver side was pointed at the black sedan, making it difficult for the men to see the occupants in the car in their rearview mirror.

"A neighbor must have called the police," the driver in the sedan said as he looked in the mirror. "Put your gun under the seat and let me do the talking. We have done nothing wrong."

"Open your car trunk, lower your windows, and place both hands on the dashboard where I can see them," a voice commanded over a speaker in the SUV.

The two men looked at each other. The driver hesitated and then reached across the dashboard and pushed the trunk release button. He pressed the window buttons, lowered the front windows, and placed his hands on the dashboard. The man in the passenger seat complied as well.

The Koreans hunkered down and braved the glaring spotlight as they tried to watch in their side mirrors. The SUV doors opened, and two men stepped out. The driver wore a uniform. He pointed a pistol at the sedan as he walked up. He stopped several feet away from the side of the black sedan. He took a long look at the driver, then nodded at the other man.

The man from the passenger side of the SUV held a metal box, slightly smaller than a typical shoebox. He cautiously approached the back of the sedan and leaned over the open trunk. He stood up empty-handed, slammed the trunk lid shut, then pulled a pistol from a holster on his belt.

He kept his pistol pointed at the car as he stepped back to the passenger side of the SUV and slid back in. The driver holstered his gun and got behind the wheel.

"You may start your car," the voice commanded over the speaker. "Leave this neighborhood and drive to Interstate 40. Get on the interstate going west and drive. I will be following you."

The driver of the sedan started the engine and slowly drove down the suburban street, then turned right onto the four-lane road that led to the interstate.

"Can the police make you drive to the interstate like this?" the other Korean asked as he scrunched down so he could look at the outside rearview mirror and study the large black SUV behind them. The blue lights were turned off.

"I don't think that is police in the car," the driver said. "That man's uniform looked different. We will get to the interstate, and then I will pull over and call Boseu. Something is not right, but they had guns pointed at us, so we could do nothing. Get your gun ready in case they try to stop us again. If they do, we will shoot them."

A few minutes later, the sedan with the two Korean men turned onto the Interstate 40 West entrance ramp. The SUV following them did not turn onto the ramp. It sped away.

The driver of the sedan drove slowly up the entrance ramp and onto the interstate. He watched in the rearview mirror, and when he didn't see the large SUV follow them, he pulled to the side and parked. He grabbed his cell phone from his pocket and dialed. Before the call went through, an explosion in the trunk rocked the sedan, followed immediately by a larger explosion as the gas tank erupted, engulfing the car in flames. Within seconds, both men were dead.

CHAPTER FORTY-SEVEN

Christopher's mind was hazy as he awoke from the anesthesia. It felt like he was swimming up from the bottom of a deep pool of water. He lifted his head and tried to figure out the large object near the lower part of his body. He shook his head to try and focus. It finally dawned on him that the thing was his right leg, in a cast from ankle to knee and elevated on a foam cushion. He felt a dull throbbing pain from the lower part of his body and his side. He craned his neck and spotted someone in the reclining chair beside his bed. It was Amy, staring at him with her arms crossed and a look on her face that alternated between worry and a pout.

"How long have I been out?" Christopher asked. His voice was dry and whispery.

"You've been in this room for about an hour. When Mom and I got here about two hours ago, a nurse told us the surgeon was operating on your leg. After that, they brought you up here. We were able to see you, but you were out cold. You know you're in St. Thomas Hospital, right? You know some bad guys beat you up, and they broke your leg?"

"Yeah, I was alert when the ambulance brought me in." His mind was foggy as he tried to remember everything after that.

"I remember the ER doc patched me up." He went to a full whisper, barely moving his lips. "They cut off my clothes. I remember the surgeon came into the room and said she probably wouldn't need to do surgery. She could just set it. Then they put me under. I don't know what happened next."

Amy stood up, went to the foot of the bed, and pointed to

Christopher's cast on his lower right leg.

"Your leg is broken right there." Her tone was matter-of-fact. "I asked a lot of questions. Because you don't have a wife, and I'm your only child, I'm next of kin. I thought I needed to be the one to know. Besides, the surgeon was cool. She talked to me mostly after I told her I was your daughter, and I was in charge. I might want to be a surgeon like her one day."

Amy reached out and touched Christopher's cast.

"The surgeon told me you had the big bone broken right there, but not the small one. I think she called it the tibia bone. Anyway, she said it did not poke through the skin, so she could set it without cutting your leg open, which is good. She told us you'll get back to normal, but you'll need about a week in bed, then four to five weeks on crutches."

"Huh? Who's us?"

"What?" Amy looked puzzled. "Oh, you mean, who was she saying this to?"

Christopher nodded.

"Well, mostly me, but Bert and Mom were there, too. They left a few minutes ago to get lunch in the cafeteria. They're going to bring me a sandwich." She folded her arms. "Bert told us your house caught on fire and you barely escaped. You have burns on your chest from some bad men, he said. He said the stove was on and gas escaped and caused an explosion. Is that what happened?"

"Yeah, that happened." He looked out the window. "And some more stuff."

"Did my things in my room burn?"

Christopher nodded.

Amy stomped her foot on the floor. "I had some good things there—clothes, my favorite boots, pictures, books...." She caught herself. "Dad, I was scared when I heard about it. I think those guys meant to kill you." Her face clouded over, and she moved to the side of Christopher's bed.

"Aw, honey, I'm going to be okay." He patted her hand,

and then he squeezed it. "They can't hurt me now."

"Bert told me they were all dead. He couldn't explain it, he said, but I think he knows something." She glanced over her shoulder and lowered her voice to a whisper. "A man came by earlier. He said he was a detective. He and Bert talked. I asked Bert again if he knew more about what happened, but he said you would tell me everything."

"I will. Tomorrow. Come see me tomorrow after school, and I'll be up for it, I promise."

As if on cue, Bert appeared in the doorway.

"Hey, man, glad you're awake." He grinned as he walked into the room. "Amy, your mother decided to eat her lunch in the cafeteria and said you should come down there and eat, too."

Amy gave Christopher a quick hug. She was careful not to press down on the bandages on his chest.

"I love you, Dad."

"I love you, too, sweetie." Christopher's eyes misted as he watched her walk away.

Bert waited until she left the room, then sat in the recliner and leaned in to talk.

"Man, they worked you over," he said, shaking his head. "You have a broken leg, cracked ribs, and some mean-looking burns on your chest, the doc tells us."

"Yeah, Amy was filling me in on the broken-leg part. It looks like I'm out of commission for about six weeks but should be okay in the long run."

Bert leaned in a little more.

"Simpson, the detective, dropped by about an hour ago. I talked with him. He told me three dead bodies were in your front yard, and one crispy critter was inside your front door. You want to tell me what happened?"

Christopher looked away for a moment, then back at Bert. "It could have been so bad. They wanted to find Kim and Gloria. They wanted you and were willing to kill Barbara and

Amy to get you. I thought I was done for. I was sure of it."

He spent a few minutes giving Bert the details and answering his questions.

"Man, how did you . . ." Bert said, "I mean, wow, to even think of that bomb and to still have the piece of paper with the phone number in your hoody pocket." He whistled low.

Christopher thought of the voice he heard, but he said nothing. He wasn't ready to talk about it, especially with Bert. He needed to process it and try to figure out if the voice was his dad or just his subconscious at work.

"I am *so* glad you're here." Bert looked away and swallowed, then continued. "According to Simpson, for now the police are viewing this as a gang war between competing syndicates over territory in the massage parlor and sex trafficking business. They also found two more dead Koreans in a burned-out car off I-40, west of Bellevue, and, of course, the bomb at the Korean's house last Friday night. All this made them think of gang or turf war."

Christopher looked at Bert and saw the slight grin. He decided to wait till later to get the details on the guys killed on the interstate. "The detective. They know the other detective, O'Reilly, was in league with the Koreans, right?"

Bert nodded. "They know he was one of the dead bodies in your front yard, and he wasn't supposed to be there. Simpson told me he knew O'Reilly was up to something. They have the cell phones, and I think once they track down phone records, they'll be convinced."

"Yeah, and I can tell them," Christopher said.

"Simpson is coming back later today. He wants to talk with you. He's a savvy guy, and he probably wonders how you were involved in this mayhem. But he knows O'Reilly had crossed over, and he knows you were tortured, so I don't think he'll be inclined to push hard."

"Good. I won't say much, just that the Koreans tortured me. I'll tell him O'Reilly was there, and after I told them about

Gloria, they all left. They told me they would burn my house down with me in it, but I got out before it caught fire. I heard explosions right after they left my house," Christopher said.

"Yeah, that's best, I think." Bert paused, looked out the window, and back at Christopher.

"I'm not telling Barbara about any of my involvement other than you stayed at our house a couple of nights, and you were concerned with Gloria's safety, so I had Greg stay over there on Sunday night. I need to not catch any attention, given the explosives. Someone could get curious if they took the time to look at my military background."

"Understood."

"One other thing. There was a *Tennessean* reporter here earlier. He wants to interview you. Given their story about you in the newspaper on Saturday, it might be a good opportunity to clear your name."

Christopher bit his lip and pondered a minute, then said, "I think I'll get him to interview Gloria. She can tell him about my involvement and clear my name. Her story of helping Kim escape is a good one, and it might help get additional funding and support for her cause. I'd just as soon keep a low profile." He was drowsy from the pain meds, and the words weren't coming out fully formed.

"I agree," Bert said. "By the way, I called Gloria and gave her the lowdown after I got to the hospital this morning. She called back a short while ago to get an update, said that Kim and June are on the bus to San Francisco, and she's on the road from Memphis back to Nashville. She'll come here this evening."

"Good, good. It was all worth it."

Bert snapped his fingers. "Oh, one more thing you need to know. I called Bruce Parsley and filled him in. He's coming up later. You can decide if you want to use him. I think you need him or some attorney around if the police want to do a formal interview with you. He wants to contact the Metro attorney and the DA's office, let them know he's representing you, and he wants to be present if they come calling."

"I guess that's okay. Tell him to go—," Christopher said reluctantly. His eyes closed before he finished the word "ahead."

▪ ▪ ▪

"I've made some calls, and here's where we are now," Parsley said when he showed up later that afternoon and paced around the hospital room. Then he stopped and asked, as if he suddenly remembered he should express concern, "You okay?"

"Just peachy."

Parsley looked at him quizzically, then resumed his pacing and arm waving.

"Metro knows O'Reilly is going to cost them a bundle. You have a strong case for false arrest and defamation. Your torture is directly related to O'Reilly telling the Koreans where you live. Simpson said he reported his concerns about O'Reilly to the Chief, but no action was taken. There were several red flags, and the police and DA's office did nothing."

The lawyer kept walking around the room. "I called the attorney representing Metro a few minutes ago. I told him we'd file suit for damages, pain, and suffering. He didn't argue much and floated a one-point five mil settlement. I laughed."

"Sounds fair. Settle it," Christopher said.

Parsley gave him a stern look. "We can easily get two million. I think we go for three."

"Take the offer," Christopher said again.

"You know you'll only get one mil after I get my third."

"I haven't agreed to any arrangement with you. I'll give you twenty percent, and that's an easy three hundred K since you do not have to work for it."

Parsley argued and continued his circuit around the room. He threw his hands in the air and talked about money left on the table, how another million is no sweat for Metro, and on and on. He finally realized that Christopher wasn't budging. He reluctantly agreed to the terms.

"Here's another way to earn that three hundred K," Christopher said. "Call the reporter from *The Tennessean*, tell him you're representing me and I'm too drugged to talk for a couple of days. Get him to interview Gloria Jean McNulty. You can mention my involvement just so my name gets cleared, but she has the better story. No one knows anything about Bert's involvement, and let's keep it that way."

"I can handle that. I'll get with Ms. McNulty, go over her story, and I'll tell the reporter I'm representing you and give a synopsis."

Christopher knew the attorney was measuring the PR value of his name and legal practice on the front page of *The Tennessean* and liked the conclusion.

"You have a Metro detective impatiently waiting outside. I talked to him briefly and told him I was representing you. Want me to send him in?" Parsley asked.

"Yeah, and you might as well hang around and see where his line of questioning goes."

"Are you clear enough after anesthesia to talk?"

"Another good reason for you to hang around." Christopher's eyes closed, and he breathed out long and hard, his head still swimming a little.

Simpson came in. He brought a strong whiff of tobacco that caused Christopher to flash back to the Korean blowing smoke in his face hours earlier. Christopher explained how the Koreans captured him before dawn and tortured him. The detective had him go through the events twice.

"So, they finally got the name and address of this lady, Gloria McNulty, but you knew by then she was on her way to Memphis with the Korean girl, Kim."

Christopher nodded.

"And then they left your house, out the front door, after telling you they planned to burn your house down with you in it. Your hands and feet were duct-taped together, and somehow you managed to get free and crawl to your kitchen door and into the back yard."

Christopher nodded again. "Yeah, I bit the tape. And I didn't crawl. I rolled."

"Someone left a bomb between your car and their car parked out front. You heard this bomb go off as you rolled out the back door. Anything I'm leaving out?"

"Well, yeah. You left out the part where O'Reilly calls the Korean dude in charge, shows up, holds my legs while they burned my chest with cigarettes, and then he tells me he's sorry, but he can't think of another way out as he heads for the front door with the Koreans." Christopher stopped to catch his breath after all the words. The memory of extreme pain and fear set his pulse galloping.

"When I told you someone was feeding information to the Koreans, you and O'Reilly arrested me for obstruction."

It was Simpson's time to nod in agreement. "I'm sorry for that," he said glumly.

Simpson thought momentarily, glanced at Parsley leaning against the windowsill on the other side of the room, and then said, "We haven't finished processing the scene, but the early evidence seems to match your story. The EMT said you had tape residue on your wrists, and your legs were still wrapped in duct tape when they found you in the back yard. I'm not sure where the bomb came from. Crime Scene techs have collected the bodies, what's left of them, and bomb fragments."

He paused again and then spoke carefully. "The bomb at the house in Brentwood and the bomb in the car beside the interstate that killed two more Koreans are loose ends we haven't tied up, and I don't like loose ends, but I'm not sorry to see these guys off the board. I suspect you're okay with it, too."

Christopher closed his eyes briefly, then tightened his lips and looked up at the ceiling. "These guys were killers, and they meant to kill me and probably Kim and Gloria, so no, I'm not sorry they're gone. Still, it haunts me that they died so violently in my front yard."

Parsley walked over toward the bed.

Christopher cleared his sore and dry throat and uttered a shallow cough. "And. It haunts me . . . that I almost died so violently in my kitchen."

"I think we're done, Detective Simpson," Parsley said.

▪ ▪ ▪

Bert and Amy returned briefly in the late afternoon but didn't stay long. Christopher ate a little hospital food, took a pain pill, and then fell into a deep sleep for several hours.

When he woke, it seemed like it was the middle of the night. The lights were out, and the window was dark. He looked at the clock on the TV. It read nine o'clock. He sensed a presence in the recliner near his head and craned his neck to look.

Gloria smiled at him as she turned on a lamp near his bed.

"Hey," he said. "How long have you been here?"

"Oh, maybe three hours."

"You were quiet."

"You were really sleeping."

"Everything went okay in Memphis?"

"The office for the temporary visa was a little crazy, but once we got through that bureaucratic maze, the bus tickets to San Francisco were a breeze." She leaned over and rested her elbow on the edge of the bed.

"When Bert called, we'd finished with the Feds and were on our way to the Greyhound station. We almost turned the car around and drove back to Nashville. Kim couldn't decide if she wanted to go to San Francisco or come back and check on you. Bert told her you were okay. He said you would want her to go ahead with her plan since people were waiting in San Francisco. She finally agreed to get on the bus."

Gloria reached over and put her hand on his arm. "I bought her a temporary cell phone at a store next to the bus station. When you feel okay, give her a call. She'll want to hear from you and know you're all right."

Christopher said, "I need to get myself a new phone first, then I'll call her."

"We were all worried. I'm still worried. I know you're downplaying it, but those guys tortured you, and you have some nasty burns and a broken leg." Gloria's face showed her concern as she talked.

Christopher looked away for a moment, then back at Gloria. "I was responsible for those guys getting killed in my front yard. I made the call that triggered the bomb."

Gloria nodded. "I know. Bert told me about it. I asked him, and he said he mistakenly left that explosive in your trunk. He said you were smart enough to remember how to set it off, and for that reason you're alive, and you saved his life, and maybe Barbara and Amy. Kim and I might have been killed too."

"They deserved what they got, but still . . . four people are dead because I set off the bomb. I'm still trying to sort it all out. I don't believe in Karma so much as I believe taking a life, even if justified, exacts a toll on your soul."

Gloria grabbed his hand and pulled it toward her. "It's not about Karma; it's about forgiveness. No matter what you've done or caused to be done, you just need to ask for forgiveness."

Christopher looked into her eyes and saw *her* forgiveness. He squeezed her hand. "I think I just did."

She leaned forward and kissed his forehead. "Give yourself the time and space to heal. You're beat up—body and soul."

"I'll be okay. I'm glad Kim and June are safely on their way."

"Let's talk about your situation," Gloria said, patting his arm. "I spoke with the surgeon when she dropped by a couple of hours ago to check on you. She said, when you want to, you're okay to get out of bed with help, but you'll need assistance for at least a couple of days, then she'll discharge you.

The cast comes off in four weeks, then physical therapy for six weeks after all that. No driving for at least two months."

Christopher had already heard this. He'd asked the hospital social worker about rehab facilities, even though he dreaded being in such a place for possibly four weeks or longer. With no house or car, he wasn't sure where he'd go after that.

"I guess I need to figure out someplace to go."

"I've got it figured out. You're moving in with me."

Even in the dim lamplight, Christopher could see her blush.

"I mean, I have a bedroom on the main level, and a bathroom in it, so it's a good setup for you. The hospital will send a nurse by every few days to check on you and change your bandages. I can drive you to doc appointments, your physical therapy, to see your mom, wherever you want to go. I'm not a bad cook, so you'll have it pretty good."

"You sleeping in that bed, too?" Christopher asked her with a faint smile.

She blushed again, but her eyes lit up. "You're in no shape for that kind of therapy. Let's give it a while."

"Just wanting to understand all the amenities," he said.

"Only room and board at this time."

CHAPTER FORTY-EIGHT

EIGHT WEEKS LATER

"I'm not sure why you're going to all this fuss," Christopher said. "We're just meeting with a Korean woman and her son. I'm in jeans and a polo shirt, but you're getting all dolled up."

Gloria looked at Christopher in the vanity mirror as she applied rose-shaded lipstick. "I like to fuss." She arched an eyebrow at him. "It's part of who I am, so get used to it." She slid the lid back on her lipstick and whirled around. "How do I look?"

Like you just got out of the sack with me, he thought, as he noticed a certain looseness of limb, a softening of the mouth, a brightness in the eyes. It had only been an hour ago, but they'd almost resumed while they were both in the shower.

"You look mahvelous," he said, faking a highbrow accent. "Let's go. Our appointment is at ten, and I'm curious to know what this is all about."

▪ ▪ ▪

"Oh, I meant to ask earlier. How was your time with Amy yesterday afternoon?" Gloria asked as they drove to the meeting in Christopher's new Ford F-150.

Christopher smiled. "We went to see a woman with a litter of English Labrador Retriever pups. Someone Bert knew."

"Why a Lab?"

"Amy's choice. She's been after me to deliver on my promise of another dog since Gracie was killed. She didn't want another Golden Retriever. Too soon after Gracie, she said. Labs are her next favorite breed."

"Okay, so how was the visit with the litter?"

"The house was out in the country, halfway to Clarksville, with lots of acreage and a long driveway. When we pulled in, two Labrador Retrievers ran out to greet us. The pups weren't far behind. There were only three left. One chocolate, a black, both males, and this small female, kind of a reddish color."

Christopher looked over at Gloria and smiled a wry grin. "I told Amy as we drove out there to not fall in love with any of those dogs. We needed to look at several litters to find the right pup."

"I think I know what happened."

"You probably guessed it right. Amy played with all three pups. The red female hung back at first. The woman said she was the smallest and shyest in the litter. Didn't call her the runt, but I knew that's what she meant. It wasn't long before Amy held only that puppy. Once in her lap, the pup stayed there like she was velcroed—never once squirmed to get down like the other ones did."

"A match made in heaven."

"After about an hour, I said we needed to go. Amy said she wasn't leaving without her pup." He chuckled.

"Sounds like it was a special day with your daughter. And your new puppy daughter."

"It was a great day."

"Where's the pup now, and what's her name?" Gloria asked.

"Her name is Lucy. I suggested it. I told Amy about another famous redhead, Lucy, from a TV show, and she liked that. Much to Barbara's dismay, Lucy stayed in Amy's room last night. I think there might have already been an accident and maybe a chewed shoe."

Gloria laughed.

"Lucy can only stay there until I get my house rebuilt. But that's at least till the end of summer. Barbara says the dog moves out of the house when school starts back. Presumably moving in with me."

"If Amy and Lucy get into trouble, they're welcome to stay at my house," Gloria said.

Christopher shook his head. "I doubt that will happen. I don't pretend to have ever understood Barbara, but for some reason she doesn't want Amy hanging out with us. Without stating it explicitly, she's worked hard the past several weeks to throw a barrier up every time I've tried to get Amy to stay overnight with us."

"I noticed that, but I don't know what to do about it. It's almost as if she's jealous of me," Gloria said, then grinned and tipped her head to the side. "Some of my church girlfriends might be a little jealous, too. They accepted you moving in with me as you healed up, but now that you are off crutches, the bolder ones are asking how much longer I will take care of you."

"The guy rehabbing the Airstream says he'll be done in a couple weeks, so I think I'll move into it temporarily. House construction starts next week. I want to be there and do some of the work during the rebuild."

Gloria wrinkled her brow. "You've said you wanted to help build your house back, but you know I don't want you to move out any time soon."

"You need the support of your friends. Let's not lose that."

They looked at each other, and Christopher added, "I can allow conjugal visits to the Airstream."

"And I'll offer outpatient therapy sessions at my condo."

Bruce Parsley waited for them just inside the lobby of the Nashville City Building, bouncing on the balls of his feet. "This is about as white-shoe as Nashville law firms get," he said, rubbing his hands together. "These Koreans must have serious dinero to have these guys representing them." He pointed a finger at Christopher. "I think you're about to get a nice settlement offer."

They rode the elevator to the eighteenth floor and were ushered into a conference room where a receptionist offered coffee, tea, or water. A few minutes later, an older man with silver hair and wearing a three-piece suit walked in, introduced himself as William Criswell, and extended his hand. He was followed by a young Asian man dressed in jeans and a dark sport coat. A middle-aged Asian woman was last to enter.

As they were settling in their chairs on the other side of the conference table, Christopher's cell phone chirped. He pulled it from his pocket, glanced at it, and silenced the ringer. It was Kim calling. Hmm, she always called on Sunday. Must be a good reason for her to call on a weekday. He decided he would let it go to voicemail and listen later.

"This is Billy Lee and his mother, Mrs. Jung Lee." The lawyer made the introductions, and both Koreans nodded their heads at Christopher and Gloria. After being assured that all present had been offered drinks and were comfortable, Criswell got down to business.

"Mrs. Jung Lee and her son, Billy Lee, have inherited the estate of the deceased Cho Lee, Mrs. Lee's brother. That includes several businesses." The lawyer waited to see if either Christopher or Gloria had any questions.

"As we understand it, both of you had an occasion to respond to a request for assistance from one of Mr. Cho Lee's employees. I am specifically talking about a young woman who worked at the Orchid Spa, which is no longer in operation."

He looked at them both expectantly. Christopher waited him out. Gloria glanced at Christopher and, taking her cues from his silence, said nothing.

The lawyer continued. "Mr. Jones, we understand that Mr.

Cho Lee was unhappy with that employee, and he and his associates threatened you because you helped her, and they eventually inflicted bodily harm on you. Mr. Billy Lee and Mrs. Jung Lee want to apologize for his actions and make sure you are made whole for any costs associated with your medical care and the loss of your home and your car. They also wish to extend a gesture of their regret by making a donation to Ms. McNulty's organization, which we understand helps women who are, uh, employed in the adult industry but may want to pursue another career."

Christopher nodded. "I think I know why we've been invited to meet here," he said. "This meeting is about liability, potential lawsuits, and protections. I suspect there are certain documents we will be asked to sign if bills are paid and a settlement accepted."

Parsley slapped a hand on the table. "We have reached an agreement with the Metro Government, but most of the blame for Mr. Jones's pain and suffering lies with Mr. Cho and his associates. Any settlement must start higher—"

Christopher held up a hand and turned to Parsley. "I want to hear what the Lees have to say."

Billy Lee leaned forward and spoke. "We're the new owners of these businesses, and we are looking at risks and rewards. These are profitable businesses, but we must understand any liabilities. You are the biggest unknown today, and we need to know your intentions."

Christopher said, "My intention is to know more about your plans with your businesses, specifically the spa business."

Criswell jabbed a finger and said, "I don't think their business plans are part of our discussion today. We're here to talk about a settlement."

"That only starts once we know your intentions with the spas," Christopher said with a soft but firm tone.

The lawyer, Criswell, opened his mouth, but before he could speak, the young Korean man swung his arm out to stop him. "Our goal—" Lee pointed at himself and his mother, "is to talk directly with you and not through our lawyer. We need to see if we can work something out together, maybe find some common ground."

"What common ground can there be between a business that trafficked women into sexual slavery and my organization, which exists to rescue women from a life of prostitution and sex trafficking?" Gloria glared at Billy Lee, then Jung Lee.

"Now, Ms. McNulty, we don't agree...." The lawyer's response died away as Billy Lee extended his arm again.

"I know what was going on in the spas my uncle operated. I also know he used violence against the women and against others who got in his way." The young man's voice grew intense, and he clenched his fists. "My mother despised that part of his business operations, and when I went to work for him, she instructed me to steer clear of the spa business. She and I eventually managed two Korean restaurants as legitimate businesses within my uncle's empire, but we had nothing to do with the spas."

"Are you shutting down his spa business?" Christopher asked.

The young man hesitated and looked over at his mother before responding. "We are not opening back up the Orchid Spa here in Nashville or any more spas elsewhere. We are selling off the spa businesses we own in Georgia. We will continue operating spas in other cities in Tennessee and Kentucky for now, but we will operate differently. The women will no longer owe any debt. They can leave. They can stay. They can live anywhere they want. We will allow them to keep most of the money they earn. We will tell them to avoid sex acts. If they don't, they risk getting arrested and losing their jobs. In other words, we plan to operate legitimately."

"So, you're no longer in the adult business at all?" Christopher tried to pin him down.

Billy Lee shrugged. "Spas are a dying business. If men want

sex, it's easier through websites and hookup links. Men under forty would never think about going to a spa for sex. It's way too risky. It may take us a couple of years, but we will transition away from stand-alone spas as a line of business." His tone was matter-of-fact as if his business model was driven solely by principles learned in business school.

"Will you allow me to meet these women who still work in your spas and talk with them, perhaps help them find other work?" Gloria asked.

Both Billy Lee and his mother nodded. "We want to expand our restaurants and open a Korean grocery," Jung Lee said, her voice soft. "We will have positions for the women if they want to leave the spas. You can help them look at other opportunities."

"First, we need to resolve any remaining issues between you and our businesses." Billy Lee looked at Christopher. "We've already paid your hospital bills as a goodwill gesture."

Christopher toggled his head. "That sounds appropriate, since it was the actions of your uncle, the business owner, that caused me to land in the hospital."

Billy Lee spread his hands. "If there are other costs for your house and car after your insurance payout, let us know. We will cover any out-of-pocket expenses, plus pay you five hundred grand for furnishings and business loss. We know you can sue us and possibly put us out of business. We've heard about the settlement with the city, and we figured we were next. What else must we do to make up for my uncle's actions and avoid costly litigation?"

His lawyer sitting next to him looked as if he was having an attack of indigestion.

Christopher nodded at Gloria. "Help fund her organization by committing to a donation of two hundred thousand annually for the next five years."

"Wait a minute," Parsley protested, but Christopher waved him off.

"Done," Billy Lee said, nodding his agreement.

His lawyer's eyes widened, but he said nothing.

"And put in writing that I will have free access to any spa or business you operate." Gloria jabbed a manicured finger at the conference table to emphasize her point. "State that I can meet with the women who work there and that they will not be subject to harassment or intimidation for meeting with me."

▪ ▪ ▪

They walked out of the law offices an hour later, leaving the lawyers behind to wrangle over the details.

"I think that was a profitable meeting, don't you?" Gloria asked. She linked her arm in Christopher's as they stopped at the corner crosswalk.

"We did okay. Could have done better, maybe, but I'm not one to drive hard bargains, unfortunately. Hopefully, they meant what they said about getting out of the human trafficking business. I'm not sure they're completely leaving the adult business, though. He hedged a little on that. He's a businessman, and I'm sure the spa business is still very lucrative. It felt like he was distancing himself to avoid any legal problems while allowing room for the girls to operate freelance if they choose."

"That part was a little muddy." Gloria nodded in agreement. "I like his mother. I think I can work with her. We'll get the girls out of the spa business."

"At least you were specific in gaining access to the girls. And you have funding to provide real assistance when needed. That's a positive outcome."

"Yes. The additional funding will help, but you shortchanged yourself. You didn't get much extra."

"Oh yeah, I did. I got you. That's extra. In fact, I'd call it extra special." He slipped his arm around her waist as they walked across the street.

CHAPTER FORTY-NINE

The woman with short gray hair sat behind an imposing but worn wooden desk and spent several minutes flipping through the completed forms in the folder in front of her. She typed on her computer keyboard and studied the results on her screen, paging down several times. She finally looked over her reading glasses at the thin young Korean woman perched on the edge of the oversized leather chair on the other side of the desk.

"You've completed all the necessary forms and documentation for admission, and you've taken the required tests, since you don't have an official high school transcript," she said in a business-like tone. "You passed the tests with no problem. The admissions committee thought there must be a mistake since you said you only completed eleven of twelve grades of school in Korea. They requested you take the tests again, and you scored even higher than the first time. Very impressive."

Kim nodded. She knew all this. The woman turned back to her computer screen again. The nameplate on the front of her desk said *Beverly Bosse, Vice President of Admissions*. Kim's face tightened as she had a momentary flashback to the man known as Boseu. This woman was stern-looking and seemed almost as old as Boseu, but not as threatening. Kim felt a moment of relief, knowing she no longer had a reason to fear Boseu or anyone else. She did not need to run from her past.

"You have been approved for admission here at the University of San Francisco, and I must say that in my years in this office, I've never seen an application move this fast."

The woman pursed her lips as she continued to study Kim. "You had some heavy hitters on your side, including your ambassador from South Korea, a city councilwoman, and a well-known female attorney, Brenda Lawford. They all made personal pitches on your behalf."

Kim smiled. "I don't know ambassador. I met councilwoman once. Brenda Lawford talked with me many times since I arrived here. She is now my friend."

"She's one of the top trial lawyers in northern California and a good friend to have in this city," Beverly Bosse said as she rubbed her chin. "She's also an alum of our law school, and a major donor." She leaned forward. "She shared your story with our president, and he shared it with me. We are glad to admit you and to offer a full scholarship."

"Thank you," Kim replied.

The woman nodded in response. "Since we're a private university, we were able to move a little faster than a state institution probably could have. In addition to your test scores and recommendations, you fit in perfectly with our stated mission. We are, after all, a Jesuit university, and one of our initiatives is addressing human trafficking."

She stood and reached across the desk to offer her hand to Kim. "Welcome to the University of San Francisco. You may enroll full-time this fall. You are also welcome to take a course or two in preparation this summer."

"Yes, I will do this," Kim said as she shook the woman's hand.

"Do you know what you plan to study?"

"I will study pre-law. I want to become a lawyer. I want to help women who are victims of human trafficking."

"Your lawyer friend must have inspired you. She is known as a champion for women's issues. We have an excellent School of Law here at USF."

"Yes, I know this," Kim said, nodding her head.

"I am not surprised," Beverly Bosse responded with a laugh. "I'll get one of our academic advisers to contact you and schedule a time to discuss the courses you should take."

--

As Kim left the USF campus near Golden Gate Park, she stopped to call Christopher. When he didn't answer, she left a message: "I have good news. I am now student at University of San Francisco. I take classes this summer. I am very happy. I will tell you more when we talk on Sunday."

Kim walked back to her new apartment in the Mission District of San Francisco. She found it two weeks ago, a fourth-floor walk-up in an old Victorian home, just two rooms and a small bathroom in what was formerly the attic. It was a long climb, but it offered a great view.

▪ ▪ ▪

She loved San Francisco from the first day of her arrival eight weeks ago. Despite the messiness of the downtown area, the ever-present homeless population, the crowded streets and sidewalks, and the unpredictable weather, the city had a contagious vibrancy. All ethnicities and languages, including a robust Korean community, seemed to be present.

Eight weeks ago, Sondra Cunningham, The Women's Shelter of San Francisco's Executive Director, met her and June at the Greyhound bus station. She already had a room rented for them with a family in the Little Korea section of San Francisco. Their thoroughly Americanized fifteen-year-old daughter treated them as new sisters and spent most of her spare minutes getting them acclimated. June still lived with the family, and Kim had dinner with them at least once a week.

With the Korean family's guidance and Sondra's help, Kim quickly got established. She opened a bank account and deposited almost fifty thousand dollars—the Min-jun money. She paid June's room and board for six months, and enough was left to cover her apartment for the next three years. June found a job as a teacher's aide at a multicultural childcare center nearby. Kim purchased new laptop computers and cell phones for her and June.

She signed up for computer classes at the Apple store in Union Square. After two sessions, the young man who taught the course offered to meet her each morning at the Starbucks next door for one-on-one training. Following the first session, he asked her to go to a movie the next night. Kim declined.

Some day she might be interested in men again, but for now, school and her future were more important. She occasionally thought about her family in Korea. She had talked with her father and learned that her mother died two years ago. Her father asked little about her life over the last four years. She decided she would return to her hometown, but only after she was a citizen of the United States. After she became a lawyer, maybe then.

Through Sondra, Kim met the city councilwoman and the attorney. Over lunch, she told her story. When she told them about shooting Min-jun, the councilwoman gasped and put her hand over her mouth. Brenda Lawford, the attorney, laughed and pounded her fist on the table three times. They both offered their help, and they jumped into action when she expressed interest in pursuing a college degree. Brenda devoted many hours to helping Kim achieve that goal. Each day was filled with applications and appointments. Kim walked all around the hills of San Francisco. Her legs grew strong as she learned to navigate around the city.

She emailed Christopher almost every day with quick notes or questions. She told him she wanted to start an exercise regimen and run at least five miles daily like he did. She said she planned to run in a marathon in the fall. He advised her on running shoes and laid out a personal training plan for her to reach that goal.

They Zoomed every Sunday at noon, Nashville time. Christopher and Gloria would listen to her excited voice and watch her face light up the computer screen with ambition and confidence. They asked questions and sometimes gave advice, but mostly congratulated her as she learned new skills, improved her grammar, made new friends, and established new goals.

▪ ▪ ▪

Kim climbed the four flights of stairs and turned the lock on her apartment door. The front room held a desk with a laptop, a large, ragged dictionary she'd found at a thrift store, and a blue couch with a flower pattern. On one side of the room was a kitchenette with a sink, refrigerator, stove, microwave, and a small kitchen table holding a sea green foil-wrapped pot of real yellow tulips, all in about a ten-by-ten-foot space. On the wall was an old clock she'd seen at the thrift store, with large numbers and the face of Jesus on it, just like the one in Christopher's house. Her bedroom was even smaller, with a single bed and dresser almost filling the space. She had a white chenille bedspread and two colorful cushions with bamboo and dogwood-blossom fabric. She loved her apartment and living by herself, taking charge of her life.

Kim glanced at her laptop on the desk and considered looking online at the course catalog for USF, but her mind was still whirling with the anticipation of going to college. She could not concentrate. Better to go for a run.

Within five minutes, she was back on the street, hair pulled back in a ponytail, dressed in maroon tights, red running shoes, and a gray, long-sleeved running top. A lightweight nylon jacket was tied around her waist because even though it was sunny and mid-seventies right now in the Mission District, as she crossed over to the Castro District and headed north to the bay area and Marina Boulevard, the temperature often dropped by ten degrees. Fog and mist could roll in and envelope her in seconds.

She started her run, feeling the muscles in her legs loosen up and stretch with a slight burn. It was a good burn, fed by a fire within her soul.

She ran at the edge of the sidewalk, passing tourists with maps and businessmen on cell phones. She dodged an Asian woman with a small child, both dawdling in front of an open-air market. A panhandler on a corner yelled at her, but she ignored him. She was a slight figure, gliding silently by, but she ran with a confident stride and focused gaze. She ran past stately Victorian homes painted in pastel colors, crowded shoulder-to-shoulder and pushed up to the sidewalk. As she topped a hill, the pointed end of the Transamerica Pyramid towered in the skyline ahead of her.

"Yes, I know this city," she whispered as she ran toward downtown.

She ran toward her future.

NOTE TO THE READER

I often get ideas for my stories from the news.

Several years ago, I read in our Nashville newspaper about a raid on Golden Massage, a spa in the tony area known as Green Hills. This massage parlor, hiding in plain sight between a liquor store and a Domino's Pizza, advertised its services through Backpage ads for "massages by pretty Asian girls" and "table showers".

Detectives raided four establishments that day, three of the four in nearby communities, and ten women were charged with promoting prostitution. More disturbing was the discovery that three women spoke no English and had no identification. They didn't know their address, and they could not identify the town where they were living.

The owner of the massage parlors, a Chinese man, lived in a large house in nearby Franklin, and when the detectives raided his home, they found that three women who worked in the spas slept on mattresses on the floor in the house's lower level. Others lived in a nearby apartment. The owner was charged with trafficking for commercial sex.

On the news that evening, I watched a gut-wrenching video of three frightened women and one man in handcuffs as police escorted them to the Criminal Justice Center.

I followed the story for a few days before it quickly faded from the news, but not from my mind. I wondered about the stories of these women and their journey from their Asian homeland to Nashville, Tennessee. I began to research the trafficking of women from China, South Korea, Vietnam, and other countries to cities across the U.S., Canada, and throughout Europe. The numbers and the stories were overwhelming.

From this real-life incident came the idea of *No Good Deed*, the fictional story about a man who unintentionally becomes involved in helping a Korean woman escape from traffickers.

If this story moves you to want to help victims of sexual trafficking, please research in your community how you can support organizations that fight this crime and help the victims.

In Tennessee, you can contact these organizations:

endslaverytn.org
nahtcoalition.org
and **thistlefarms.org**

If you like this story, please consider posting an honest review on Amazon or Goodreads. Your review will guide me in my future endeavors. If you want to chat more, please email me at jack@jackwallaceauthor.com. More of my writings and information about my books and short stories are on my website: jackwallaceauthor.com

ACKNOWLEDGMENTS

I'm indebted to so many people who have encouraged me and assisted me in writing and crafting this novel.

Two writing groups worked through each chapter with me: The Nashville Writers Alliance members Ed Cromer, Rita Bourke, Phyllis Gobbell, Doug Jones, Will Maguire, Shannon Thurman, Mary Buckner, Mary Bess Dunn. The Vine Street Writers members Greg Rumburg, Melanie Gao, Jim Carls, Kristin Harney, and Heather Hendrickson. Your critiques and support helped me grow as a writer. I am eternally grateful.

Thanks to Darnell Arnoult for the early instruction on the craft of writing a novel. Without your patient guidance and feedback, I would have given up many years ago.

Thanks to the team at Atmosphere Press for shaping and polishing this story into a real novel. Y'all delivered everything you promised.

Most of all, to the love of my life and soulmate, Joanne. Thanks for believing in me.

ABOUT ATMOSPHERE PRESS

Founded in 2015, Atmosphere Press was built on the principles of Honesty, Transparency, Professionalism, Kindness, and Making Your Book Awesome. As an ethical and author-friendly hybrid press, we stay true to that founding mission today.

If you're a reader, enter our giveaway for a free book here:

SCAN TO ENTER
BOOK GIVEAWAY

If you're a writer, submit your manuscript for consideration here:

SCAN TO SUBMIT
MANUSCRIPT

And always feel free to visit Atmosphere Press and our authors online at atmospherepress.com. See you there soon!

ABOUT THE AUTHOR

Jack Wallace holds degrees from Gateway College and the University of Tennessee. He's written stories for many years about growing up in the "Christ haunted" South and has one published novel, *The Unrighteous Brothers*, and many short stories, several of which have been published in literary journals.

Jack lives in Nashville, Tennessee, with his wife, Joanne, and his red Lab, Lucy. He also spends many weeks at his Flat Rock, North Carolina, cabin. He is most at home on a trail or fishing a stream in the mountains of North Carolina or Tennessee.

Printed in the USA
CPSIA information can be obtained
at www.ICGtesting.com
LVHW041447280224
772927LV00006B/681

9 798891 320529